Dear Reader,

I'm very excited about this book, which revisits *Class Act's* Keystone School. When I finished *Class Act* (Harlequin Superromance #803) I hated to walk away and leave Pam Carver, the attractive head of the English department, without her own happily-ever-after romance.

Bless her heart, she'd been looking in all the wrong places. Sometimes, you know, love is right under our noses, and if we're very, very lucky, we get to marry our best friends. So it is for Pam.

And so it was for me. Larry was my CPA, my fellow church member and my sounding board at a difficult time in my life. In short, he was my friend. I can pinpoint the exact moment in our relationship when I looked at him and something went "zap." My "friend" had morphed into something more—much more. And nothing was ever the same. Only better!

Like Grant Gilbert, the hero of this story, Larry welcomed my family without reservations—including my three children. I don't want to spoil the ending of the book for you, but Andy, Grant's teenage son, has truths to tell about the meaning of family—truths Larry and I learned through living them.

With best wishes,

Laura Abbot

P.S. Readers' comments are important to me. Write to me at P.O. Box 2105, Eureka Springs, AR 72632 or e-mail me at LauraAbbot@msn.com. And don't forget to check out these Web sites: www.eHarlequin.com and www.superauthors.com.

ABOUT THE AUTHOR

A Kansas City native, Laura graduated from Kansas State University with a bachelor's degree in English literature, later studying at the graduate level at the University of Central Oklahoma. She spent twenty-five years as a high school English teacher in Kansas and Oklahoma, finishing her career as the advanced placement senior English teacher and dean of Faculty at an independent college preparatory school in Oklahoma City. Along the way, she and husband Larry reared five children—her two daughters and one son, his daughter, and his orphaned nephew. In the mid-seventies, Larry and Laura discovered Beaver Lake in northwest Arkansas and began working on a plan to move there permanently. Their dream was realized in 1992 when Laura took early retirement and the couple built a home overlooking the lake near Eureka Springs, Arkansas. It was then that Laura began pursuing her own dream—nurtured since grade school—of writing fiction. She sold her first novel to Harlequin Superromance® in 1994 and has been happily writing for the line ever since. Between entertaining the couple's children and thirteen grandchildren, curling up in the hammock with a good book, and spinning stories that always end happily, Laura says life doesn't get any better.

Books by Laura Abbot

HARLEQUIN SUPERROMANCE

You're My Baby
Laura Abbot

HARLEQUIN®

TORONTO • NEW YORK • LONDON
AMSTERDAM • PARIS • SYDNEY • HAMBURG
STOCKHOLM • ATHENS • TOKYO • MILAN • MADRID
PRAGUE • WARSAW • BUDAPEST • AUCKLAND

ISBN 0-373-71059-3

YOU'RE MY BABY

Copyright © 2002 by Laura A. Shoffner.

Visit us at www.eHarlequin.com

Printed in U.S.A.

With respect, affection and appreciation,
this book is dedicated to my editor, Laura Shin,
whose discerning eye, steady editorial hand
and understanding heart have challenged me to
reach beyond my self-imposed limitations.

CHAPTER ONE

YOU THOUGHT you were so careful? So smart? That things like this only happen to other people?

Pam Carver slumped against the bathroom counter. With effort, she swallowed an onslaught of nausea, then studied the white-faced, big-eyed image staring back at her from the mirror. A stranger.

She could maybe have found comfort in the familiar reflection of a thirty-plus, rosy-skinned redhead, with hazel-green eyes and laugh lines. She knew that woman. Good old Ms. Carver, popular spinster English teacher. *Spinster.* She'd grown to hate the prudish, spitlike quality of the word. It sounded like a woman who didn't want a man and had never known one. Certainly not in the Biblical sense.

A ragged snort escaped the stranger's mouth. Pam leaned closer, mocking the shocked reflection in the glass. "Well, think again, sweetie. Condoms aren't foolproof." Her voice, unnaturally loud, reverberated off the ceramic-tile walls. "I wonder, is 'pregnant spinster' an oxymoron?"

A fat tear oozed out of the left eye of the figure in the mirror. Pam swiveled, grabbing the cardboard remnants of the EPT kit, and in slow motion sank onto the plush bath mat.

A baby. Oh, God, a baby. Just when she'd about given up hope of ever being a mother. This was not at all the way it was supposed to happen. She was supposed to be married to a man who adored her, who wanted children as much as she did, who would cherish this new life growing within her.

But that could never be. Not with Steven. Nor, in fairness, could she blame him. From the beginning, he'd been totally honest with her, and they'd both agreed there could be no follow-up to their summer together. She had accepted her responsibility in the matter, just as he had. He was a fine man. He would've been a fine father. A happily-ever-after love. In another time. Another place.

Yet every nerve in her body urged her to pick up the phone. To tell him. But that was not an option. All he had ever asked of her was that she respect his situation.

No, she couldn't betray his trust. His right to know about her pregnancy was far outweighed by the devastation the truth would cause.

Even if it meant her child would be fatherless.

Even if that reality left her heart in tatters.

Fumbling in the pocket of her robe, she located a crumpled tissue, wiped her nose, sniffled a few times, then shakily got to her feet.

Now the woman in the mirror cradled her abdomen, the regret and fear in her face turning to resolve. Child support wasn't the issue. She was capable of taking care of the baby, and she would. "I didn't mean for it to be this way, my sweet little one. I'm all you've got. And that'll have to do. Somehow."

Pam splashed cold water on her burning cheeks. Right now, she had no idea how she would manage, but there was no question of choices. She was keeping this child. However, she couldn't continue teaching. The parents and administrators at the private school where she taught would hardly consider an unwed mother an appropriate role model.

She wiped her face, then wandered into her bedroom, where she flopped on the bed, a forearm shielding her eyes. School was starting in less than two weeks. Was there a way she could carry on, at least for a while? Before anyone knew? She needed the time to rearrange her life. How long did it take before you could no longer conceal a pregnancy? At that point, she would resign. She had no intention of embarrassing herself or the school by forcing the issue of her employment and possibly getting involved in a discrimination suit. But what about her health insurance if she quit?

She felt a slight bounce and, looking up, welcomed Viola, her velvet-gray cat, who studied her with knowing green eyes. "Am I in a fix or what, Vee?" As if intuiting her anxiety, the cat stretched, then settled in the crook of Pam's arm, her steady purr a calming influence. Drawing a ragged breath, Pam stroked Viola, willing away panic. The problems, which at first had seemed insurmountable, could surely be handled. One by one.

Lulled by Viola's reassuring presence, Pam concentrated on the child within her. Wonderingly she caressed the flat of her stomach, imagining the microscopic being growing and developing there even now. Boy or girl? Would the baby have her red curls? Or Steven's black hair? So many questions. So many surprises to come.

And then she felt it—the smile softening her mouth, relaxing her features. And with it, a humbling rush of gratitude.

A baby. My *baby.*

FORTY-NINE, FIFTY. Grant Gilbert replaced the weights in the rack and, using the tail of his T-shirt, wiped the

sheen of perspiration from his face. At least he was in
the school's air-conditioned weight room, not on the
football field with the kids, broiling under the Texas
sun, enduring the afternoon segment of their two-a-day
preseason practices. At times like this, it paid to be the
basketball coach.

This year, though, he had bigger problems than a
winning season. No amount of sit-ups, curls or leg work
had driven away the worry settling in his gut. His ex-
wife Shelley demanded an answer, and to do the best
by his son, Andy, Grant had to find a solution. Immediately.

In the coaches' locker room, he undressed, then
stepped into the shower. Steamy water eased tension in
his shoulders he knew wouldn't disappear until he figured out what he was going to do.

Although he and Shelley had been divorced for thirteen years, she still manipulated him and Andy to suit
her own selfish needs. This latest caper was no exception. Already divorced from husbands two and three,
she was currently in hot pursuit of number four, a
wealthy businessman—*read "Sugar Daddy,"* Grant
thought bitterly—who, she had just learned, was spending the upcoming year on assignment in the United
Arab Emirates. Of course, didn't Grant understand, she
had to go along. And, "of course," it would be im-
practical to take Andy.

Damn right!

Emerging from the shower and toweling down, he
couldn't rub away the memory of her patronizing voice.
"He's fifteen. The ideal time to go to boarding school
where he can begin making those all-important contacts.
I've found the perfect place in New England. I suppose

maybe he could come visit you out there in Texas for vacations.''

For vacations? After intense, sometimes acrimonious negotiations, he'd finally convinced her that maybe, just maybe, it made better sense for Andy to come live with him while she was gone. But ''sense'' wasn't a concept customarily part of Shelley's modus operandi.

Heck, it had made ''sense'' for him to be involved all along with Andy. But Shelley was the master of excuses and evasions, moving whenever she had a new love interest, shifting Andy from school to school. Though she talked a good game about ''roots,'' Shelley interpreted that to mean Andy should rarely have to make further moves simply to visit his father. With few exceptions, whatever contact they had resulted from Grant's traveling to Florida. During the school year, that was difficult, and even summers were restricted by coaching summer leagues, running basketball camps and taking college courses.

He'd been nuts not to appeal the custody arrangement. But who could've foreseen how difficult Shelley would be? There was a time early in their marriage when she'd seemed sweet, gentle. Even accommodating. But that was before she fixed her sights on what she chose to call ''more promising opportunities.''

Disgusted, he threw the towel into the laundry bin, then sauntered to his locker. Dressing slowly, he tried to analyze why being separated from Andy hurt more with every passing year. Obviously part of it was regret for what he'd missed. Firsts. Fun father-son times. A bonding that had never happened. In fact, he often thought Andy resented him, and Grant suspected Shelley preferred it that way.

Now, after weeks of wrangling, she was handing him

a golden opportunity. He could have Andy for one year. At least this was a stage on the growth and development charts he ought to know something about. His son would live with him here in Fort Worth, attend Keystone School, maybe even try out for the basketball team.

If.

Grant buttoned his shirt, feeling in his pocket the weight of the letter that had arrived today. He grimaced, recalling the dispassionate legalese. Count on Shelley to require an attorney instead of handling communication about Andy like a civilized adult.

He shook his head. Typical. As usual, she'd found a way to stick in the knife, as she had later in their marriage when the ''new'' had worn off. She had expected a husband to arrive home before dinner and stay there, dancing attendance on her throughout the evening. Late practices, road trips and school events were not part of her plan. In retrospect, it was a wonder the marriage had lasted even four years.

As he walked toward the exit, he heard the clatter of cleats hitting the cement floor. He backed up against the wall to let the football team thunder by. Sweat poured off their wet heads, and several grunted with each step. Two or three mustered a tired grin and a ''Hey, Coach G.'' as they passed.

Jack Liddy, the head football coach, paused beside Grant. He sniffed the air. ''Hey, Gilbert, you smell way too good.'' Then he grinned. ''I'm still lookin' for some help with the ends. Sure you're not interested?''

Grant laid a hand on the younger man's shoulder. ''You know darn well the last time I played football was in high school. You can't be that desperate.''

"I'll remember that when you're scrounging for a seventh-grade basketball coach."

"Seriously, I'll be pretty tied down this year."

"How come? They giving you extra classes?"

"Nothing like that." Grant raked a hand through his still-damp hair. "My son's coming to live with me."

"Hey, that's great!"

"Maybe."

Jack frowned. "What's to doubt?"

"My ex has laid a little stipulation on the deal. I have to locate a live-in housekeeper in the next several days, or she's sending Andy to boarding school."

Jack slapped Grant on the back. "Surely there are some honeys who've been tracking a bachelor like you." Then the coach sobered. "All kidding aside, do you have any prospects?"

"I've called a couple of agencies and I'm putting an ad in the paper this weekend, but I'm not optimistic. I mean, it can't be just anybody."

"No, of course not. Hey, I'll talk to my wife, ask around." He glanced over his shoulder at the assistant coaches coming in from the field, clipboards tucked under their arms.

"I'd appreciate that, Jack." Belatedly Grant thought to ask about the prospects for the football team.

"We could win a few, if we get some breaks."

"Like Beau Jasper's eligibility?"

"That would sure help. He's okay for now, but I've gotta have him at the end of the season, after midterms."

"I need him for basketball, too. I hate to say it, but without him, we could be in deep trouble."

"We'll be set if we can just get him through Pam Carver's senior English class."

Grant grinned. "I don't even want to think about it."

"Pam's a good egg. Maybe she'll cut him some slack."

"If anybody can pull him through, she can." Half the boys in school were in love with Pam. Grant hoped that would be sufficient motivation for his high-scoring forward to make a decent grade. He turned to leave. "Hey, Coach, you, too, can smell good. Have a great shower."

Jack laughed, then joined his assistants headed for the locker room.

Grant ambled to the door, stepping out into the sultry August afternoon. The low whir of a riding mower cruising between the lower and middle schools, the splash of sprinklers and the smell of new-mowed grass had him pausing for a cleansing breath. His gaze fell on the upper school building, its red-tile roof highlighted by the angle of the sun. Late August—the calm before the storm of the school year. Although he enjoyed the more relaxed pace of summer, he was always eager for school to start.

Despite Shelley's dim view of his calling, he couldn't imagine doing anything else. Working with teenagers kept a guy young. Every day was different, and it was never dull.

As schools went, Keystone was special. He glanced fondly around the campus—attractive, colorful landscaping, architecturally pleasant Southwestern-style buildings, well-maintained playing fields.

Gosh, he hoped Andy would come to love it, too. But how many new schools had the poor kid attended? Could this one be any different for him?

Grant turned abruptly and walked to his car. He could skip the daydreaming. Andy's satisfaction would be a moot point unless he could find—and afford—the cool teenager's version of Mary Poppins.

Hell.

PAM GRIPPED her straw purse and rounded the corner of the brick wall encircling Ginny Phillips's patio. A profusion of colorful sundresses and the babble of high-pitched laughter greeted her. She faltered, a wave of stage fright threatening her composure. *Act normal,* she told herself, before sweeping across the lawn to join her female colleagues at Ginny's annual back-to-school brunch.

The first to greet her was henna-haired Jessie Flanders, self-proclaimed grande dame of the faculty. "Making a big entrance, Pamela?" Heads turned at the shrill of Jessie's voice.

Pam spread her arms and struck a pose. "Hello, dahlings," she cooed, batting her eyes. Then she relaxed. "What else would you expect of the drama coach at our beloved Keystone?"

A smiling Ginny hurried toward her. "I'm so glad you're here. I was afraid you weren't coming."

"What? And miss all of this?" Pam gestured to the pool, sparkling in the morning sun, and the lavishly spread buffet table. She could hardly tell Ginny she'd been delayed by a bout of morning sickness, even though Ginny, the upper school counselor, would be more understanding of her predicament than most.

Ginny ushered her toward the beverage table. "You're way behind the rest of us. Would you prefer chardonnay or white zinfandel?"

Pam's stomach did a half-gainer. Fortunately, just beyond her hostess, she spotted Connie Campbell. "Nothing right now, thanks." She waved at Connie, who excused herself and walked toward them.

Pam embraced her closest faculty friend. "Long time no see. How was Canada?" Connie and her husband Jim, the Keystone headmaster, had been married only a short time, and the trans-Canada rail trip had been their first true vacation.

Ginny chuckled. "Don't ask if you don't really want to know. She'll give you an hour's worth of travel information."

"Listen to the woman." Connie affected sternness. "You're just jealous, Ginny, that you were stuck here in simmering Texas all summer."

"That makes two of us," Pam said.

"How *was* your summer session at U.T., by the way?" Connie asked.

You'd be surprised. Really surprised. "Okay. I had a so-so seminar in literary criticism, but a dynamite course in post–World War II American fiction."

Just then the caterer appeared at Ginny's elbow. "Excuse me," Ginny said. "I'm needed in the kitchen. Help yourself to the wine."

Darn. Pam had hoped she'd sidestepped the issue of drinking. Her TGIF buddies Connie and Ginny would be the first to suspect something when she turned down chardonnay. She poured herself a glass of ice water.

"No wine? You must be sick." Connie made a show of laying her palm on Pam's forehead.

"Maybe later. I'm really thirsty from my rush to arrive more or less on time."

"Well, now that you're here, let me introduce you to our new faculty members." She leaned closer. "Is it my imagination, or do they get younger every year?"

Pam raised her eyebrows in mock horror. "Surely it couldn't be that we're getting older?"

Grateful to be led away from the wine and the potential for discovery, Pam circulated through the crowd. Without fail, several colleagues asked her the standard question: "Are you ready for school?" Ready? It would be miraculous if she could overcome her morning sickness each day before her first-period class.

By the time the food was served, Pam had no trouble downing the curried chicken salad, fresh fruit compote and three of the lemony poppy-seed muffins. She refused to feel guilty about her gluttony—she was eating for two, after all. Thankfully no one noticed that water remained her beverage of choice.

Jack Liddy's very pregnant wife, Darla, sat at Pam's table, reveling in talk of babies. "The only problem is that Jack'll be in the middle of football season when Junior makes his appearance. Let's hope I don't deliver on game night."

"Not the best planning, huh?" Carolee Simmons, the French teacher said.

Darla winked mischievously. "You have to do *something* in the off-season, you know."

"Will you be teaching until the baby comes?" Pam asked, as much for herself as because of her interest in Darla.

"I'm trying to make it to the end of the first quarter, then a substitute will take over until I can return at the semester."

Carolee, single herself, leaned forward. "Won't it be hard to leave the baby to come back to work?"

Darla shrugged. "It'll be awful. But what choice do I have? We'll need the money."

Pam pursed her lips. "Occupational hazard of educators.'' She, too, would have no option but to work. Otherwise, how could she afford her condo, car, insurance and day care?

"Anyway," Darla continued, "my doctor says I should be fine by January."

Pam's mouth felt dry. "Who is your doctor?"

"Belinda Ellis. She's wonderful!"

Pam stored the name in her memory. Initially she would have to find a doctor in another part of town, one with no connections to the school—if that was possible. So Dr. Ellis was out. At least for now. Despite the Texas sun, her hands had turned to ice.

When the party broke up, Connie fell in beside Pam as they walked to their cars. "Inquiring minds want to know. Did you meet any interesting men in Austin?"

Pam knew Connie and Ginny worried about her. Each had tried sporadic matchmaking attempts, with disappointing results. Finally she *had* met someone—a man she could happily have followed to the ends of the earth. And she couldn't say one word. Even to her best friend. "Interesting? They were *all* interesting, sexy, and, naturally, hot for li'l ole me."

"Give me a break," Connie said, calling her bluff. "No one?"

Pam opted for a half-truth. "There was one."

"And?"

"He's gone home, I've come home, and that's that."

"No letters? No scheduled visits?"

Pam shrugged. "Nope. The cookie has crumbled, as they say."

Connie laid a comforting hand on Pam's shoulder. "I'm sorry. Someday your prince will come. I just know it."

Well, he'd better hurry the hell up. Pam mustered a

laugh. "Hope springs eternal. See you at the opening faculty meeting?"

"Sure thing. I've told Jim to make the headmaster's address short and sweet."

"Gee, you have that kind of influence?"

"It's amazing what the love of a good woman can accomplish."

Pam hugged Connie, then climbed into her hatchback. Connie was, indeed, a good woman. Before she married Jim, she'd been single for many years, supporting her mother and daughter Erin. If Connie could do it, Pam reasoned, so could she. But Connie hadn't had to give up a job she loved.

With a sinking heart, Pam acknowledged that she herself faced exactly that eventuality.

GRANT PAUSED in the doorway of his sterile classroom, looking at the blank, freshly painted walls, the student desks shoved into the corner, the newly carpeted floor. He crossed to the windows, raised the blinds, then stood, hands on his hips, studying the boxes and rolled posters piled along one wall. Time to tackle decorating his room, if you could dignify what he did by that term.

Tearing open the top box, he began stacking supplementary geometry texts in the built-in bookshelf. Next week teachers' meetings started and he didn't want to wait until the last minute to bring order to his space. Besides, he needed to be organized if Andy came. But that continued to be a big "if." So far, responses to his ads had been discouraging. Few applicants wanted to live-in, and, of those, they either demanded exorbitant wages or had personalities that never in his wildest dreams would be considered adolescent-friendly.

Savagely he attacked the next box. Shelley was pres-

suring him for an answer, and if he didn't find someone
from the ad running this weekend... Surely she
wouldn't follow through on her threat to send Andy to
boarding school. Maybe, since it wasn't basketball season yet, she'd let Andy come whether or not a housekeeper was in place. Doubtless, in a matter of weeks,
he could locate a suitable person.

By the time he arranged his texts between the book-
ends on his desk and finished tacking up the exhibit of
geometric forms on his bulletin board, his stomach was
growling. Taking one last glance at the transformed
classroom, he stepped into the eerily quiet hall and
locked the door behind him.

He ran down the stairs and passed the first-floor office
before becoming aware of music emanating from Pam
Carver's room. He'd thought he was alone in the building, but apparently not. He'd stop by, say hello, find
out about her summer. Pam was one of his favorite co-
workers—devoted to her students, realistic about school
politics, often the voice of reason amid the cacophony
of rumor and complaint and, besides that, fun to be
around. Who else could have talked him into making a
fool of himself annually in the faculty pep skit?

Outside her classroom Grant paused, hearing above
the soft strains of classical music the muffled sounds of
weeping. Her door was ajar. Slowly he eased it open.
Pam sat hunched over her desk, head cradled in her
arms, shoulders shaking. Sure, she taught drama, but
this was way too convincing to be an act. He took a
tentative step forward. "Pam, are you all right?"

Her head shot up, revealing a tear-streaked face.
"G-Grant?" She grabbed a tissue from the box on her
desk and hastily blotted her eyes. "I didn't know anyone else was in the building today." Her voice, usually

warm and vibrant, sounded thin, and he had a sudden urge to protect her.

"I wanted to get my room set up."

"Me, too." She hiccuped, then flung an arm in the direction of the books and boxes piled haphazardly along the far wall. "The summer painting project is wreaking havoc, though. It's been years since I've had to box up my stuff."

"Is that what's upset you?"

She glanced away briefly, before turning back, a watery smile in place. "Stupid, isn't it, to let something so minor throw me."

He watched her mask of bravado slip back into place. He'd bet it would take a whole lot more than a little mess to shake Pam Carver. "I'm willing to help."

"Somehow I can't imagine you draping my bookcases with Indian shawls or putting together a montage for my bulletin board."

He pointed to a stack of cardboard leaning against a file cabinet. "Maybe not, but I can certainly assemble your Globe Theatre replica."

"You've just made me an offer I can't refuse. I never was any good at inserting tab A into slot B."

They worked quietly side by side for half an hour. Every now and then she'd stifle a sigh. Her shoulders, usually held back confidently, sagged periodically, as if she bore a huge weight. He didn't want to pry, but something was going on with her.

She finished with the bulletin board about the same time he put the flag atop the Globe. He stood and faced her. "Feeling better?"

Her eyes were too bright, her smile too brittle. "Much. I needed a little nudge, that's all." She laid a hand on his sleeve. "Sorry if I upset you."

He put an arm around her and snugged her close. "What are colleagues for, anyway? Remember, our school motto is Caring, Character, Curiosity. This was the caring part." Then, struck by a new idea, he laughed. "And curiosity, too, I guess. Pam Carver reduced to tears? I couldn't picture it."

"If you live long enough, you see everything."

Although her tone was light, he had the disturbing sense she was making a joke of something very serious. Then he became aware he still had his arm around her waist, his hand on her hip.

She moved away at the same time he dropped his arm. "Thank you, Grant. I'm fine now. Really."

"Take care, then. See you at Tuesday's meeting?"

"Sure thing." She extended her arms, more like the old Pam, and said, "Let the games begin."

He chuckled at her final remark as he left the school. But gradually his smile faded, replaced by a sadness he couldn't identify. He had always been fond of Pam. Heck, tell the truth. He was attracted to her. But she was like a tropical bird—colorful, flamboyant, dramatic. He'd always figured she'd never go for a plodding, meticulous math teacher who just happened to be tied up several months a year with a high school basketball team.

Driving home, he couldn't shake the feeling that her brave front had been just that. A front. He didn't think she was fine. Not at all.

And he didn't like that. He wanted her to be fine.

PAM BANGED AROUND the small kitchen of her condo, fixing a salad and warming leftover corn bread for dinner. What kind of idiot Grant must think she was! All afternoon she'd replayed the scene in her mind. Why there? Why then? To fall to pieces like some fragile Melanie Wilkes. Unthinkable.

It was the notes that had done it. She'd been rummaging in her desk drawer for the key to her filing cabinet when she'd come across them. She made a habit of saving complimentary correspondence from students and parents. Then on bad days she'd pull them out and read them to remind herself why she loved being a teacher. She'd been okay until she came to Cissy Philbin's scrawled message. Poor Cissy, who struggled to make B's and had been devastated by the death of a sibling and later by her parents' divorce.

"Dear Ms. Carver,
I couldn't have made it through high school without you. You always believed in me and demanded my best. You knew what I was going through and willed me through bad time after bad time. You wouldn't let me quit. Or be a crybaby. You made me believe that like the saying says, there can't be a rainbow without the storm. You are my rainbow. Thank you."

Now, recalling the words, Pam felt a flood of emotion similar to what she'd experienced at school. It wasn't just hormones, although they were certainly doing a number on her. When she'd read Cissy's words, she'd felt a painful void. If she had to quit teaching because of the baby, she wouldn't be there for the Cissys of the world, nor would they be there to infuse her life with purpose and meaning.

Picking up her plate, she moved to the living room couch and turned on the evening news. But she scarcely heard the newscaster. Grant, of all people. They'd worked on faculty committees together. She admired his no-nonsense approach to problems and his well-deserved popularity with the students. Several years ago she'd toyed with the idea of exploring a relationship with him. But they were very different. He was quiet; she was not. He was steady; she was mercurial. Finally she'd concluded it would be foolish to risk a valued friendship in the unlikely search for romance.

Any other time she might have found it comical to watch him sitting on the floor of her classroom, his rangy six-foot-four body hunched over the myriad components of the Globe replica. But today she had studied him intently out of the corner of her eye, noticing how his big hands worked dexterously with the tiny tabs, grateful for his understanding and concern.

After supper she settled on the couch with the book she'd stopped to purchase on her way home. *What to Expect from Your Pregnancy*. She'd had no idea it would be so thick, so full of information. As she read, she found herself almost unconsciously rubbing her palm back and forth across her still-flat stomach and humming along with the *Phantom of the Opera* CD playing in the background.

She was intently studying diagrams of the stages of fetal development when the doorbell rang. She jumped up, curious. She wasn't expecting anyone. She ran a hand through her hair, then stuffed the book under a pillow. At the door she peered through the peephole. Grant?

She undid the chain and unlocked the dead bolt before easing the door open. He loomed above her, his eyes twinkling, his mouth quirked in a grin. "You're probably wondering what I'm doing here, right?"

She held the door open wider, by way of welcome.

"It had crossed my mind. I would think you'd had enough of me for one day."

"Apparently not. May I come in?"

"Of course." She ushered him inside, then pointed at the only easy chair in the room. "Have a seat. Can I get you anything? A soda? Iced tea? Sorry, but I'm out of beer." *And will be for nine months.*

"A soda would be fine." When he followed her into the kitchen, the room seemed to shrink.

She took her time at the refrigerator, bewildered. Grant Gilbert had never been to her home. Why was he here tonight? When she turned back, he was leaning over the counter, his chin propped in his hands, studying her. Maybe it was because they were at eye level, but she'd never noticed before what gentle blue eyes he had. Or how his short, wavy brown hair was silvering just a bit above his ears. Flustered, she handed him a Sprite and watched him pour it over the ice. Then with the grace of a born athlete, he moved back to the living room and eased into the armchair.

She sat back down on the sofa, then decided to get to the heart of the matter. "About this morning—"

He waved his hand in dismissal. "I'm glad I could help with the theater. Were you able to get your room finished?"

Had he deliberately misinterpreted to help her save face? "Finished? You know better than that. My room is a constant work in progress."

"Speaking of works in progress, I'd like your advice about one of my own. That's one reason I came over."

One reason? Were there others? "How can I help?"

As he talked, he slowly rotated the glass between his palms, every now and then pausing to see if she was following him. The need in his eyes was apparent as he explained how much he wanted to have his son with him for the year. Pam had had no idea his ex-wife was such a bitch, nor that she had made it so difficult for Grant to be with his son. "...so I'm desperate. I'm asking everyone I know if they can recommend somebody. Anybody."

She smiled. "Not just anybody, I hope."

He shrugged, then grinned ruefully.

She thought for a moment. "Have you contacted area colleges? There might be an older woman going back to school who would need some extra income."

He brightened. "I hadn't thought of that. It's worth a try. Finding a qualified person within my budget will be a problem."

Like having a baby within my budget. "I can imagine." Although he had obviously accomplished what he came to do, he didn't seem inclined to leave. In truth, she found his presence welcome.

They sat quietly for a few moments. "Nice music," he said. "What show is that?"

She told him.

"I like show tunes, but I'm more of a jazz buff myself. Vintage Erroll Garner is about as good as it gets."

The longer they talked, the more she relaxed, even enjoyed herself. Usually all colleagues wanted to talk about was school, but Keystone hadn't been mentioned since the beginning of their conversation. She was delighted to discover he enjoyed movies as much as she did and was something of an expert on Jack Nicholson. They disagreed on whether Anthony Hopkins should make a third Hannibal Lecter appearance, but both thought *Schindler's List* was a work of genius.

"And all along, you probably assumed I was just a dumb jock," Grant joshed.

"No telling what you think of me. An artsy, impulsive broad, maybe?"

"Don't put words into my mouth." He stood and placed his empty glass on the kitchen divider. Then, to her surprise, he sat down next to her. Not too close, but definitely not at the other end of the sofa. "Pam, I had another reason for dropping by."

Something shifted in the vicinity of her stomach. "Oh?"

He bent one leg and stretched his arm along the back of the couch so he could face her. "Those tears this morning? I don't think they had much to do with a messy room."

His sensitivity nearly did her in. She owed him some kind of answer. "I have...things going on in my life right now. Things I can't talk about. Not yet." She looked into his eyes. "It's not just you. I can't talk about them with anyone. They're...very personal."

"I respect that. But whatever is upsetting you, maybe I can help. You don't have to go it alone."

Oh, but I do. "Thank you. That means a lot." She didn't know what to say next, how to break the thread of intimacy his offer had woven. Fortunately she didn't have long to worry about it. The ringing phone saved her. Quickly excusing herself, she took the call in the kitchen. It was her widowed father in West Texas, who phoned her nearly every Saturday night. She loved him for the gesture. Undoubtedly he thought his call made her feel less dateless, less lonely.

After concluding her conversation, Pam returned to the living room, surprised to find Grant standing, his hands behind his back. "That was my father. He—" She faltered, the perplexed expression on his face stopping her in her tracks. She stared at him, confused.

He took a step toward her. "I—I was looking for the TV remote. You know, to catch the ball scores." Slowly he brought his hands in front of him. "And I found this instead." He held up the book she'd hidden beneath the sofa pillow.

The walls whirled and his voice seemed to be coming from a great distance.

"Pam, you're not just doing research, are you?"

There was no turning away from the question, nor from the compassion in his eyes. "No." Helpless, she felt tears threatening once more. She gulped, then, for the first time, whispered the words aloud. "I'm pregnant."

CHAPTER TWO

WHERE THE HELL was Ann Landers when a guy needed her? Grant stared at Pam, questions racing through his head. Carefully he set the book on the arm of the sofa and moved toward her. "That's good news, er, isn't it?"

She lowered her eyes, standing before him defenseless and vulnerable. "Yes," she said quietly. "Just wonderful."

The hitch in her voice tugged at him. "Come here." Before he could stop to think, he had wrapped her close, cradling her head against his chest.

He held her for long minutes, feeling her shoulders tremble beneath his hand, listening to the muted sounds of her weeping. She had to be scared to death. How could this have happened? Pam was smart, savvy. She had to know where babies came from.

He scanned her living room, desperately trying to focus on something besides the feminine body pressed against him. Okay, two cats reclining on the window ledge, books piled randomly in the bookcase, a baker's rack crowded with candles and figurines, multihued pillows everywhere and an eclectic collection of prints and pictures on her walls. Nothing matched, but it was somehow…homey. Comfortable. The same way she felt in his arms.

The faint citrus scent of her hair and the way her

cheek nestled against him stirred a surprising hunger. *Gilbert, don't be a jerk. The last thing this woman needs is you coming on to her.*

He stepped back then and tilted her chin so he could look at her. "Are you okay?"

She ran her hands down his arms, then, clutching his wrists, ducked her head. "I'm sorry. Tears are stupid. They don't accomplish a thing." She let go, then turned away from him. "Two times in one day. That must be something of a record for you."

"Probably, but who's counting?"

"I promise not to make it three."

"Sure? Third time's the charm, you know."

"There isn't any charm to help with this."

What did a guy say to that? He led her back to the couch, then wrapped a purple mohair throw around her. "Sit down and let me fix you a cup of tea. That was my mother's solution to everything."

"It can't hurt. Tea's on the top shelf of the pantry." Almost without seeming to notice what she was doing, she picked up the baby book but didn't open it, her fingers tracing a path around the edges of the cover.

While he waited for the water to boil, Grant paced, considering his options. Should he keep his big mouth shut? Or ask the tough questions? Like where the father was. Who he was. There had to be a rational explanation for this bombshell. He was no dummy, he'd read about the biological clock. Maybe she'd deliberately gotten pregnant. But then what about her job? Talk about an awkward, potentially litigious situation.

The whistling kettle startled him. He was in way over his head. He hadn't a clue how to help her.

When he presented her with the steaming cup of tea, she took two dainty sips before setting it on the antique trunk that served as a coffee table. Then she gave him a wan smile. "Your mother was right."

Holding his cup and saucer carefully, he lowered himself into the easy chair. And waited. A car horn sounded outside; inside, the ticking of a wall clock created a hypnotic rhythm. The bigger cat, a black one with white spots, leaped from the window ledge and hopped into Pam's lap and curled into a ball.

"Who's your buddy?"

"This is Sebastian." She nodded toward the window. "And that's Viola. They were littermates."

Cat names had always struck him as pretentious. He was a dog man himself. Dogs had forthright names like Buster and Max. "Where'd you get those handles?"

"The bard. Viola and Sebastian are the sister and brother in *Twelfth Night*."

"Oh." Shakespeare. It figured. If he ever had a cat, God forbid, did that mean he should call it Euclid?

They sat in silence, slowly drinking the tea. She appeared lost in thought, but finally looked up. "I'm scared."

That was an admission he'd never have anticipated from the Pam Carver he knew. "You don't need to tell me, if—"

"It's time I talked to somebody, and it looks like you're elected."

"You can trust me, Pam."

"I do."

Her sincerity touched him. "Is there a man in the picture? Are you planning to marry?"

"No man." Then she gave a short, derisive laugh. "Obviously there *was* one. But marriage isn't an option."

Grant was confused by his reaction. How could he be relieved to hear that? "Does he know?"

"No. And he's not going to."

"Is that fair? Maybe he would want to be involved. Help."

"Please." Her eyes begged. "You'll have to take my word for it. I'm in this by myself. For good."

The enormity of her predicament was hard to imagine. "It'll be tough being a single mother. I'm sure you've thought of that. Have you considered...you know...?"

Her cheeks flamed. "That's not an option. I want this baby very much. This may be my only chance to become a mother. You've surely noticed I'm not getting any younger." The edge in her voice cut off any inept, glib response. "So I simply have to figure out where to go from here."

"Does anyone else know?"

"No. And I don't plan for them to until it has to come out." She drew the throw closer around her shoulders. "I'll have to resign then."

That would really be a blow for her. She was a born teacher, but schools—especially private schools—couldn't overlook what might be viewed as "immoral" behavior. And Keystone? For the second time that day, the school motto came to him. Caring, Character, Curiosity. Jim Campbell, the headmaster, was big on character, but even if he found a way to ease Pam's situation, would the trustees go for an unmarried, pregnant English department chairman? Pam was in a no-win situation. "Jeez, I suppose you're right. What then?"

She looked directly at him. "I don't know. I wish I did." She crossed her arms over her stomach, as if protecting her womb. "But I'll tell you one thing." Her voice held the old spark. "I will do whatever I must to love and support this baby."

"You've got guts." Pam had always been a fighter. She'd need to be now.

"I figure I'll be able to make it at school until Thanksgiving, at least. That should give me time to line up some other type of work."

"Have you seen a doctor?"

"I'm not very far along. Except for morning sickness, I feel fine. I'll try to locate a doctor this week. One that has nothing to do with Keystone School." She reached for her cup, then took several sips. "I'm sorry to burden you with this."

He rose to his feet. "It's no burden." He picked up his cup and saucer and carried them to the kitchen divider, then returned to her. "You're brave. You'll manage." He stood awkwardly, feeling helpless. "What about your family? Can they help?"

"Not really. My mother's dead. My father and I are very close." She ducked her head. "He'll be disappointed in me at first."

He waited.

Then she looked up. "But he'll love this baby."

"I'm sure he will. What about sisters? Brothers?"

"One sister. I can forget about any help from her."

The uncharacteristic bitterness surprised him, especially in light of the bond he and his brother Brian had shared. "Why's that?"

"We rarely see each other. I think it's safe to say Barbara doesn't have much use for me. She has her life in California with her dentist husband and her three children. For as long as I can remember, she's made it clear I'm the baby sister who made her life miserable. Never mind that we're grown-ups now. Supposedly."

He identified with the hurt in her voice. He knew from his own father and from Shelley what rejection felt like.

She placed Sebastian gently on the floor and stood. "If you don't mind, I'd like to be alone now."

Every instinct said, *hug her,* but instead he nodded his head. "I understand."

She accompanied him to the door. "Thank you for coming. It helps just knowing I can talk to someone if I need to."

He hesitated in the doorway, admiring the way she stood tall, determined, as if she could take on the world. "Call on me anytime if there's something I can do."

"I will."

He studied her coppery hair, her wide hazel eyes, her full lips—as if he'd never seen them before. She was not only courageous, she was beautiful. "Good night," he finally managed, turning to leave.

"Good night. And, Grant?"

He paused. "Yes?"

"The father is a good person. I knew what I was doing. But accidents happen." She studied the floor and he knew she was going to say something more. Finally she raised her eyes. "But this is the last time you or anyone else will hear me refer to this precious child as an 'accident.'"

Then she came closer, stood on her toes and kissed him on the cheek. "Thanks for being my friend. Now, go," she said, gently nudging him in the small of his back.

He stood on her walkway long after she had closed the door. The night was warm, and above him a nearly full moon was on the rise, the stars hidden beyond the city lights. The universe was as it eternally had been, its orbits fixed.

But something—Pam—had knocked him out of his.

HOLDING THE BASKETBALL in the crook of his arm, Brady Showalter gaped toward the azure swimming pool, bordered by palm trees swaying in the Florida breeze. "Your mom's a fox."

Andy Gilbert shot his friend a disgusted look. "So?"

"It's cool, that's all. My mom, all she wears are these dumpy-looking pantsuits. And I don't even wanna tell you about her swimsuit."

Andy knew what Brady meant. His friend's mother wasn't the hottest babe he'd ever seen. Still, it was embarrassing to have your own mother parading around the pool in her bikini, kinda like she was deliberately showing off her bod for his buddies. "Gimme the ball."

Brady bounced it to him and Andy feinted, then lofted a shot that whistled through the hoop. Diving after the rebound, he whirled and went in for a layup. "Four points!" he crowed.

"You gonna play basketball in Texas?"

Andy banged the ball off the backboard. "You gotta be kidding. Play for my father? No way in hell." What was with Brady? He oughta know the last subject in the world Andy wanted to discuss was this freakin' move to Fort Worth! It was bad enough he couldn't stay here where—finally—he would've been eligible to try out for the varsity. But play for his dad? No way.

"You're weird, Gilbert." Brady stole the ball from him and darted to the basket.

Andy stood, rooted. *Weird.* That was the truth. His whole life was weird. Mom was running off to some stupid foreign country with Harry, the biggest dork so far of Mom's boyfriends. Which was saying something. Harry had a gut-busting paunch, fuzzy gray chest hair and a pinkie ring like some Mafia mobster. And he insisted on calling Andy "Sonny." Like in "Hey, Sonny, how's it goin', big guy?"

"Andy? You wanna play or not?" Brady held the ball in front of his chest, waiting to pass off.

"Nah, I'm going inside. Mom's been on my case. I gotta start organizing my stuff."

"For the move, you mean?"

"Yeah. So I'll see you later."

"Here." Brady tossed him the ball. "Call me if you wanna go with the guys to crash Liz's slumber party."

"Okay." Andy dribbled angrily along the sidewalk to the back door of the house—the third one he'd lived in in two years. What was the point of going with Brady tonight? He'd never see any of these kids again after next week. Oh, no. He had to go live with his dad, Coach Cheeseball of Keystone School. The father who'd walked out when he was three.

What did Dad know about him, really? Maybe he'd squeezed in some visits between teaching, coaching and running basketball camps, but it wasn't like they ever spent any length of time together. Dad had never once made it to one of his basketball games.

His mom kept telling him just to forget about it. "He's devoted to that school, Andy. You have to understand. Everything else comes second. Maybe it's better this way. Just you and me, sweetie." Yeah, you and me and whatever dickhead was after Mom. He didn't want to go to the friggin' United Arab Emirates and he sure as hell didn't want to go to Fort Worth. But did he have a choice? No, he was just the kid. The victim.

He slammed the back door on his way to his room. Divorce sucked.

GRANT USHERED the smilingly officious woman out the front door, closed it and sagged against it, the headache he'd had all day continuing to play racquetball against his temples. How many applicants was this? Seven? Two who spoke minimal English, one who smoked like a chimney and had insisted she be allowed to bring her bulldog with her, two who claimed they'd had no idea he actually expected them to stay over the weekends, and one—the only real possibility—who wouldn't be available until at least November.

He walked toward the kitchen, wiping his palms on his pants, aware of a buzzing in his ears and an uncomfortable shift in his stomach. He was running out of ideas, and he had to let Shelley know something by Friday. Before the upcoming Labor Day weekend. Because, if all went well, Andy would arrive Labor Day evening. And school started the day after.

But all wasn't going well. He'd interviewed everyone who'd applied through the agency or the newspaper ad. Texas Christian University and U.T. at Arlington had both been dry holes. So where did that leave him?

Desperate.

He reached in one of the cupboards and pulled out the aspirin bottle, shook out two tablets and chased them with a glass of water. He had so much riding on this year with Andy. Although he knew he couldn't make up for all the time he'd missed, he hoped to God they could build their relationship. The boy needed a family. Stability.

A family. It had all been so promising in the beginning. Sure, he and Shelley had been young and naive, but when Andy was born, he'd been certain they could raise a fine son, have more children. Live happily ever after.

But that hadn't happened. He could never please Shelley. And Andy, poor kid, had been the one who'd suffered most. Damn.

Grant had to do something. He couldn't let this opportunity pass him by.

A family. More than anything, that's what Andy needed.

Prickles cascaded down Grant's spine. A hammering sensation reverberated in his chest. No. It was a crazy idea.

Lunacy.

Grant raked both hands through his hair. But if...?

Pros and cons rocketed through his brain. He shook his head. "Crazy" didn't even begin to get it.

Somewhere outside a neighbor's dog barked. The air-conditioner compressor cranked on. But Grant didn't move. Maybe, just maybe, it could work.

He turned and grabbed his car keys from the counter and, before he could reconsider, strode toward the garage.

Hell, what did he have to lose?

PAM SAT on her living room floor, the multiple pages of her senior English syllabus spread all around her. Collating was hard work when Viola and Sebastian insisted on regarding the papers as playthings. Finally she'd had to close the cats in the utility room. She compiled one complete set, tamped it on the coffee table, then stapled it. As she gathered the next sheets, she deliberately avoided looking at the headings, especially those for second semester. It hurt too much to realize that someone else would be teaching the Romantic poets, Thomas Hardy and Wilfred Owen.

Sorting and stapling, she mentally reviewed her search through the Sunday want ads. There were openings for secretaries, of course, and receptionists. She'd thought about real estate, but what would she live on while she took the licensing course and established her clientele? College teaching might be a possibility, but openings were scarce.

She sighed. Tomorrow teachers' meetings started. And after that when would she have time to follow up on job opportunities? She'd read in the pregnancy book that the lethargy she was experiencing was common in the first trimester. How ironic that when she most needed her energy, she was so bummed out.

She scooped up the collated syllabi and got to her feet, feeling oddly top-heavy. Eventually she'd have to tell her father she was pregnant. Although he might not approve, she knew he'd stand by her. That's just the way he was. She smiled fondly. He'd be the greatest grandpa. Soft-spoken Will Carver had a heart as big as the West Texas skies.

In fact, it would be far easier to tell him than her sister, twelve years older than she and impossibly narrow-minded and sanctimonious.

Barbara, who'd always blamed her for their mother's death. No doubt her sister had suffered a devastating loss at an impressionable age. But Pam had never understood how she could continue to hold an infant responsible for the difficult delivery, the hemorrhage, the loss. Barbara had, though, apparently steeling herself against any show of affection for her baby sister. Finally Pam had had to make up her mind not to let her sister's indifference matter. But it still hurt. Big time.

Overwhelmed with helplessness, Pam set the syllabi on the counter. She'd never know the comfort of a mother's love and advice during this pregnancy. Or a sister's.

Maybe it would be a blessing when her condition became known. She hated hiding things. Perhaps from her friends would come the support Barbara couldn't give. Above all, Pam didn't want the baby to suffer—not from lack of affection and certainly not from stigma. Whatever it took, she'd protect this child.

She liberated the cats from the utility room, then changed out of her jeans into her pajamas. She wanted to get to bed early. She'd need all her strength for the teachers' meetings tomorrow—and for the days ahead.

Curling up on the sofa with a copy of the English lit text, she yawned as she reread—as she did each fall—the introduction to the first unit of study. Keeping her eyes open was a challenge, and the book slid out of her lap.

When the doorbell rang, she reared up, looking around dazedly. What? Who? Had she fallen asleep? The bell pealed again.

She tiptoed to the door, amazed to find Grant Gilbert standing outside. Again? She reached for the robe lying on the back of the sofa and, glancing in the hall mirror to be sure she was presentable, opened the door.

Whatever Grant had intended to say had been lost apparently. "Oh. I...I'm sorry. You were in bed? I'd better leave."

She checked her watch. It was only eight-fifteen. "I was planning an early evening, but not this early. Please come in."

He hesitated. "You're sure? I don't want to intrude. I should've called first."

She hid a smile. It amused her to see the normally self-possessed Grant flustered. She resisted the impulse to take his face between her hands and tell him it was all right. "Please. Come in."

When he stepped across the threshold, Viola emerged from under the couch and twined herself between his feet, purring audibly. The look on his face was priceless. Pam chuckled. "You're not much of a cat lover?"

"Does that make me a bad person?" His features relaxed into a sheepish grin.

"Not exactly. But you'll have to demonstrate other redeeming qualities."

He studied Viola, who refused to budge. "I would if I could move."

Scooping up Viola and cuddling her, Pam settled cross-legged into the armchair. "There. You're free. Have a seat and tell me what brings you out on D-Day eve."

"D-Day?" He plopped onto the sofa. "The invasion doesn't really start until next Tuesday when the students show up."

"Okay, then. D-Day minus seven." Despite the bantering, he seemed uncomfortable, crossing and recrossing his legs, then stretching them out in front of him, his arms spread-eagled along the back of the couch.

"Did you get to the doctor?"

"Not yet, but I will. Soon."

"It's important to take care of yourself."

For some reason, he seemed nervous, plucking the sofa fabric between his thumb and index finger. Surely he hadn't come over merely to inquire about her health. "How's the interviewing coming?"

"You don't want to know. 'Disaster' about sums it

up. Nannies expect babies, not a hormone-driven fifteen-year-old.''

She leaned forward, clutching her knees. "So what are you going to do?''

''Throw myself on Shelley's mercy, I guess. Unless...'' He shifted his weight and turned to look directly at her.

''Unless what?''

''I don't quite know how to suggest this.''

''Spit it out, that's how.''

He rose to his feet. ''Nah, it's a crazy idea. I don't know what I was thinking.''

She went to him and guided him back to the sofa, then settled beside him. ''Get it off your chest, Gilbert.''

''I didn't want to do it like this.'' He looked miserable.

''Do what?''

He lifted her hand, studying her fingers, then said in a hoarse voice, ''Propose.''

Her ears echoed with the word—a preposterous word. *Propose?* ''Come again?'' She leaned forward to be sure she had heard correctly.

''I should get on my knees, present you with a rose or something,'' he went on lamely. ''Isn't that how it's done?''

She held up her hand, as if asking for a time-out. ''Wait a minute. Are you actually suggesting we get married?''

''I told you it was a crazy idea.'' His shoulders slumped. ''But I thought maybe we could work out some sort of arrangement. You need a father for your baby, I need a housekeeper. I know it wouldn't be easy, but...''

Chaotic thoughts whirled in Pam's head. "Marriage? That's a pretty extreme solution."

"It was just a thought."

For one idiotic moment Pam actually considered the idea. "Why would you be willing to marry me?"

"You'd be a great influence on Andy. Not a housekeeper, really. But Shelley would be off my case. Besides, if we were married, you could keep your job and you'd have a name for your baby's birth certificate."

She sat speechless, skeptical, but helpless to ignore the benefits of his idea. Marriage was sacred. It was about much more than mutual convenience.

"We're friends," he continued.

"That's a start," she conceded.

"I'm suggesting a kind of open-ended arrangement, but it would help me out if we could agree to live together for at least a year. After that, Andy'll go back to his mother. So, come September, we can terminate our formal relationship. You know, we can—"

"Divorce?"

"Yes."

"I don't know, Grant. It's a drastic step." Just then, he put his arm around her shoulder. The embrace made her feel warm, protected—and unexpectedly fluttery, like when she was in junior high and the boy she had had a crush on smiled at her.

"It would be what we make of it."

She looked up into his eyes, so serious yet hopeful. "Even if I were to entertain the notion, how would we ever carry it off?"

"You're the drama teacher. The imaginative one. Surely we could think of something." He massaged the sore spot between her shoulders as he went on speaking.

"Somehow we'd have to convince everyone at school that we're so in love we acted on impulse."

"What do you mean?

"It would make sense for us to be married this weekend. Before school starts. Before Andy comes. We could pass it off as a whirlwind courtship."

"But...but..."

"You're right, they'd suspect. It's not like we have a dating history." His hand stilled on her back.

"Weren't you here in town all summer?" She couldn't help herself. She was actually playing out the scenario in her mind.

"No. I attended a three-week coaches' clinic in Austin the end of July and the beginning of August."

Pam studied the ceiling, wondering why fate was playing into their hands when she desperately needed a reason to say no. "I was there, too," she said quietly.

"In Austin?"

"For summer school."

He smiled for the first time since he'd arrived on her doorstep. "Do you think we might have fallen in love there?"

Her heart thudded. "It's possible," she found herself whispering.

"I don't want you to think I'm using you. I would never do that. I would genuinely welcome your baby for whatever time we're together. In fact, if the kid needs a father—" He stopped as if he'd realized he was presuming too much. "I mean, well, my name would be on the birth certificate."

Pam studied his face—the plane of his cheeks, the set of his mouth, the depth in his eyes. Implicitly she knew he would never hurt her or her baby. Outlandish as it was, his offer was tempting. A momentary panic fluttered in her stomach. She needed time. "You've given me a lot to consider."

He smiled. "Then you're not rejecting the proposal outright?"

"I should." She took a deep breath. "But I can't."

"If we're to pull this off, we don't have much time."

"I know."

"Tomorrow evening, then?"

Twenty-four hours to make a life-altering decision? Impossible. "Okay."

He nodded thoughtfully, then excused himself. She trailed him to the door, her emotions in turmoil. Before leaving, he paused to say one last thing. "I would take good care of you, Pam." Then he was gone.

She wandered back to the sofa, pulling the throw around her as a shield against all the doubts, anxieties, questions.

She had some serious thinking to do. Fast.

CHAPTER THREE

THE ONCOMING HEADLIGHTS, the flashing neon of fast-food joints, the intricacies of traffic—none of it penetrated. Grant drove more by instinct than conscious action. Had he made an utter mess of things? What had seemed like a reasonable, if somewhat far-out suggestion an hour ago now could be categorized as sheer idiocy. Although he'd wanted to help Pam, too, she had to interpret his proposal as self-serving. And it was.

But not entirely for the obvious reasons.

The idea appealed to him on another level, one he wasn't yet ready to put into words. He'd dated lots of women since his divorce, one or two rather seriously. But none had been as fascinating to him as Pam, who embraced life and didn't give a darn what other people thought.

Turning onto his street, he tried viewing his neighborhood as Pam might. An older section of town with taller trees, these few blocks were in the process of making a comeback. Most of the houses, like his two-story, had been rehabbed by young professionals interested in preservation and renovation. A few, though, bore signs of neglect—fading paint, overgrown yards, seedy porch furniture. Would she be willing to move into his home? He hadn't even mentioned that restriction, but Andy needed the yard and neighborhood, not a cramped condominium. And what about the sleeping arrangements? Swerving at the last minute to avoid a neighbor kid's bike abandoned in the gutter, he pulled into his driveway.

Sleeping arrangements? A sudden image of Pam's smooth, rosy-hued skin and full breasts unnerved him. He was a red-blooded male, for Pete's sake. Could he withstand the temptation? There was a vast difference between being a husband in name only and the real McCoy.

He parked the car and sat brooding. Was he nuts? He was acting as if this was a done deal when, in fact, Pam had to be wondering if he'd lost his mind. Heck, he was wondering that himself.

Well, the die was cast. He walked toward the house, experiencing the same kind of jitters he felt before a crucial game. While he was still unlocking the back door, he heard the phone. He caught it on the fourth ring. "Hello?"

"Where have you been? I've been trying to reach you for over an hour."

Typical Shelley, always diving right in. No pleasantries. "I'm home now." Darned if his whereabouts were any of her business. Especially tonight.

"We need to talk about Andy. Are we all set?"

"I think so." He took a deep breath. "But I may have a delay on this end."

"Delay?" With her emphasis, she managed to convey both incredulity and exasperation. "What delay?"

"I'll have someone, but she may not be in residence right when Andy comes."

"We have an agreement, you know."

"I know, but surely a few days won't matter. It's important that Andy begin school with the others. Basketball practice for me doesn't start until mid-October, so I'll be around to supcrvise him.''

"Grant, don't you be pulling a fast one."

Ordinarily he'd resent the hell out of that remark, but is that what he was doing? Pulling a fast one? "Like you, Shelley, I have Andy's best interests at heart."

"I certainly hope so." He could hear her long fingernails rat-a-tatting on the receiver. "All right, then. But as soon as you employ a housekeeper, I expect you to give me and my attorney the particulars—her name, social security number, and so on."

For the first time since Grant had entertained the wild hope that Pam would accept his offer, he had an admittedly unworthy thought. He'd sacrifice a first-place finish in the prep league to see Shelley's face when he told her his housekeeper just happened to be his wife. "I'll be in touch." He pulled a kitchen stool close and sat down. "Is Andy there? Could I speak to him?"

He waited for what seemed a long time while Shelley went to find their son. When Andy finally picked up, Grant could hear the frantic beat of a rap tune in the background. "Andy?"

"Yeah."

"It's Dad. How're you doing, buddy?"

"Okay, I guess."

"Looking forward to the move?"

"Oh, yeah, I'm jumping through hoops."

So that's how it was. "It's gotta be tough, leaving your friends and all."

Nothing.

"I think you'll like Keystone, once you get used to it. I'm really looking forward to having you live with me this year."

"Well, I have to stay somewhere."

Like Fort Worth was the last alternative. "I'm glad that 'somewhere' is with me."

"Whatever."

Andy wasn't going to let his father slip easily into his life. Hopefully things would be better when they could communicate face-to-face. Grant had dealt with surly, unhappy kids before, but the challenge was different when it was your own son. Could he rise to it? He had to. He might never have another chance. They talked then about the arrangements for meeting at the airport. Finally there didn't seem to be anything further to say. "Good night, son."

"See ya."

Grant hung up. Pam had to say yes. For so many reasons. Not the least of which was how lonely and helpless he felt.

TUESDAY MORNING the Student Council officers, the boys dressed in crisp khakis and sport shirts and the girls in sleeveless sundresses, greeted the teachers as they slowly filtered into the cafeteria for the coffee-and-doughnut reception preceding the kickoff faculty meeting. Pam stopped to chat with Brittany Thibault, the StuCo secretary, who had been in her junior English class last year.

"Can you believe it?" The girl gestured to the other officers. "We're actually seniors."

Pam smiled. "Yes, I can believe it. The faculty's expecting great things from you."

"We won't let you down."

"Good. I'm counting on a nice, easy year." At least at school. It was a cinch nothing else in her life would qualify as easy.

Connie caught up with her at the food line. "You're

in luck, Pam. They've got your gooey doughnuts with those disgusting sprinkles,'' she said, reaching for a maple stick.

Pam eyed her favorite confection and realized that the nauseating whiff of freshly brewed coffee was upending her stomach. ''I've eaten, so I'll settle for an apple.'' She plucked the piece of fruit from a tray and bypassed the coffee.

Connie stirred a packet of sugar substitute into her own coffee. ''What's up with you, caffeine addict?''

Pam waved her fingers airily. ''Didn't I tell you? I'm on a health kick. All those veggie, whole-grain restaurants in Austin convinced me.'' Surely that inspired explanation would satisfy Connie, because nothing right now sounded more purely revolting than black coffee.

''Gee, we'll have to be careful in the future about letting you out without a keeper. No coffee? That's practically sacrilege.''

Pam chomped down on the apple. ''But think how healthy I'll be.''

After ten minutes of chitchat, Jim Campbell stepped to the microphone and asked everyone to take a seat. Out of the corner of her eye Pam saw Grant enter with a group of coaches. Why had she never noticed him before? Really noticed. He was by far the best-looking. He was the same tall, attractive, loose-limbed man he'd always been, but this morning she reacted to him in an entirely different and disturbing way. A physical way.

Before she could process that reaction, Jim Campbell began his opening remarks. He was a good speaker, mixing humor with motivational anecdotes. But today she couldn't concentrate on a word he was saying. A single thought kept drumming in her brain. Grant Gilbert was willing to marry her.

Looking around the room at her colleagues and the self-important Student Council officers, she was moved by a wave of love, nostalgia and regret that tripped her breath. How could she leave all of this?

But people don't get married to fulfill a bargain. She'd lain awake until the wee hours of the morning considering what was best for her child. If Grant was willing to give the baby his name, how could she refuse? Yet the logistics were overwhelming. How could they live together with Andy? Convince their friends and colleagues that they'd had a mad summer romance culminating in an elopement? And then carry on the charade every day for a year under intense scrutiny? She was a good actress, but this was an impossible role.

She studied Grant's profile. And what about him? He was candor personified. Such duplicity wasn't in his nature. They'd be discovered. And never mind that Andy sounded like anything but the ideal teenager. She wasn't afraid of that, exactly, but he was a big unknown in the equation.

No, it was too complicated, too devious, too desperate.

Then she thought about the tiny person growing in her womb. Who was she kidding? Was there such a thing as "too desperate"?

GRANT COULDN'T HELP HIMSELF. The first thing he did when he entered the cafeteria was scope out the room for Pam. She was sitting next to Connie Campbell, her face animated. From his vantage point, no one would guess Pam was weighed down by vital decisions.

Grant moved toward an empty row of seats near the podium. Just in time. Jim Campbell had begun his address—the usual welcomes and platitudes about having a great year—but Grant had difficulty concentrating. All he could think about was his offer to Pam. Had expediency overwhelmed reason? Had he crossed some line between right and wrong?

Finally Jim's words penetrated. ''…and so I urge you to give equal attention—or more—to the kids in your classes who, let's face it, try your patience. There's an old saying, 'Children need love most when they seem not to deserve it.' It's easy to single out and enjoy the friendly, cooperative, motivated youngster. But as teachers, we have to go further. The boys and girls who need us most are often least capable of reaching out. They feel unappreciated, alienated, lonely. So here's my challenge to you for the coming year. Reach out to your students—all of them—so not one leaves us at the end of the day feeling ignored or unworthy.''

Grant shifted uncomfortably. Jim's remarks were hitting way too close to home. Parents could heed his words, as well. Is that how Andy felt? Alienated? Unappreciated? Would one year be enough to make a difference in their relationship?

He turned slightly in his chair to glance at Pam. She was staring at her lap, her shiny hair obscuring her face. Was it fair to burden her with his problems? Marriage was a huge step. Was he trying to kill a wasp with an atom bomb? Beside him Jack Liddy coughed. Sitting here, surrounded by his co-workers and friends, Grant felt truly crummy. How could he ever have entertained the idea of deceiving so many who trusted him? Sure, he wanted to help Pam. No infant deserved to come into the world with the label ''illegitimate.'' But he'd insinuated his own situation with Andy into her life. That wasn't fair.

With a sick feeling in the pit of his stomach, he made

a decision. His "solution" sucked. They'd have to find another way.

The meeting broke up shortly, and he managed to locate Pam in the hallway on her way to a department meeting. He fell in beside her. "Could we meet for dinner tonight?" Up close, he noticed the dark shadows under her eyes, the uncharacteristic paleness of her complexion. He felt like a cad. His proposition had probably led to a sleepless night for her, as it had for him.

She continued walking, looking straight ahead. "If we make it early."

"How's six? I'll pick you up. Maybe I'll show off my barbecue skills." Home would be good. They certainly didn't need to have their discussion in a public venue.

She paused outside her classroom and looked up at him. "Okay. We do need to get some things straight."

He was drawn into the amber depths of her eyes and realized belatedly that he needed to say something. "Yes, we do. I'm afraid—"

"Is this where the English department meeting is?" A young man who looked scarcely old enough to shave paused in the doorway. "I'm Randy Selves, the new journalism teacher."

"Yes, please go on in." Pam shrugged apologetically. "Sorry, Grant, but I need—"

"No problem. See you tonight." He watched her adopt a professional face and turn to address her department members.

He headed down the corridor toward the math meeting, for once not caring that he'd be late. Pam deserved the best. A man who would love and honor her.

His proposal had been ill-conceived. Unworthy of

her. But at least he'd figured that out before he made a huge mistake.

GRANT HAD BEEN ten minutes late to pick her up, but that had suited Pam fine. She'd laid out three different outfits, but none of them worked. They were too frilly or too loud or too...something. Then her hair decided to have a mind of its own. Finally in desperation, she'd pulled on purple crinkle-cloth slacks and the matching boat-necked caftan top, knotted her hair on top of her head, put in big gold hoop earrings and called it good. All the while, though, she'd wondered why she was going to such trouble. After all, Grant saw her every day at school. What difference did it make how she looked tonight?

Her attempts at small talk in the car had gone nowhere. He had seemed unusually preoccupied, though that was understandable given the nature of the serious conversation looming ahead of them.

"Here it is. My neighborhood." He glanced at her, apparently expecting some sort of reaction.

"I love it when people rehab these beautiful older areas. There's much more individuality and artistic expression in these homes. I've never been a cookie-cutter subdivision kind of person. I bought my condo because it was the one thing close to school I could afford."

"I needed a yard for the rare occasions when Andy visits. Although I had to do a lot of painting and refinishing, the basic structure of the house is sound." He slowed in front of a two-story brick home with a full front porch and a detached garage. "Here we are."

Tall trees shaded the yard and a hardy arborvitae hedge obscured the foundation. He pulled in the driveway beside the kitchen door.

"Aha! I knew it. There it is." She pointed toward the backyard, half of which was devoted to a large concrete patio with a basketball hoop at the far end.

He chuckled. "What'd you expect? This way, when I miss a shot, I'm not visible from the street."

"You? Miss a shot?" She poked him playfully. "Your secret's safe with me."

He ushered her to a chaise longue near the grill and excused himself. When he returned, he carried a glass of lemonade for her and a beer for himself. "I guess you're off alcohol now?"

"Yes, thanks. That's thoughtful of you." She didn't have the heart to tell him that citrus ate at her stomach lining.

He busied himself at the grill, while she studied the yard. It could do with a feminine touch. No flowers had sprouted here in a long time and the patio furniture was rusty and mismatched. She studied the lawn, trying to visualize a sandbox or a swing set. It was odd that he hadn't invited her inside. Maybe that would come later.

When, at last, he finished swabbing the chicken pieces with a lemony sauce that smelled wonderful, he pulled up a chair at right angles to her and sat down.

She smiled. "All set?"

"For now. I hope you don't mind not going out to a restaurant." He folded his hands, nervously circling his thumbs.

"We can talk better here."

"That's what I figured." He drew himself upright. "I've been doing a lot of thinking—"

"Me, too."

"I owe you an apology."

"What on earth for?"

He placed his hands palms-down on his thighs. "For

assuming you would welcome my crazy idea. You must think I'm about as self-centered as they come.''

The lemonade soured in her throat. ''Wait. What are you trying to say?''

''This isn't a business proposition. You need a real family. Not—what do they call it—a marriage of convenience.''

Pam could literally feel the color draining from her face. ''Are you reneging?''

He leaned forward, his expression anguished. ''I would never do that. It's just that...I took advantage of your...position.''

''And you don't think my marrying you would take advantage of yours?''

''Jeez, Pam, I never should have mentioned it. Logically, I suppose, it made sense, but marriage has to be about more than what's good for Andy, what's good for the baby. It would need to be about us. Otherwise, we could never pull it off.''

''Are you afraid?''

''Of course I am. Aren't you?''

''Is that why you're calling this off?''

His jaw dropped. ''Are you saying what I think you are?''

She closed her eyes briefly, then looked straight into his. ''I'm saying yes, I'll marry you.''

''But—''

She swung her legs to the ground to face him. ''It *can* be about us. It can be about two friends who have mutual respect for each other. Love may be an overrated emotion. I can't speak for you, but I've never had much luck with it. Surely we can reach an understanding, somehow compromise to make this work.'' She hesitated. ''Unless you've totally changed your mind.''

"You're certain about this?"

"My baby needs a name. And I can't think of a better one than yours. But I do think it would be prudent to put our understanding in writing. Just so we're clear."

"You mean some kind of contract?"

"Exactly."

He took hold of her hands, then rose to his feet, pulling her up, too. He took a deep breath, then said in a husky voice, "I'll do my best to make this arrangement as comfortable for you as I can."

They stood motionless, their eyes locked. Pam's face was flushed with an emotion she couldn't name. It was beyond gratitude, beyond fear. Finally she broke the spell. "Looks like we have an agreement to formalize and a wedding to plan, Mr. Gilbert."

PAM AMAZED HIM. Calmly, confidently, she'd agreed to marry him. With a tectonic shift, his plan had lurched from the theoretical to the actual. Detecting the odor of seared meat, he edged toward the grill. "We'll think better on full stomachs." Grateful for the excuse to turn his back, he took the chicken pieces off the fire, all the time trying to master his confusing emotions—relief mixed with panic, excitement tempered by anxiety. And fear. Not of the day-to-day stuff—that he could handle. But fear that the unexpected elation welling within him would be short-lived. He'd promised not to hurt her. But, he suddenly realized, he'd given her the power to hurt him, if he let himself care—and it was going to be almost impossible not to.

Over dinner they agreed to obtain the marriage license in another county the next morning and be quietly married on Saturday. Further, she consented to live in his home. Naturally they would maintain separate bank accounts and, for legal purposes, Pam would retain her maiden name. Besides, all the school rosters would already list her as Carver. That way, she said, it would be easier when...

But he noticed she didn't complete the sentence.

Then, clearing his throat nervously, he said, "I guess I need to reassure you about something. This is a business deal. I wouldn't expect we'd, uh, have—"

"Sex." She completed his thought. "Of course not. That never crossed my mind. We're just friends, and friends we'll remain."

With all the details committed to writing, they dug into the meal with gusto. Pam even apologized for her hearty appetite. "The little guy needs to grow," Grant suggested.

"Little guy?" She looked up with a smile that turned him to mush. "It could be a girl, you know."

"Do you have a preference?"

"Healthy. That's my preference."

He couldn't get over it. Here they sat, talking babies, as if it was the most natural of conversation topics. He hadn't discussed babies, not really, since Shelley was pregnant with Andy. And to tell the truth, for all his brave front, the thought of Pam's pregnancy terrified him. What if something went wrong?

"How about the house tour? We'll have to figure out where to put your stuff and where you'll...sleep." Leading the way toward the house, he cursed under his breath. The word "sleep" echoed and reechoed with each step he took. And the visuals were equally disturbing.

Pam stopped at the kitchen stoop. "That's a problem, isn't it?" She furrowed her brow. "Unless you plan to tell Andy about our little charade."

He groaned. "No, that can't happen. Everybody, and I mean everybody, has to believe we're for real, especially for you and the baby."

"Then we'll simply have to work something out."

He held open the back door and she stepped into the small kitchen and stood, speechless, studying the aqua sink and countertop, the cocoa-brown appliances, the wallpaper sporting aqua and brown steaming coffee cups on a yellow background. With a sinking feeling, he saw it from her fresh viewpoint. "Uh, I haven't gotten around to doing much with the kitchen."

She tried a smile. "Vintage 70s decor. All we need is the Brady Bunch."

"Maybe, um, we could redecorate."

"Don't be silly, it's only for a year."

"Oh, yeah." Why hadn't he realized how dated and ugly his kitchen was? He hastened to put distance between him and the Martha Stewart disaster. "Down this hallway on the left is the dining and living room combination." He stopped and made a vague gesture. "The master bedroom, bath and den are on the right. What first?"

"And up there?" She gestured at the staircase.

"Two bedrooms and a bath."

"Where does Andy sleep?"

"Upstairs."

"I guess, then, you'd better show me the master bedroom."

He stood aside and let her precede him. The plaid bedspread was drawn barracks-tight over the king-size mattress. His dresser top was bare except for a pewter dish for pocket change, a small portable television set and a basketball trophy. The bedside table sported a lamp, an alarm clock and the biography he was reading.

The bare wood floor suddenly looked utilitarian. When, after a few moments, she hadn't said anything, he couldn't stand it. "Well?"

She screwed up her face as if searching for the word. "Spartan. Masculine."

"Is that bad?"

She shrugged, then smiled. "C'mon, you've seen my place. The kindest thing that can be said of my taste is organized chaos."

"But you can bring your things." He looked around helplessly. "Do whatever you like."

"Plants?"

He nodded.

"Wall hangings?"

"Sure."

"A big, old braided rug?"

"Why not?"

"A nest for Viola and Sebastian in the corner?"

"In *here?*"

"My kitties always sleep with me."

That stopped him. The darned felines were going to be better off than he was. "Uh, where did you have in mind for us to sleep?"

"Show me the den."

He led her through the bathroom to the small room crowded by his desk, bookcase and a beat-up daybed. He noticed her studying the bed. "I suppose I could sleep in here," she said, eyeing the sagging mattress dubiously.

"I thought I would."

"Grant, look at it. You're a foot taller than that thing is long. If anyone's going to sleep in here, it'll be me."

"Okay, we'll try it that way, but I don't want you and Barney to be uncomfortable."

"Barney?"

He reddened. "You know. The baby."

She shook her head, seemingly bemused. "Or Bar-nette, don't forget." She started back through the bathroom, then stopped. "Are you sure you're ready to share a bathroom with a woman again?"

He had a sudden disturbing image of wet hosiery, like slimy tentacles, draped all over the towel rack and shower curtain rod. He gulped. "I'm sure."

By the time they reached the living room, which she proclaimed "austere," he was worn-out.

"I don't want to intrude into your lifestyle, but—"

"Nonsense," he said. "This will be your home, too. I want you to be comfortable."

She sank down into the brown tweed sofa he'd bought at a going-out-of-business sale. It had been cheap and matched his cushy, man-size rust recliner.

She eyed the mantel. "Do you think we could get a shelf for those?" Move his team pictures and state championship trophies? He enjoyed looking at them while he watched TV. "Sure, if that's what you'd like."

Her eyes, like some malevolent detecting device, raked the room. "And maybe we could move your chair and turn the sofa this other way, so my chair would fit."

"I guess." What was it with women? Did they come wired with the rearranging-furniture gene? Just as he acknowledged his irritation, she relaxed against the sofa, spreading her arms in a gesture of contentment. "It's going to be fine, Grant, really fine."

He sought the comfort of his recliner before answering. "I hope so. But it may require more patience than we imagined."

She eyed him thoughtfully. "Having second thoughts? It's not too late."

Second thoughts? Not about her. She looked just right sitting in his living room, even if she was discussing upsetting his ordered existence. "No. I want to marry you, Pam." Then, grinning, he added, "And that's my final answer."

She pulled her knees up to her chest and propped her chin on them, a peaceful expression on her face. "Good," she said softly.

They sat in silence for several minutes, and he thought how pleasant it was to have this kind of quiet companionship. Finally she spoke up. "If we're going to hit the county clerk's office before our eleven-o'clock upper-school meeting, I think you'd better take me home soon."

"I will, but first..." Curiosity had been eating at him for several days, waiting to be satisfied. "Could you tell me about the man? The father?" Needing to risk the rest, he blurted out the difficult question, "Do you love him?"

CHAPTER FOUR

SLOWLY PAM EASED her feet to the floor, caught off guard by the question, by Grant's sudden earnestness and by her own disturbing flashbacks. Steven—devilishly handsome in an intense, scholarly sort of way. High cheekbones, dark eyes, thick black hair, and long, tapering fingers with a magic of their own. She couldn't resist him, even after he told her the truth. But love?

In fairness, she owed Grant an honest answer. This man, not Steven, would be the baby's father on record. She focused on the emotions Grant's question had aroused—joy, passion, sadness, resignation. "In a nostalgic, romantic sense, a part of me will always love him. I would never have been intimate with him otherwise."

She paused, remembering the yearning and pain in Steven's brown eyes, recalling the apology he'd tried to voice before she had hushed him—before they had come together in mutual need and desire. Pam looked directly at Grant. "I was not promiscuous. Nor did I intend to get pregnant."

"Have you reconsidered telling him about the baby?"

"No." She paused, letting the sound of the word die away. "And I won't. Fate threw us together in unusual circumstances. But he never deceived me."

Grant appeared to be mulling over what she'd said.

He probably wasn't even aware of the furrow on his brow.

She pulled forth her deepest, most painful memory— one she'd never considered sharing. Until now. "I knew he was married. That he had two daughters, ten and twelve. He'd told me all about Julie, his wife." Why couldn't she catch her breath? "But what he said didn't register until I saw her for myself."

So vivid and distressing was the memory she was hardly aware of her surroundings or of the man sitting across from her. She struggled to go on. "He was being honored by the university. His family had flown in for the occasion. I hadn't intended to go, but at the last minute, I couldn't help myself. That's when I saw her. That's when I truly realized why he could never see me again. Never have anything further to do with me."

"If this is too difficult, Pam—"

"No. I need to tell you." She drew a deep breath, then went on. "He loves his wife. Dearly, devotedly. I saw that when he pushed her wheelchair onto the platform. When he leaned down to kiss her so very tenderly." Tears filled her eyes. "Grant, she's paralyzed from the shoulders down. A skiing accident." She pulled a tissue from her pocket and dabbed her cheeks. "Now do you see? I was lonely. He was a kind man with needs. I guess you could say nature took its course, and here I am—pregnant. Even so there's no decision to be made. What do you suppose knowing about the baby would do to her? To him?" She let the question hang in the air before continuing. "I've given this considerable thought, and I know the time may come when, either for personal or medical reasons, my child will need the truth. But I'll wait until that day arrives."

He ran his hands up and down the arms of the recliner

LAURA ABBOT   65

before speaking. "Thank you. I know it wasn't easy for you to talk about this. After tonight, I won't ask you any more questions about him. It's just that, well, for the baby's sake, I didn't want there to be, you know, complications down the road."

His earnest, troubled face swam before her. She was missing something implied by the faltering nature of his explanation. Was he prepared to care for this baby? To want to claim more than merely the title of "father"? Could he be thinking beyond the one year limit of their agreement?

SUNDAY AFTERNOON of Labor Day weekend Pam stood in her living room knee-deep in boxes. It was difficult to know what to take with her and what to put in storage. As if sensing an impending shift in their tranquility, Viola and Sebastian scampered from chair to table to windowsill, unsettled by the disruption of their space. Pam could empathize.

She studied the solid gold band on her left hand as if it were an encoded alien object. Though small, it served as the exclamation mark on her life-changing circumstances.

The wedding had gone off flawlessly, if you could call a three-minute ceremony in a farmhouse living room with two elderly ladies as witnesses—one playing a dirgelike rendition of "Oh, Promise Me" on a wheezing pump organ—a wedding. But it would do, Pam rationalized. She was beyond virginal wedding dresses, a flower-bedecked church and multiple chiffon-clad bridesmaids. At least she would be able to tell her son or daughter about the ceremony. About the champagne-hued tea dress she'd worn, about Grant standing tall and resolute in his navy suit and about the chaste kiss he'd dropped on her cheek at the urging of the beaming justice of the peace.

But the wedding night was a different story. Nontraditional in every sense of the word. After an awkward dinner at one of Dallas's finest restaurants, Grant had delivered her to the condo and gone home to begin sorting his things to make room for hers. Since no one knew yet about their marriage, they'd decided to postpone her move until Tuesday evening to allow Andy to settle in and Grant to break their news to him in person. Meanwhile, Pam would see about leasing her condo.

Sun streamed through the picture window, illuminating the dust motes stirred by the packing. What next? The chore seemed suddenly overwhelming. Nor could she continue to ignore the difficult task she'd been putting off—telling her father about her marriage. Even though hers hadn't been a normal wedding day, not having him by her side had hurt.

She picked up the phone, settled in her cozy chair and summoned the kitties to her lap for moral support. She uttered a silent prayer, then dialed, waiting patiently for several rings. Her father's knees weren't what they once were and he moved slowly. Finally he answered.

"Daddy, it's Pam."

As it always did when she called, his monotone voice brightened. "I've been wondering when I was going to hear from you, since I couldn't get hold of you yesterday."

Oh, yes. The ritual Saturday night call. "I was out."

"On a date?" he asked hopefully.

She gathered her courage. "Not exactly. But something like that." She hesitated, then, before she lost her nerve, rushed on. "Daddy, I have some news. Are you sitting down?"

"I don't like the sound of that."

"It's not bad. Just something that may surprise you."

"Girl, the cows'll come home before you get around to telling me. What in tarnation is it?"

"There's no easy way to say this, so here goes. I got married yesterday." No response. Darn, she should've cushioned the shock somehow. "Dad, are you all right?"

"A Texas tornado gives more warning to a fella than you do. Gimme a minute." There was a long pause, then he said, "Did you say 'married'?"

"I did."

"Who the hell to?" His voice betrayed the bafflement and hurt she'd been worried about.

"A good man, Daddy. His name is Grant Gilbert and he teaches with me at Keystone."

"Why haven't I heard anything about him before?"

"Well, this has been kind of a whirlwind relationship."

Her father snorted. "That's putting it mildly." He was quiet for a time. Then he said, "I would have come, you know. If you'd invited me."

Pam bit her lip. She'd disappointed her father, and the sadness in his voice spoke volumes. "I know you would have. But we...eloped. It was a brief ceremony, just the two of us, and now we're getting packed so I can move in with him, so it just seemed—"

"Better to take the biggest step in your life without your old dad?"

She pinched her forehead and searched for the right words. "There wasn't time. School starts Tuesday, Grant's son is coming to live with him and—"

"Son? What son? Slow down and start over."

So she did, telling him about Andy, about Grant, about everything except the baby.

When she finished, in a low voice he said, "Do you love him?"

She had never lied to her father. Could she start now? "He's a wonderful, caring man, Daddy. You'll love him as much as I do." That was close to the truth, wasn't it?

"Well, then." He sighed heavily. "That's all that matters. When do I get to meet my son-in-law?"

"Soon. Let us get school underway and my move completed. Then we'll all come visit you."

"Honey—"

She sensed he was about to ask a question, perhaps the dreaded "Are you pregnant?" But he must've reconsidered, because all he added was "Be happy."

After she hung up, she sat for several minutes, absentmindedly stroking Viola and Sebastian. Eventually she'd have to tell Barbara. But not right now.

Her father's acceptance had reinforced her obligation to commit to this marriage, in appearance if not in fact.

SUNDAY EVENING Grant called Jim Campbell to ask if he and Pam could drop by on a matter of school business. The Campbells needed to be told first, not only because Jim, as headmaster, needed to know, but because Connie and Jim were their friends. But now, approaching their attractive ranch-style home near the campus, Grant had a walloping case of stage fright. This would be his and Pam's first attempt to pull off their fabricated story. Could they possibly convince anyone they were in love?

He glanced at Pam, who was giving undue attention to the passing scenery. His eye caught the gleam of her wedding band and, with his left thumb, he fingered his. "Nervous?" he asked.

"Try terrified. Connie has a radar capability metropolitan police would envy."

"Things'll go smoother after we get the telling over with."

"I hope so. Dad wasn't easy, and when I called my sister, she wasn't very understanding, much less congratulatory. She'll freak out when she learns I'm pregnant."

"My folks didn't have much reaction when I told them, but after thirty years in the military, little fazes them. They couldn't have come to a wedding on short notice anyway." Time enough later to reveal "strained" accurately described his relationship with his hard-nosed father.

"Do you have any brothers or sisters?"

Her question stopped him short. How little they really knew about each other despite working together for several years. "I had an older brother." He swallowed, the memory still painful. "He died of brain cancer when he was twenty-nine."

She laid a comforting hand on his thigh. "I'm so sorry. How devastating for you and your family."

"Yeah, it was. Brian and I were eighteen months apart. We shared a room, played together on the high school team, fought over the same girls. I guess you could say he was my best friend." He didn't add that Brian had also served as a buffer between him and his father. From the time his dad had returned from Vietnam, he'd been difficult, distant. Brian had been the golden boy who could do no wrong. But Grant? In his father's eyes, he'd never been anything but a disappointment. And the hell of it was, he'd never understood why.

"Your family's had a lot to deal with in recent years."

He smiled ruefully. "So maybe a baby'll help, huh?"

She looked thoughtful. "Maybe," she said quietly, removing her hand from his leg.

Why had he gone and said a fool thing like that? As if he had any claim to the baby beyond next September. He couldn't start thinking of the child as his in any way except name.

"Here we are," he said, pulling to a stop in front of the rambling brick home. On the porch was a white deacon's bench illuminated by an antique lamppost. He turned off the ignition and sought her eyes, which reflected the same uncertainty he was feeling.

Neither of them moved. Finally she drew a deep breath and jabbed him on the shoulder. "Show time!"

"Is this where I say, 'Break a leg'?"

"This is where," she answered just before he left the car to come around and escort her up the walkway.

After greeting them, Jim ushered them into the inviting family room, displaying many of the primitive American pieces he and Connie collected. When Jim had first filled the interim headmaster position, before accepting the job permanently, the faculty had been stunned to find out he and Connie had known each other in their distant past. It hadn't taken long for them to renew their friendship, culminating in a marriage much approved by Connie's mother, daughter and the entire Keystone community.

Jim settled in a wing chair, and Grant and Pam sat together on the sofa. "I gather there's some urgency to the matter you want to discuss," Jim began.

Grant found his voice—and Pam's hand. "There is."

Pam looked around. "Connie needs to hear this, too."

"I'll get her." Jim stepped down the hall and summoned Connie, who took a seat in the antique rocker by the hearth.

"Pam, Grant? You're sure this isn't confidential?" she asked uncertainly.

"We're sure. In fact, we imagine everyone at school will know in a matter of days," Pam said.

"Well, don't keep us in suspense." Connie eyed Pam curiously, as if unsure whether concern or elation was the expected response.

Grant seized the initiative. "Although this may come as a shock, yesterday, happily, Pam and I were married."

Connie's eyes widened in bafflement. "Wait. I'm having trouble taking this in."

"It's true." Pam cast Grant an adoring look—a convincing, adoring look.

Jim glanced from one to the other. "Married?"

Connie studied Pam as if searching for a key to the mystery, before facing her husband. "That's what they said."

"It's understandable," Grant managed, "that our news is a surprise."

"You can say that again, but surprise or not," Connie said over her shoulder as she moved toward the kitchen, "this definitely calls for champagne. And then—" she paused for emphasis "—we want to hear the whole story."

She returned bearing a tray of filled champagne flutes, which she distributed, then indicated they should all stand up. With a bemused smile, she raised her glass.

"To our friends Pam and Grant. May their love grow with each day they spend together and may their home be filled with joy and peace."

"Hear, hear," Jim said, as the four touched their glasses and drank.

Grant noticed that Pam took only a token sip.

"Okay, then," Connie said, settling back into the rocker. "Start at the beginning. Tell us everything."

Pam leaned forward. "First let me apologize, Connie, for not telling you sooner. But Grant and I only decided last week to go ahead and get married before school started."

"But how did you get together? Why didn't I know about it?"

Facing her friend, Pam undertook the carefully rehearsed explanation. "We were both at the university this summer. And, somehow, being away from our daily lives—" she put her arm around Grant's shoulder in a loving caress "—we suddenly saw each other in a new light. Isn't that right, honey?"

Lord, she was feeding him lines like a pro. "I'll say. For whatever reasons, we just…connected."

"Then," Pam continued, "you were on your trip so I couldn't tell you. Anyway, we decided we'd test the relationship back here in Fort Worth before we made any decisions."

"But when we got back home, everything seemed right." Grant nearly choked on another swig of champagne.

"So it seemed silly to wait. When you know, you know," Pam said, snuggling closer to him. So close he could smell her wonderfully arousing fragrance.

Jim, who had been surveying the situation, managed to get a word in. "Of course, Connie and I are happy for you. You're two fine people, and you make a great couple." Then, with a grin playing over his face, he added, "This bombshell will create quite a stir on campus."

"There's one favor we'd like to ask, Jim," Grant said.

"Name it."

"As you know, my son Andy will be a new student at Keystone. He arrives tomorrow. Pam and I have decided he needs to be told and have a chance to get used to the idea before we make any kind of public announcement, so could you keep our news quiet for a little while?"

"Naturally. Just tell me when you're ready."

An awkward silence followed. Pam looked at Grant. He looked at her. *These are our friends,* she seemed to be saying. The unspoken communication helped him make up his mind.

"There's one more thing. Something we don't plan to share with anyone else yet."

Pam gripped his fingers. "But you two are our dear friends and..."

Before she could go on, Grant made the announcement for her. "Pam is pregnant."

No one moved. Then Connie, her eyes filled with tears, knelt beside Pam. "Oh, honey, it's what you've always wanted."

Grant stood, awkwardly awaiting Jim's reaction. "I hope this won't make you think less of us."

Jim rose and clapped an arm around Grant's shoulder. "These things happen," he said. Then slowly a smile broke across his face. "Looking at how happy you both are, I can see it was hardly a shotgun wedding."

Later when the Campbells walked them to the door,

Grant tried to focus on what Jim was saying, but off to the side he heard Connie whisper urgently to Pam. "I'm surprised, of course, but I'm sure you must know your own heart."

Grant managed a perfunctory "uh-huh" to whatever Jim was saying, all the time straining to hear Pam's response. It floated to him on the gentle summer breeze. "I knew exactly what I was doing. You'll see."

Pam's words caused his throat to tighten. Yes, all of them would see. Come September.

GRANT GRITTED HIS TEETH and pounded the steering wheel, but the traffic ahead of him only inched along before feeding into a single lane. He checked his watch and swore under his breath. No way would he get to the airport in time unless Andy's plane was late.

He didn't need this aggravation. As if he wasn't already as nervous as a rookie playing in his NBA season opener. He wanted Andy to like it here, but being stood up at the airport would be a lousy welcome.

He found himself wishing Pam were with him. But they'd agreed Andy would have enough of an adjustment without immediately being introduced to his— jeez, it sounded odd—stepmother. Yet he'd have to tell his son about Pam as soon as he found an opening. Today if possible. Once Andy learned about the marriage, he'd think it was weird if Pam lived somewhere else.

Seizing an opening in traffic, Grant edged into the line of moving vehicles. Sure enough. Up ahead he saw it. A truck jackknifed on an overpass. Cops everywhere. He hated the thought of Andy having to wait—and wonder.

Poor kid. He'd have a lot to get used to in a short

time. Grant had a sudden image of his own bedroom overrun with lingerie, lava lamps and cats. And one warm, gorgeous woman.

Andy wouldn't be the only one doing some adapting.

THE MINUTE the aircraft rolled to a stop at the gate, Andy jumped to his feet, relieved to escape the old lady in the window seat, who'd asked him dumb questions all the way from Atlanta. Like his life was any of her business.

As the line of passengers moved toward the exit, he maneuvered to the overhead bin and extracted his backpack and tennis racket, then joined the crowd inching toward freedom.

It hadn't been too bad a flight. The worst part had been his mother making a big scene in the Orlando airport. Which was kinda funny when you thought about it. It was her idea to go to Dubai, not his. But you'd have thought he was shipping out for World War III the way she carried on.

Well, screw it.

He shouldered his backpack and walked into the jetway. That's where the blast furnace hit him. Great, it must be a hundred ten degrees. He'd been to Fort Worth a coupla times before. It might be okay if you were a cowboy, but he missed the ocean and the palm trees.

When he stepped into the concourse, he scanned the crowd for his father. All around him were these freakin' family reunions, and several freckle-faced, snot-nosed kids were hugging the old lady who'd driven him crazy. Like seeing her was a big deal.

As groups of people moved off toward the baggage claim area, the crowd thinned. Still no Dad. He usually drove Andy wild with his Mr. Punctuality routine. Not today. It figured. Andy tossed his backpack onto an empty chair and slumped into the adjacent one. Prob'ly his father was all tied up with important matters at that candy-assed school. How hard could it be teaching math and coaching basketball? It wasn't like it was a real job or anything.

The tennis racket had been a great idea. He'd tell Dad he was going out for tennis in the spring. That'd get the guy off his case about playin' basketball. No way was he going to consider that. About the last friggin' thing he needed was to be the coach's son and play on his team. It was gonna be bad enough to go to the same school. At least he wouldn't have his father for a teacher. He'd already taken geometry and wasn't ready for calculus.

Maybe Dad'd let him have a dog. That would be kinda cool. And when he turned sixteen next spring, he'd get Dad to buy him a car. Wheels. Freedom. He couldn't wait.

"Son?"

Andy looked up. There was Dad, with this big dopey grin on his face. Taking his time, Andy rose to his feet and was engulfed in a bear hug. "Where ya been?" he muttered into his father's shoulder.

"Sorry. There was a wreck on the freeway. Say, looks like you've grown another six inches since Christmas."

His dad stood back, studying him. Andy shrugged, then picked up his backpack and tennis racket.

"C'mon, then. We'll get the rest of your bags."

As they made their way to the baggage claim area, Dad kept up this running monologue about how glad he was to see him and how he had everything arranged at Keystone about enrollment and all.

Once they were in the car and Dad was weaving through the traffic, he didn't say much. But when they turned into the neighborhood, ol' Coach G. dropped the bomb. "With that additional height, I can really use you on the basketball team."

Might as well get it over with, and Dad'd never know the difference, since he hadn't made it to a single one of his games last year. "About the basketball... Dad, I'm gonna play tennis instead. I know you were a high school hoops hotshot and all, but I'm no good. Last year I mostly sat on the bench." Which wasn't true, but how would his father know?

Then his dad gave him one of these you've-let-me-down looks that was supposed to make him feel guilty. "Son, I'm really disappointed. You can play both basketball and tennis, you know."

"I hate basketball!" The words just slipped out, but they sure as hell got a reaction from the old man.

"That's no way to—" Then his dad seemed to catch himself. "I'm sorry to hear that. I was hoping it was something we'd have in common."

"No chance," Andy mumbled.

The rest of the way to the house, neither one of them said anything.

Crap. It was gonna be one long year.

THANKS TO THE SODA CRACKERS she'd eaten before she got out of bed, Pam actually felt halfway decent this hot, sunny first day of classes. But no way could she go near the teachers' lounge before school. Even during the best of times the acrid pungency of stale coffee was a fixture there. No, any tummy flutters she had today would be a result of nerves. Grant had called her late last night with the discouraging report that Andy had arrived not only with all his luggage, but with a capital *A* attitude. He'd made it known in no uncertain terms that he was not in the mood for a father-son chat. So their news remained to be told.

Walking toward the office, she nodded at Ralph Hagood, the principal, who stood in the intersection of two halls, greeting the students and giving bewildered freshmen directions. Pausing by the bank of faculty mailboxes, Pam pulled out her updated class rosters to scan before heading for her classroom. Then she saw the name. Just when she'd thought she had her stomach under control. Sixth period sophomore English. Andrew Paige Gilbert. Of all the luck. She had only one section of sophomores. What if she asked for him to be changed? But what reason could she possibly give Ralph?

Around her, the students' voices swirled in an upbeat symphony of sound, charged with the contagious energy and excitement of the first day of school. Although she hadn't met Andy yet, she empathized with him. If half of what Grant had told her was true, the poor kid's first day at Keystone would be just another in a long line of disruptive changes.

A round-faced, curly-headed young man caught up with her as she walked down the hall. "Ms. Carver, when are auditions for the fall production?"

Oh, Lord, the play. That was so far down on her list of priorities, she hadn't given it much thought. "I don't know yet." She beamed at the eager youngster. "But I hope you'll try out."

"Are we still doing *Our Town?*"

"You bet."

"I'm your man, then." He ducked into the French room. "See ya later."

When she entered her classroom, most of the seniors, many of whom she'd had as students in the past, were already in their seats. They greeted her with familiarity. "You gonna be rough on us, Ms. Carver?" "Tell me this course isn't as hard as last year's seniors said." "Let's just ease into this year, huh?"

With a knowing smile, she introduced her class guidelines, handed out the syllabi and then launched into a lecture on the origins of Anglo-Saxon literature. After class, Brittany Thibault stopped at Pam's desk. "I think I'm really gonna enjoy English lit." Before Pam could respond, the girl hurtled on. "Could I ask you a huge favor, Ms. Carver?"

"Fire away."

"Would you be willing to write my college recommendations?"

"I'd be happy to. Bring them to me when you're ready."

Watching Brittany leave and the students in her second English lit class arrive, Pam had the urge to put her head down on her desk. Plays to direct, college recommendations to write, lectures to prepare, tests to administer, papers to grade, committee meetings to attend—it hadn't taken long for her airy, hopeful balloon to settle back to earth. And she hadn't even listed the most important job of all—a baby to nurture.

The first day of classes was always exhausting, and by noon her adrenaline supply had dwindled. But she still had to face her afternoon class of sophomores. And Andy Gilbert.

Looking around her classroom at the restless sea of sophomores, she identified several unfamiliar faces. Which one was Andy? The burly Scandinavian-looking boy by the window? The short, tense little guy with wire-rimmed glasses? Then she spotted him. She'd have known Andy anywhere, with his rangy body, deep blue eyes and Grant's thick brown hair falling over his forehead. He sat on the back row, his long denim-clad legs sticking out into the aisle. With an air of detachment, he had his nose in a Stephen King paperback. His body language sent a clear signal—leave me alone.

Her heart went out to him. He must be a master of camouflage. Sure enough, none of the other students was paying him the slightest attention.

She allowed herself a glimmer of hope. If he was a Stephen King fan, maybe she could capture his interest with Edgar Allan Poe. She always started the sophomore year with Poe's classic short story ''The Tell-Tale Heart.''

Only when she began speaking did he put aside the novel, but he never once looked at her, instead studying his fingernails with the intensity of one discovering the Rosetta stone.

When the class ended, she stopped him at the door. ''Andy, you're new here, right?''

''Yeah.'' He fidgeted with the strap of his backpack, as if he was late for a pressing appointment.

''I just wanted to extend a special welcome. I hope you'll enjoy Keystone.''

''Thanks.'' He shifted from one foot to the other. ''Is that all? Can I go now?''

''Yes, that's all. Bye.'' She watched him walk away, eyes averted, melting into the river of students flowing toward the next class.

She leaned wearily against the doorjamb, then closed her eyes. Thank God her planning period was next. She didn't know when she'd ever been so tired.

"Pam, are you all right?" Connie's voice brought her to attention.

"Oh, sure. It's been a long day, that's all, and I just met Andy Gilbert for the first time."

Connie stepped inside the empty classroom. "And?"

She sighed, rubbing her hands together, oddly aware of her vacant ring finger. "I think Grant and I have our work cut out for us."

"When does Grant plan to tell Andy about you?"

"Sometime today. Before I move in."

"Are you scared?"

"Stepmother is a role I haven't played before."

"It's a challenging one, but if anybody can pull it off, it's you."

"I wish I shared your confidence." Added to the demands of the day was the overwhelming sense that she had gotten herself into something way beyond simply providing a father for her unborn baby.

A bell shattered the air, and Connie patted Pam's shoulder. "I'm late. Not setting a great example, huh?" Then she hurried off toward her history class, leaving Pam wondering how she and Grant could have been so naive.

IMMEDIATELY AFTER SCHOOL Andy disappeared upstairs, claiming homework. He'd spent most of last night unpacking and arranging his room. Then on the way home from school today, when Grant had hoped to tell him about Pam, he'd pulled out a portable CD player, plugged in the headphones and played air drums on his knees to music Grant could hear only as a disjointed metallic beat.

Grant found himself prowling through the house, unable to settle to any task. How long was the kid going to shut him out? He knew better than to pry. Yet he had to tell Andy about Pam. Hell, she was supposed to move in tonight. Maybe the family dynamic would change for the better with her around. He'd never met a kid who didn't warm to Pam. Surely Andy would be no exception.

Okay. He'd bite the bullet at the first opportunity.

That settled, he wandered into the kitchen and began patting out hamburgers for the grill. Then he tossed a can of pork and beans into a dish, stirred in some brown sugar, catsup and pickle juice and put the casserole in the oven to bake. That plus the deli potato salad he'd picked up yesterday ought to do it.

Grant made himself watch the evening news, then went upstairs and knocked on Andy's door. No answer. He rapped louder. He heard a shuffling, then Andy opened the door, his head phones eased away from his ears. "What?"

"I'm putting on the burgers, son. Dinner'll be ready in ten minutes."

"Good. I'm starving." Then Andy shut the door, leaving Grant standing in the hall feeling helpless.

Fortunately the dinner was a hit. There was nothing wrong with the kid's appetite. He'd even extended Grant a grudging "good beans."

Grant made small talk about a late-breaking national news story, then began inquiring about Andy's day at school. "Did you find your classes all right?"

Andy lifted his eyes from the hamburger he was devouring. "It's not that big a place, Dad. We're not talking electronic circuitry."

"Meet any of the other kids?"

"The principal introduced me to some guys, but I

can't remember their names. I checked out a coupla chicks in Spanish, but mainly I just hung loose.''

"What about lunch?''

"You call that sewer cuisine 'lunch'?''

"I meant did you sit with anyone there?''

"The jocks were all in one big group. I wasn't about to crash that. And I sure as hell wasn't going to sit with the dweebs, so I ate by myself.''

"I guess it takes a while to get used to a new school.''

Andy shot him a look as if he'd just made the dumbest remark of the century. "Uh, Dad, that would be a big 'Roger.'''

"So basically your day—''

"Sucked. There. Are you satisfied?''

"No, Andy. I want you to enjoy your year here. But you'll have to make some effort. You can't rely on everyone else to make you happy.''

"Oh, believe me, I know that.''

They ate in silence broken only by the snap of corn chips and the crunch of dill pickles. Grant chewed mechanically, swallowing with difficulty. Andy's belligerence hurt. But the hell of it was, in the long run it would probably hurt the boy even more than it did him.

He had a sudden wild need for Pam—for her common sense, her ability to laugh, her understanding. But needs like that were dangerous.

"Is there any dessert?''

Grant pulled some store-bought cookies from the bread box. "Try these. Remind me to pick up some ice cream at the store.''

"Dad, pick up some ice cream at the store.'' The glimmer of a smile shone in Andy's eyes. A tiny, but significant breakthrough.

Grant seized the opening to ask one more question. "What about your teachers? Like any of them?"

Andy popped an entire cookie into his mouth, but managed between bites to say, "They're okay, I guess. Except for world history. Old lady Flanders is screwy. She's so ancient she prob'ly witnessed Custer's last stand."

Smothering a grin, Grant agreed. "She is a bit long of tooth, isn't she?"

"Actually, there was one teacher who seemed really cool."

"Who was that?"

"English. Hot-looking redhead."

Grant couldn't have said it better himself, but he had more important things to think about than Pam's tantalizing physical features. "Ms. Carver, you mean?"

"That's her."

He had an opening. "Er, about Ms. Carver..."

"What?"

Forcing himself to look directly at his son, Grant continued. "I have something important to tell you, and there's no easy way to say it."

Andy looked mildly curious. "Yeah?"

Grant waited a beat for his heart to stop threatening to explode in his chest. "Uh, she's my wife."

CHAPTER FIVE

ANDY STARED at his father, dumbfounded. "You're kidding, right?"

"No, Pam and I were married Saturday."

"Well, ex-cuze me, but isn't this kinda sudden?" Jeez, that was only—what?—three days ago. You'd think somewhere along the line his old man could've given him a clue, for cripe's sake.

His dad pushed his hands through his hair, like he always did when he was frustrated. "I know it seems that way, but—"

"If you're married, how come she isn't here?" He might not be a certified adult, but he knew newlyweds slept together. "Does Mom know?"

"Hey, son, one question at a time. Pam will come over later with the first load of her stuff. We thought it would be better for you to get settled before she moved in. Kinda get used to the idea."

Get used to the idea? It was bad enough he had to stay in Fort Worth with his dad for a whole year, but now he had to live with honeymooners, one of whom was his friggin' English teacher! Ol' Mafia Harry was looking better by the second.

"Son?"

Andy shook his head, trying to clear his brain. "Tonight? She's coming tonight?" His father was staring at him, a tight-ass expression on his face. "Oh, yeah," he nodded wisely, "I guess the sooner the better, huh, stud?"

"Andy, please. That's no way to talk."

"No way to talk? How'd you like to be me? I hafta go live with my old man that I hardly ever see and after I get there, he throws in a small detail he's forgotten to mention. 'Oh, by the way, I'm married.' Whaddya expect me to do? Turn handsprings?"

"I know it's a shock, but you like Pam, don't you?"

"It's not about 'Pam.' Oh, hell, that's great! Am I supposed to call my teacher 'Pam' or call my stepmother 'Ms. Carver'? And, anyway, what does it matter if I like her? It's not as if I have a choice."

"Can you help me out here? At least try to make her welcome?"

Andy crossed his arms and stared icily over his father's head.

There went his dad's hand through the hair again. "Let me try to explain this better." He sucked in a big breath like he was about to shoot a game-winning free throw. "Pam and I have been friends and colleagues for several years. This summer we, er, we were both in Austin for summer programs, and, well, we suddenly saw each other differently."

Oh, brother. He could go a long time without hearing the details of his dad's hot romance.

"When we got back here," his father's voice droned on, "it didn't seem practical to wait to get married."

Then it hit him. Of course, it didn't. "Especially when you needed a housekeeper for me, right?"

If Andy had slapped him, his father couldn't have looked more stricken.

"Jeez, Andy—"

"Sorry," he mumbled. It *was* kind of a cheap shot. "But, Dad, this is nuts!"

"I suppose it seems that way now. But Pam is a wonderful woman, and she's really looking forward to getting better acquainted with you. Please, give her, give *us,* a chance. That's all I ask."

All? He felt dizzy, as if he'd stumbled into a crazy movie of his life, sorta like *Pleasantville* or *The Truman Show.* "What about Mom?"

"I plan to call her tomorrow."

She would freak out. Would she make him go to Dubai or, worse yet, to that snobby prep school she'd talked about? Andy stood abruptly, nearly knocking over the kitchen chair. "I'm goin' up to my room."

His dad got to his feet. At first Andy thought he was going to lay a fatherly hand on his shoulder, but instead, he kind of shrugged helplessly. Like he didn't know what to do. "Will you come say 'hello' to Pam when she arrives?"

Andy shrugged. "Do I have a choice?"

"Let me rephrase that." His father squared his shoulders and fixed him with that schoolteacher glare of his. "I expect you to come greet Pam. I'll let you know when she gets here."

"Fine." Andy edged toward the hall, desperate to get away. "Fine, you do that."

He took the stairs two at a time, stomped into his room, threw himself on his bed and covered his ears with headphones. The driving beat of the heavy metal band matched the angry throbbing of his heart. He'd thought his life couldn't get much worse. Well, he'd thought wrong. He was screwed. Totally.

PAM SHOULDERED her overnight bag and started up the walk toward her new home. Pausing on the deep front porch, she wondered for the umpteenth time whether she was doing the right thing. But it was way too late for second thoughts.

Just as she rang the bell, the door swung open, and there stood Grant, his thin smile betraying the same awkwardness that was rendering her speechless. "Welcome," he said, taking the bag and holding the door for her. After depositing her bag in the bedroom, he joined her in the living room. They stood staring at each other, as if waiting for a prompter to throw them their lines.

"Do you suppose this is the first day of the rest of our lives?" she finally managed to say.

"Maybe. Feels weird, doesn't it?"

"Very." She sat primly on the sofa, watching him as he retrieved an envelope from the top of the bookcase.

"Here." He laid the envelope in her lap. "These are the keys to the house and my car."

"Thanks." She glanced around. "Where's Andy?"

"In his room."

Grant didn't need to say anything. She knew. "It didn't go well, huh?"

He shook his head. "I'd hoped for a more positive response, but he's pretty hostile."

"You can't expect him to be thrilled. He thought he'd have you all to himself. I'm an intruder."

"No, I don't think it's that. I—" his voice cracked "—I don't think he likes me."

Pam had never seen Grant vulnerable. "Nonsense. We've upset his expectations, that's all." She willed him to understand. "Give him time, Grant. Love you can easily give, but patience may come harder."

"How'd you get so wise?"

She chuckled mirthlessly. "It's a whole lot easier when you're the observer, not the parent."

He shifted uncomfortably from one foot to the other. "Uh, there's something else."

"What's that?"

"He thinks we're like honeymooners. You know…" A faint flush highlighted his cheeks.

She cocked an eyebrow. "Hands on, you mean?"

"Uh-huh."

"Can you fake it?"

"We'll have to. At least sometimes."

"Play the part, Olivier. Just play the part." If only it were that easy. A drama had three acts, five at the most. This was reality theater, 24/7.

Grant shrugged. "I'll get Andy. We need to put this first family meeting behind us."

Pam stood, laid her hands on Grant's shoulders and tried an encouraging smile. "Curtain's going up, Gilbert." Then she gave him a stage-wifely peck on the cheek.

ANDY CRANKED DOWN the volume when the doorbell chimed. *She* was here. He could hear the low murmur of voices, soon followed by the ominous sound of his father's footsteps on the stairs. He still couldn't figure it. His dad, *married.* He guessed he didn't have anything against Ms. Carver, but the whole thing was weird. His dad was a cautious guy. Going off and getting married—it just didn't sound like him.

His father tapped on the door, then opened it a crack. "Son? Pam's here. C'mon downstairs and join us."

"Cool your jets, okay? I'll be there." He took his sweet time turning off the CD player, straightening his rumpled bedspread, even lacing up his Nikes.

Downstairs his dad was sitting next to Ms. Carver on the sofa. She looked different, younger, than she had at school, what with her hair up in a ponytail and wearing jeans and all. "Hi," Andy said, standing awkwardly in the doorway, feeling like a jackass.

Ms. Carver had this big smile on her face. That's one of the things he'd liked about her in class. Her smile. "Andy, I'm so glad to see you again. I know these are much different circumstances, but I'm happy about them. I hope in time you will be, too."

"Yeah, well, I guess I should say congratulations or something." He noticed his dad's arm snake around his teacher's shoulders.

"Thank you." She gestured toward the ugly recliner. "Come sit down, so we can get better acquainted."

Uh-oh. The inquisition. "I've got a lotta homework, Ms. Carver." He sat tentatively.

"Just for a little while. And please call me Pam, at least at home."

"I hope I don't goof up."

"It won't be the end of the world if you do."

His father just sat there, letting Ms. Carver—Pam—talk, which she did. "I noticed today that you're a Stephen King fan. Do you have a favorite?"

"I like them all, but my favorite is *Salem's Lot*."

"Have you read the Poe I assigned?"

He felt a slow burn splotching his face. He hadn't done any homework. And he didn't have any plans to. "Not yet."

"If you like King, I predict you'll like Poe. He's the father of the mystery story."

Andy was mildly interested, but darned if he'd let her or his father know it. Maybe later he'd take a peek at his English book.

"One of his eeriest is 'The Black Cat.' Speaking of which—" she grinned at his dad "—the cats are still in the car. Will you help me get them, Andy?"

"What cats?"

"Viola and Sebastian. My kitties. You'll love them."

He got up to follow her. "I dunno," he said. "I've never had any pets. Unless you count goldfish. Which I don't."

"Well, then, you have a treat in store."

He helped her lug a big cage inside. When she unlatched the door, a black-and-white fur ball dashed under the sofa, while a silky gray cat with huge green eyes hunkered inside the cage, eyeing him curiously.

"C'mon out, Viola," Ms. Carver urged. Finally the cat crept forward, sniffing the air in a finicky way. "Meet Andy," Pam said, scooping up the cat and gently placing it in his arms. It lay there, all soft and furry. Then he felt the rumble against his chest. The cat was purring. For a moment he felt peaceful. Hey, no way. The woman wasn't going to win him over with a stupid cat. "Here," he said, handing the creature back.

His dad had sidled away from the cage, obviously content to let them deal with the animals.

"Grant, why don't you fix us all some sodas? Maybe some chips. I imagine Andy could eat something." She winked at him.

He realized he was kinda hungry. After his dad left the room, Pam sat down again, still cradling the cat. She motioned him to join her on the sofa. "Viola is a very particular cat. You should feel honored. She likes you." Before he could think of an answer, he was startled to discover the cat creeping toward him, then kneading his thigh with her forepaws. "Now, Sebastian, he takes to everybody. But he doesn't like new places."

She laughed. "He may not come out from under the sofa for days."

He couldn't freakin' believe it. He was sitting here involved in a conversation about her pets. He didn't even like cats. "Yeah, it's kinda hard to change homes." Crap. He hadn't meant it to come out like that. He sounded like a big crybaby.

"I imagine it is." She hesitated. "Especially when you arrive to find a complete stranger married to your father."

What was he supposed to say to that? *Damn right?*

She reached over and ran a hand down Viola's back. "But I'm hoping you and I can be friends and that you won't be too hard on your dad. I think he's been lonely for a long time."

Her voice sounded sad. Come to think of it, he hadn't ever considered that. About Dad being lonely. It always seemed like he didn't need much of anybody, except for his team and stuff.

"We'll all just have to work it out. How to become a family. As for school, I know it will be awkward at first to have me for a teacher, but I checked your schedule. There's no way for you to take driver's education without having English sixth period. I hope you don't mind."

"It'll be okay, I guess."

"I'll work hard not to show favoritism, and I hope you won't let our relationship interfere with your learning."

"The other kids'll prob'ly call me teacher's pet."

She chuckled. "We'll have to be sure that doesn't happen."

She had a nice laugh, too. Maybe it wouldn't be too

bad having her around. But of course she was sucking up now. She needed her stepson to like her.

"Here we go." With a bag of chips clutched under his arm, Dad juggled three glasses of soda. While they drank, they worked out when they'd bring over Pam's boxes and furniture. Dad seemed kinda nervous about her plans for sprucing up the house, but Andy thought they sounded okay. Dad was a tan-and-gray kinda guy, but Pam was red, orange and yellow. After he'd scarfed down the last of the chips, he excused himself. Maybe he'd actually read "The Tell-Tale Heart."

Later he sprawled on his stomach across his bed, the lit book propped on the pillow. This was good stuff. He could almost hear the beating heart. *Whoa.* He *could* hear it. Then he realized it was Viola. Purring. While he'd been absorbed in the short story, she'd nudged his door open and now snuggled beside him on his bed.

Cool.

GRANT HELPED PAM bring in the rest of her stuff, including litter boxes, one of which she placed beside the tub in the downstairs bath they would share. And he'd thought wet panty hose would be the most offensive addition to his bachelor quarters! He'd made room in his closet for her hanging things. Now, though, he could see he'd probably have to move his wardrobe to the upstairs spare bedroom, at least if he had any hope of leaving any space between garments. It had been a startlingly swift and complete invasion of his space—her robe hung from a hook beside the shower, the kitty nest was wedged between the bureau and the wall, assorted colognes were aligned on the dresser top and shoe boxes too numerous to contemplate were stacked on the floor. On the bedside table, as if it had always been there was a dated photograph of a smiling young couple, her parents he presumed.

He could hear Pam in the bathroom, rearranging the medicine cabinet to make room for her cosmetics and medications. He flopped on the bed, hands cradling his head. In retrospect how simple it would've been to ensconce a housekeeper in the guest room, close his bedroom door at night and relax in his masculine sanctuary. Now he was practically going to have to make an appointment to step into his own shower.

Then there was Andy. Not only understandably upset and confused, but also on the lookout for evidence that he and Pam were behaving like a horny teenager's version of newlyweds. He rolled over on his side, sat up and grabbed the bedside phone. No point postponing the inevitable. He punched in Shelley's phone number, steeling himself for her reaction.

Which was every bit as histrionic and patronizing as he had anticipated. Ten minutes later, after hearing how disappointed Shelley was that now Andy wouldn't receive all of his father's attention and being berated for putting his new wife's needs ahead of his son's, he managed to beg off and call Andy to the upstairs extension. That conversation had been pure Shelley! The very accusations she'd tossed at him were what she'd been guilty of for years. With her, men came first. Andy, second.

He sat, head down, hands dangling between his legs, the weight of the day's events cowing him. A few minutes after he heard the shower shut off, he mustered the energy to rise and knock on the bathroom door. "Pam? Are you about finished in there?"

When she opened the door, a misty cloud of steam hit him in the face, along with a smell like June roses.

His vision cleared, and he gawked. Standing before him in a fluffy peach-colored terry-cloth robe was Pam, her head wrapped in a towel, her smooth, clean skin flushed from the heat, her tawny eyes fringed with long lashes. "I'm done. Do you need in?"

He gulped. "In a while. I thought maybe we ought to settle a few things before we turn in."

"Like?"

"Our morning routine, for starters."

She edged past him toward the bedroom, where she sat at the foot of the bed toweling her hair dry. "As you can see, I'm an evening shower person. I'll need about fifteen minutes in the bathroom in the morning."

He couldn't take his eyes off her. When she raised her arms to massage her scalp, the robe gaped, revealing a sheer nightie it would be folly to think about. Tendrils of hair trailed down the nape of her neck, and he wanted nothing more than to throw off the towel and plunge his hands into her hair and...

"What about you?"

Me? "What about me?"

"The bathroom," she prompted.

"Oh, yeah. I get up at six. I'll be cleared out of there by six-thirty." He stuffed his hands into his pockets to have something to do with them.

"You know I've been thinking," she went on. "If we're to pull this off, we need to know a little more about each other. Our histories, likes, dislikes, that kind of thing."

It made sense. "We haven't had much time to consider stuff like that, have we? But what about Andy? He'll suspect, if we talk around here."

"I was thinking maybe we could slip off campus for our lunches this week."

Now her hair fell to her shoulders and she worked on drying the ends. Without makeup, she looked younger. Something about the intimacy of her sitting on his bed in her nightwear tangled his tongue. "Sounds good. Tomorrow then?"

She nodded. "Also we have to think about how to make the announcement of our marriage." She lowered her hands and spanned them across her abdomen. "The sooner the better," she whispered.

That made sense. You didn't have to teach in the math department to compute nine months. "What about the all-school assembly day after tomorrow?"

"That would certainly kill all the birds with one stone." She looked up, her eyes holding a spark of humor. "Or we could just tell Geraldine Farley."

He grinned. Mrs. Farley, one of the school patrons, was notorious as Keystone's number one gossipmonger. "The assembly's far safer. Besides, we wouldn't want Andy to think our marriage is a secret. I'll tell him in the morning that we're making the announcement Thursday."

Pam stood, her bare feet unaccountably arousing. Grant resisted the urge to let his gaze lift to her bare knees. "Tonight went better than I expected," she said. "With Andy."

"I wish I could say the same for my conversation with his mother. No telling what poison she fed him when they talked."

Pam moved closer, the heady fragrance of rosebuds disarming him. She laid a hand on his arm. "Don't borrow trouble."

"I'll try not to." He stepped around her to turn down the bedspread. Then he hesitated. "Are you sure you don't want this bed?"

"I'm sure. See you in the morning." At the door, she paused and turned back to him. "Thanks, Grant. For everything."

Later, lying in bed, he longed for the oblivion of sleep. It had been an exhausting day—school starting, telling Andy, moving Pam, calling Shelley. Heck, Pam was right. He didn't need to borrow trouble. He already had plenty.

The ex-wife from hell.

A son who barely tolerated him.

And a pregnant wife-for-a-year. One who aroused in him emotions long dormant and potentially dangerous.

"HEY, GILBERT, wait up." A string bean of a kid with a blond buzz cut and hands the size of fielders' mitts grabbed a notebook out of his locker, slammed it shut and loped after Andy. "Aren't you Coach G.'s son?"

This guy was only about the thirtieth jerk who'd asked him that same question. As if he didn't have an identity of his own. "Yeah, I'm Andy."

"Hey, welcome to Keystone. I'm Chip Kennedy. Are you a sophomore?"

Andy grunted assent, wishing the creep would leave him alone.

"So am I. I'm hoping to start this season. I'm a forward. How about you?"

"I don't play basketball," Andy said, frowning.

"No kidding? You look like you'd be a natural. What are you? Six-one?"

"Six-two."

"How come you don't play?"

Chip was a regular Regis Philbin with the questions. What answer would he buy? "I've been living with my mother. She's not into basketball." That was an understatement. Last year she'd made it to only one of his games and had been more interested in flirting with their center's divorced father than in watching him score nineteen points.

"Maybe you could come out for the team here. Give it a try."

"No." Andy didn't even bother to be polite. Chip was bugging him. Gratefully, Andy realized he was at the door of his English class. "Gotta go."

"Good to meetcha. See ya tomorrow." Chip moved on down the hall and Andy slipped into his seat at the back of the class. He opened his textbook at random and pretended to study a chart called "Elements of the Short Story." It was getting harder and harder to be anonymous around here, and after tomorrow's assembly, there'd be no hiding, especially in this class where all the kids would figure he was getting special attention from the teacher.

Ms. Carver was talking in her chirpy voice about the dude who wrote "The Tell-Tale Heart." He sounded like a screwball, but, man, could he write. When she finished, there was a kind of interesting discussion he pretended not to listen to about how Poe's choice of words enhanced the dramatic impact. Out of the corner of his eye, he noticed this one chick wearing jeans and a tight purple T-shirt. Her straight glossy black hair was tucked behind her ears. He could tell from the way she sat—straining forward eagerly—that she was a good student. Not to be confused with him. He had no intention of doing any more than necessary.

"…so for Friday, I want you to write a paragraph about a place that's special to you. In it, try to use words that convey the sights, sounds and smells particular to the scene you're describing." Ms. Carver was a slave driver—for Friday they also had to read Poe's "The Masque of the Red Death." Andy snorted under his breath. This great writer dude couldn't even spell "mask."

When the bell rang, she flashed the class that big smile he'd noticed. It was like she really enjoyed teaching. Maybe even liked the students. Some of them. But he had to watch out. Just because her cat was okay didn't mean he had to like her, because, bottom line, it was weird to see his dad with her. Maybe it was because he was living with them, but his father and...Pam... seemed sort of stiff.

God, he dreaded tomorrow. He'd feel like a freak when the whole school found out that his dad had married Ms. Carver. Prob'ly then old Chip would ask even more questions.

He picked up his books and sauntered toward the door, not looking to one side or the other. In the hall, waiting for him, was the dark-haired girl he'd eyeballed in class. "Andy?"

"Yeah?"

She grinned, and he noticed the bands on her teeth. A lotta kids wouldn't smile for months after they got braces, but she didn't seem to mind. "I'm Angela, and we have Algebra II together next period. Wanna walk with me?"

She wouldn't try to talk him into playing basketball and she was kinda cute, so what could it hurt? "Okay."

While she talked, she nodded and smiled to other kids passing in the halls. "You going to the football game Friday night?"

Right, like he was gonna get all hyped up about the Keystone Knights. "I don't know."

"Everyone goes. We're supposed to be pretty good this year. See that guy standing at the water fountain?"

Andy took in the form of a solidly built kid about six-five who looked about twenty-three. "What about him?"

"That's Beau Jasper. He's a senior. Last year he broke the school scoring records in both football and basketball."

Andy hated the worshipful look on her face. Girls. They were always after popular jocks. He doubted his tennis playing was in the same league with Beau Jasper's accomplishments.

"Here we are." Angela paused outside the math class, looking at him as if wanting him to say something. What?

"Maybe I'll see you around."

He found his desk, aware she was trailing after him. "Yeah, maybe."

She sat down and started pulling her homework out of her notebook. He couldn't figure it. For some reason, she'd seemed kinda sad. What could he possibly have done to upset her?

Heck, he upset everybody these days.

THURSDAY MORNING Pam had an even bigger case of stage fright than when she'd played Auntie Mame in a local little theater production. The assembly was between second and third periods. She didn't know which would be worse—this awful anticipation or the aftermath when the reactions came. She and Grant had agreed to sit together, since it might look odd if they didn't. After what seemed the longest second period class she'd ever endured, the bell rang and she made her way toward the auditorium, scarcely aware of the jostling students, banging locker doors or buzz of conversation. Near the back of the auditorium, she spotted Grant. He signaled her and she slipped into the seat beside him. "Ready?" he said under his breath.

"No, but do we have a choice?"

He didn't answer her rhetorical question, but merely shrugged. Ralph Hagood calmed the crowd and then introduced Jim, who traditionally talked with the students at this first assembly of the year.

The tension in Grant's body was almost palpable. But it was no match for hers. Once Jim shared their news, there would be absolutely no turning back.

Pam gripped the armrests and waited. How would she and Grant pull off the masquerade? They were still tiptoeing around each other at home, being excessively polite, each taking care to observe the other's space and privacy. Even roommates weren't so formal with each other. Fortunately Andy seemed lost in his own world, so perhaps he hadn't noticed the strain. Lunch yesterday with Grant had helped some, but it was going to take more than a few meals to establish routine familiarity.

He could be very sweet. Although he clearly had no affinity for cats, she had found him yesterday, his face screwed in distaste, holding at arm's length a pooperscooper. When she'd asked him what in the world he was doing, he'd said, "I remember Jack Liddy complaining about having to empty their cat's litter box while Darla's pregnant. Something about a disease cats carry. I figured with all that's on your mind, you didn't need that worry."

Out of the corner of her eye, she glanced at Grant. To all outward appearances, he would seem to have his attention glued to the headmaster. But what must he be thinking? Did he want to bolt and run? She wouldn't blame him.

For a fleeting moment she thought of Steven. For the first time, she had a flare of anger. She wouldn't be sitting here with a teeth-rattling set of nerves if only... She hugged herself against the chill of the air-conditioning. But there was no *if only*. Never had been. There was merely Jim Campbell's voice, now moving from a serious to an upbeat tone. Then she heard the words "I have an announcement to make." She found herself clutching Grant's arm in the effort to still the pounding of her heart. "...so I ask all of you to join me in a congratulatory round of applause for the happy couple."

The buzzing in her head was replaced by a roar of approval, then by deafening applause. Grant reached for her hand and drew her to her feet. For a moment she wanted to believe in happy endings—all around them students and faculty were grinning delightedly as if each of them had personally been the matchmaker.

"Hey, Coach! Aren't you gonna kiss her?" The suggestion spread like an August grass fire. "Kiss, kiss, kiss!" The chant reverberated throughout the auditorium.

Grant looked down at her, a shy grin creasing his mouth. He raised his eyebrows in question.

She took a deep breath. "Act 1, scene 2," she whispered as his arms went around her and he bent his head. Then his mouth was on hers, his hands caressing her back. With a jolt, she realized that he was an accomplished actor. Her hands twined behind his neck as if they'd been choreographed to do so. The part of her not blushing with embarrassment at the spectacle they were making of themselves made an important, unexpected observation.

This didn't feel like any stage kiss she'd ever experienced.

AFTER THE WAITER SET their lunches on the table, Grant bit into his burger. "Food. That's better."

Pam smiled. "Didn't you eat breakfast?"

"I was too nervous." That was the truth. The thought of the assembly had destroyed his appetite.

Forking up a bite of salad, Pam nodded appreciatively. "Soda crackers were all I had, but, wonder of wonders, I didn't get sick."

Grant studied her full lips closing over her fork. She had a wonderful mouth just made for kissing, as he had discovered this morning. He shifted against the leather booth back. She hadn't fought him at all. If he didn't know she was a fine actress, he could almost convince himself she'd enjoyed the kiss. The students had reacted with wild applause, crying out "More, more!" He wouldn't have minded in the least indulging in an encore, but discretion had triumphed and he and Pam had shooed the kids off to class.

"Now that the word is out, maybe you can make a doctor's appointment."

"I did. Yesterday. With Belinda Ellis, Darla's doctor." She set down her fork, her forehead furrowed. "The next hurdle will be when we reveal the rest of our news."

"There's no point in waiting too long." He grinned wickedly. "We'll just let everybody believe we worked fast."

"Pretty sold on yourself, huh?"

The glow in his eyes faded. "Lady, it's been so long

since I've had any practice, at least let me nurture my illusions.'' The illusion he was having right now was a full-blown fantasy that would make Pam blush if she could read his mind.

- ''Nurture away,'' she said. Then she looked up as if she'd just thought of something. ''I guess maybe I ought to give you, er, permission. Other women, I mean. You know, during this year, it's not like I expect you to be a monk. So if—''

''Forget it. For one year I promised to make this marriage work. Look, I know it's not like other marriages, but that doesn't mean I want to set tongues wagging.''

''You're sure?''

He hesitated, knowing full well the only woman he wanted to go to bed with was the one sitting across from him. Pam had no idea how tough it was going to be for him to remain a husband in name only. ''Sure.'' Before any other disturbing images came to his brain, he needed to change the subject. ''Are you getting more comfortable with the idea of being pregnant?'' He dipped a French fry in catsup and waited for her answer.

''It still seems odd. And sometimes for a few minutes, I even forget. My biggest fear is the risk involved in having my first child after age thirty-five.''

''The doctor should be on top of those things. That's one reason I'm glad you're seeing her soon.''

''There's…one other thing.'' Piece by piece, she gradually shredded the paper napkin she was holding. When she stopped, she gave a shuddering little sigh and said, ''My mother died having me.''

He looked into Pam's haunted eyes, desperate to reassure her. ''God, I'm so sorry. But that doesn't mean—''

''That I'll have complications. I know.'' She managed a halfhearted chuckle. "That was nearly forty years ago. Times have changed."

Boy, that explained a lot about Barbara's resentment and Pam's hurt. He set his uneaten French fry on the rim of his plate. "I'm not a 'real' husband, Pam, but you don't have to worry all by yourself."

She reached across the table and squeezed his hand. "Thanks, Grant. No one could ask for a better friend."

"It's easy." Darned if he wouldn't be the best friend she'd ever had. Since he couldn't be her husband.

THIS MIGHT POSSIBLY HAVE BEEN the next-to-worst day of his life. Andy sat at his desk staring out the bedroom window, an unopened pile of schoolbooks at his left elbow. A stiff breeze ruffled the leaves of the oak tree, and down the street he could see some guy in an undershirt mowing his lawn. Maybe this *was* the worst day, though, because he couldn't actually remember much about the day his father had moved out. Except for crying himself to sleep.

But today had been pure hell. All these kids he'd never seen before treating him like a celebrity. Acting like they knew him. Asking him all these questions about how his dad had popped the question and what it was like to live with Ms. Carver.

He knocked the books on the floor. It wasn't bad enough that he'd been exiled to Fort Worth. No. Now he had to hear from all these Keystone geeks about what a great guy his dad was, how lucky he was to have such a cool family. Family? He wondered what that might be like. Not that he'd ever know.

In the distance he heard the phone ring, but he didn't pay any attention. No one would be calling him. Unless it was Mom. But today she and Harry were flying half-way around the world. It wouldn't be her.

A tap on his door startled him. "Yeah?"

"For you," his dad said.

"Okay." He walked to the bedside table, picked up the extension, then flopped on his bed, wondering who the heck wanted to talk to him. "Uh, hello?"

"Andy?" It was a girl. He struggled to sit up. "It's Angela. Remember? From English and math?"

He couldn't believe it. The rah-rah-football girl. Phoning him? "I remember."

"I, uh, wondered if you got the answer to problem number four in algebra?"

She sounded breathless. "No. I haven't started my homework."

"Even English?"

"I guess you think since Ms. Carver's my stepmom that I hurry right home and dig in."

"Well, yeah. If it was me—"

"It isn't. But you may have a point. I don't need to volunteer for any more trouble than I've already got."

"Especially if you're going to be driving soon. You'll need a B grade average to get the car insurance break. My folks said I'd have to pay my own premiums if I didn't make the grades."

He hadn't thought about that. He *did* want to get his license. And he wanted his father to buy him a car. Ticking the old man off about his studies might not be the greatest idea. "I didn't realize, about the grades and all. Guess I'd better look at problem four after all."

"Have you written your paper for English yet?"

She didn't seem to get it. He hadn't turned a tap except for reading Poe. "I'll whip it out tonight."

"I've heard she's a tough grader."

How much more bad news could Angela lay on him? "I'm good in English."

She didn't answer. It was like neither of them had anything to say. He couldn't figure out why she'd called him in the first place, unless...

"About tomorrow night?"

Tomorrow night? What did she mean? "What about it?"

"I thought if you were coming to the game, well, maybe you'd like to sit with me."

He'd had no intention of going to the stupid game, but Angela *was* kinda cute. "Sounds good. I'll see you there."

"Okay." Her voice lifted on the "kay." Then after a long pause she said; "I've gotta go finish my math. Bye, now."

He hung up, but continued staring at the receiver. Had she sorta asked him for a date? He could halfway get excited except for the fact now his dad and Pam would know everything about his life.

He reached across the bed and scooped his English notebook off the floor. He supposed he had to make at least a halfhearted effort to write the stupid paper about his favorite place.

Just where the hell would that be? He glanced around the room. Not here, that was for sure.

He hunched up against the headboard and opened the notebook. He picked up the pen that fell out of it and stared at the blank page. Nothing was coming to him.

A special place? One with good memories? He couldn't think of a thing to say.

CHAPTER SIX

THE KEYSTONE COACHES traditionally met to play poker following home football games. On Friday night the odors of cigar smoke, stale beer and lukewarm barbecued ribs greeted Grant along with ribald comments. "Hey, Gilbert, surely a newlywed has better things to do on a Friday night than hang out with us" and "Pam worn you out already?"

Amid the knowing grins, he could hardly confess he and his new bride slept in separate rooms.

He endured the card game but was relieved when Jack Liddy called it an evening, pleading the need to start early in the morning reviewing game films. The two men left together. The football coach paused before getting into his SUV. "You know, it's about time you settled down. Pam's a great gal. I'm happy for you both."

"I appreciate that."

"By the way, how's your son getting along?"

Grant leaned against the hood, arms folded across his chest. "It's hard to say."

"How'd he take the news?"

Grant thought about the question, unsure how to answer. "He was surprised, but at least he's not taking it out on Pam. So far. I'm the one he's mad at. Told me point-blank he hates basketball."

"Weren't you counting on him coming out for the team?"

Grant shrugged helplessly. "I thought he liked basketball. He did as a little kid. Things change, I guess."

"That's gotta be disappointing."

Uh, yeah. "He's going out for tennis in the spring."

"That's something." Jack raised a finger in farewell. "Hang in there, man."

Grant stood quietly, trying to ease the tension in his gut before heading for home where his pregnant wife and surly teenage son awaited him. Andy seemed determined not to let him get close, holing up in his room except for meals. The two of them had exchanged only the most cursory of words in the past few days. It was anybody's guess what the kid was thinking, but, as Pam reminded him often, Andy needed time to adjust.

Grant knew he should stop tiptoeing around his son. Discipline and love, as he well knew from teaching, were the keys. But, jeez, it was a precarious balancing act.

At least things were going okay with Pam. The lunches had been a good idea. He'd been able to tell her about his father being in Vietnam when he himself was a kid. About how he couldn't remember his father approving of anything he did or his mother ever going against her husband's orders. He'd confessed how, as a kid, he had never felt he measured up. He probably should have resented Brian, but his brother had been his advocate, his idol. When Brian joined the army, following in their dad's footsteps, Grant had felt as if he'd lost part of himself, and since Brian's death, Grant had maintained only a tenuous connection to his family.

He'd admitted to Pam how, even as an adult, he'd been a disappointment to his father. "Teaching? What kind of life is that for a man?'' Those few words summed up his distant relationship with Lieutenant Colonel Jarvis J. Gilbert.

Despite Shelley's dissatisfaction, it was little wonder his attempt to create a family had failed. He'd had no model. Maybe ''happy family'' was nothing more than a myth. But that didn't prevent him from wanting one.

From Pam, he'd learned more about the emotional distance between her and her sister—how, as a child, no amount of good behavior or beguiling smiles could win over Barbara, frozen in grief and resentment. On a cheerier note, Pam told of her closeness to her rancher father, her days as an undergraduate at U.T., her roles in theater productions, her love of American literature. But nothing more about this past summer, about her love affair. For the life of him, he couldn't fathom why thinking about her with another man bothered him so much.

It had only been a week since their marriage. Fifty-one to go. The way he felt right now, though, the time could only grow more torturous, because with every passing day, despite his history, he was becoming more and more invested in the idea of family. His family. This family.

But he'd made a bargain. And he was a man of his word.

SUNDAY AFTERNOON Pam curled up on the sofa with two stacks of student papers. Grant watched a pro football game, seemingly unaware that Viola was perched on the back of his recliner.

Saturday had gone better than expected. Andy had slept late, and when Grant had returned from a morning at the gym, Pam had put them to work bringing over the rest of her belongings from the condo and then re-arranging furniture here and hanging her prints. Luckily she'd leased her condo to Randy Selves, the young journalism teacher, for the school year.

Grant asked her if the audio of the game was disturbing her, and although she said no, she nonetheless found her attention straying from the papers. Glancing around the room, she allowed herself a satisfied grin. It no longer seemed stark and utilitarian. Her collection of wooden candlesticks looked great on the mantel, and the colorful Southwestern throws and pillows brought color where there had been drabness.

At halftime Grant muted the TV and moved to the sofa. "How do you think it's going? Our arrangement?"

"Okay. Maybe we're at our best when we forget we're married and try just to be friends."

"This is harder than I thought."

"That's because we can scarcely ever let our guard down."

"Maybe we'll settle into a routine soon."

"Let's see, you do Sunday breakfasts, I cook dinners, I do Andy's laundry, you do your own." She continued ticking items off on her fingers. "We take turns cleaning the bathroom. You vacuum, I dust. How am I doing so far?"

"Sounds like a game plan to me."

"Would you mind if I planted some bulbs in the yard?"

He chuckled apologetically. "It's pretty barren out there."

"All it needs is a woman's touch." Should she have mentioned flowers? Was it presumptuous to put such a permanent stamp on his territory?

He stood. "Can I get you anything? A soda or something?"

"No, I'm fine."

He hesitated, then went on. "Is it next week you go to the doctor?"

"Yes. Wednesday after school."

He didn't say anything, just nodded. But there was something in his body language that suggested uncertainty. Surely he didn't want to go with her. That would be way too weird. Besides, she had lots of questions to ask Dr. Ellis, and her privacy was important. He didn't need to feel any obligation to carry their charade that far. "On second thought, a glass of iced tea sounds good."

"Sure," he said, heading toward the kitchen.

Had it been fair to entangle him in her personal affairs? With perseverance he could surely have located a housekeeper. Then he and Andy could have bonded without the complication of her presence in their midst. For Andy, though, the biggest surprise was yet to come.

Lost in self-recrimination, she didn't hear Grant return. "Here." He handed her the tea. "Okay if I watch the second half?"

"Go ahead." He shooed Viola away and settled in his chair.

She held the icy glass to her cheek, relishing the cool. Finally she set it on the table and picked up the papers still awaiting her attention. This early in the year she took particular care with her grading, making more than the usual number of comments in the effort to reassure the students. The senior essays had been, by and large, proficient, but, as expected, the level of quality among the sophomores was all over the board. When she came to Andy's paragraph, she took a sip of tea before beginning to read.

Halfway through, she closed her eyes, fighting tears. His heart lay there on the page, bleeding.

A special place? Where would that be? A guy'd have to stay long enough in one spot to feel at home. So it can't be my house in Florida with all those smelly, hothouse plants and my mother's stupid macaw who woke me every morning with his squawking. It sure isn't hot, dusty Texas where I'm forced to go to a school where my dad is this big cheese. Keystone. The kids look like sitcom actors and the buildings resemble some architect's idea of hacienda-land. I suppose a lot of students will pick their bedroom to write about, probably 'cuz they have stuff around them like photos and posters and dorky stuffed animals that they've had all their lives. Me? I've got my music, my clothes and a tennis racket. You want to know what a special place would be? One where I don't have to answer to anybody. Where adults aren't always expecting something from me. Where I can just hang out and be me.

She set the paper in her lap, awed by Andy's self-revelation and wondering how on earth she would find the words to respond. Her love went out to him with a fierce protectiveness that caught her utterly by surprise.

ANDY SAT CROSS-LEGGED against the headboard of his bed, listening to a new rap CD and staring at the phone. Should he call her? And say what? "Angela, this is Andy"? And then what? No way could he ask her for a real date, not before he had his own wheels. He could just picture it. His old man chauffeuring them to a movie. Sneaking peeks in the rearview mirror to see if he'd made any moves on Angela. Nah, better to remain just friends.

He did like the way she smiled at him, though. And her long black hair was shiny the way wet pavement was after a rain.

But the football game had been weird. He'd felt like an alien. All the other kids knew one another. Heck, some had been at Keystone together since kindergarten. He didn't have a clue who they were talking about or what they were laughing at.

But Angie—that's how he liked to think of her— hadn't seemed to mind. In fact, after one big score, she'd slipped her hand into his, like they were a real couple. Yeah. Angie and Andy. That sounded cool. She was friendly, nice. Not like some of those snobby girls with the tight skirts, French braids and designer purses. He closed his eyes, picturing the two of them kissing. Would her braces get in the way? He hoped not.

The phone sat there. Waiting. Maybe she wouldn't be home. Worse, what if her father answered?

He flung off the headphones and crossed to look out the bedroom window. Downstairs he could hear the drone of a sports announcer. Outside, the next-door neighbors were setting up for a backyard barbecue, across the street some little kids were running through a sprinkler and a fat bald guy with a fire-engine-red face was jogging slowly down the street.

But he didn't have a place. Not out there. Not in here. Certainly not at Keystone.

He turned back to stare, once again, at the telephone. *Forget it, Gilbert. Don't let yourself get sucked in.*

THE WAITING ROOM with its pastel color scheme was intended to be soothing. But Pam felt edgy and nervous. All around her sat women in various stages of pregnancy, one so huge Pam feared she might give a birthing demonstration any minute. Pam laid a hand across her flat stomach, finding it hard to believe she'd ever look like that.

She turned her attention to the new-patient questionnaire the receptionist had given her, cringing when she came to the section concerning the father's medical history. Every time she thought she'd moved beyond Steven, something like this blindsided her.

She swallowed back a sob. Damn. She hated being so emotional. It wasn't like her at all, but these days every little thing set her off. Like Andy's paragraph and Grant's thoughtfulness in tending to the litter boxes.

"Mrs. Gilbert?" A nurse clutching a clipboard smiled into the waiting room.

Pam rose to her feet and followed along. To her surprise, the nurse ushered her, not to an examining room but to a beautifully appointed office. "Dr. Ellis would like to visit with you before the exam," the nurse explained, directing Pam to a wing chair. "She'll be with you shortly."

On the chair-side table lay several pamphlets and the latest issue of *Parent's Magazine*. Pam thumbed idly through one of the pamphlets in which terms like amniocentesis, alpha-fetoprotein and blood sugar seemed like a foreign language. What if something went wrong? Miscarriage, she knew, was a definite threat during the first trimester. What if—

The door opened and a petite, middle-aged woman with sparkling dark eyes and short-cropped black hair

breezed in. "Mrs. Gilbert? Sorry to keep you waiting."
She held out her hand. "I'm Belinda Ellis."

Pam didn't know quite what she'd expected—maybe
a tall, horsey-looking woman with a bun—but she was
immediately disposed to like her obstetrician. "It's
good to meet you."

"We'll be seeing quite a bit of each other in the next
few months," the doctor said, taking her place behind
her desk. "I like to get to know my patients. That way
we can work together so that you have a happy, fulfill-
ing experience. And a healthy baby." She glanced
down at the questionnaire Pam had filled out. "I see
you're a teacher. Will you be working throughout your
pregnancy?"

"I plan to." Pam gave silent thanks to Grant, who
had saved her from having to resign.

Dr. Ellis continued gently probing, and Pam gradually relaxed as she noticed how intently and empathet-
ically the doctor listened to her answers. At last the
obstetrician set the chart aside and folded her hands on
the desk. "Since you're over thirty-five, I'll be asking
you to take certain precautions. Later, if it's indicated,
I may recommend a couple of special tests. But right
now, I don't want you to worry about anything. From
what you tell me, your pregnancy is proceeding quite
normally."

Pam expelled a sigh of relief. "That's good news."

"I'm sure you'll want to share it with your husband."
The doctor leaned forward. "You know he's welcome
to come with you for your appointments. In fact, I en-
courage it."

Pam gave fleeting thought to what it would be like
to have a doting husband at her side, but that was more
than she could ever ask or expect from Grant. "He, uh,

he's a coach. It's hard for him to get away. He won't be coming with me.''

Belinda Ellis narrowed her eyes in concern. "Have I said something to make you uncomfortable?'' She hesitated. "I see a lot of women, and I can generally tell when there's something I need to know regarding the baby's father. You are married, aren't you?''

Pam thought again about the questionnaire and the answers she'd fabricated for the section about the father. She couldn't go on with the lies, not when her baby's health was at stake.

Forcing her body to relax, Pam looked straight into the doctor's warm eyes. "Yes, I'm married, but..." She bit her lip.

"Go on,'' the doctor urged softly.

"My husband is not the baby's father.'' Pam had thought the world would cave in if she ever said those words aloud. Instead, she felt as if a heavy weight had been lifted.

"Tell me about it, if you'd care to. Whatever you say to me is in strictest confidence.''

Unburdening herself to this woman was easier than she would ever have imagined. Only when Dr. Ellis handed her a tissue halfway through the telling did Pam realize her cheeks were wet with tears. Finally she managed the part about Grant and their arrangement. When she finished, she awaited the doctor's judgment. A verdict and sentence she knew she deserved.

Instead, Dr. Ellis smiled a gentle smile and said, "Grant sounds like quite a man. Pam—may I call you Pam?—why don't you let him be as much a part of this pregnancy as you and he are comfortable with? You could use the support and if, as you say, he's a good friend, he might like to help you through this special time in your life. What about it?''

Pam nodded mutely, blew her nose, then smiled in relief.

The doctor rose. "Feel better now?" She moved to the door. "Let's get you into an examining room and find out how that precious little one is doing."

Later, lying on the examining table with Belinda Ellis's comforting hand on her abdomen, Pam could truly begin to believe that she was going to be a mother and that everything just might turn out all right.

ANDY HAD FIRST SPOTTED IT late Sunday afternoon when he'd borrowed his dad's bike and taken a tour of the neighborhood. A park tucked behind a row of scraggly cedar trees. He'd known the basketball court was there before he saw it because he could hear guys talking trash. He'd stopped to watch for a while, a hard lump rising in his throat.

So what the heck? Today Pam had some appointment after school and, after delivering him home, his dad was off helping officiate a middle school football game. They'd never know if he sneaked out to shoot some hoops. He missed playing basketball, but he'd never give his father the satisfaction of knowing that. He went out to the garage, hopped on the bike and pedaled down the street.

In this multiethnic neighborhood, it was no surprise to find the players at the park included a couple of awesome black dudes, several tough-looking white kids and a short Hispanic guy who could dribble like greased lightning—probably all from the large public high school nearby. Andy's hands itched for the ball. But he knew he had to hang around until he was invited.

Finally one of the black guys turned to him and said, "You play hoops?"

"A little," Andy said modestly.

"Here." He tossed Andy the ball. "Show us your stuff!"

Andy threw a head fake, dribbled through the first two defenders, reversed, stalled, then quickly pivoted and drove toward the basket. Then up, up he went for two, count 'em, points. "Hey," another kid laughed, "You're good, man. Can you do it again?" And they were off and running. The best games, the ones where Andy felt most alive, were pickup contests with guys whose hearts, like his, beat to the tattoo of a basketball bouncing on asphalt.

After an exhilarating few minutes, they chose sides. Howie, one of the white kids, and Andy were teamed with Andre and James, the black guys. The other three white guys and Juan squared off against them. Once they started, it was war. Nobody called any fouls and you had to be tough to keep up. Half an hour later, Andy wiped sweat from his face, then rubbed the bruise on his elbow he'd picked up when he'd gotten knocked on his ass defending under the basket. "I gotta go," he said.

"You come back anytime, dude," James said. "You can *play,* man!"

Hot and dirty, Andy pedaled away as fast as he could. He needed to beat Pam and Dad home and get a quick shower so they'd never know he'd been gone. But, jeez, that had been a blast. Maybe he could survive this crummy place if he could sneak away and shoot hoops every now and then. So long as his dad never found out.

For some reason, thinking about basketball reminded

him of his paragraph for English. How stupid would it have sounded to tell Pam that his special place was a basketball court? Worse yet, what if he'd written that and she'd told his dad? Actually he'd been kind of amazed to get a B on the paragraph. She'd liked his description of the flowers and bird. She said he had a strong "voice," too, whatever the heck that was. But one of the things she'd written made him feel kinda squirrelly. He put on the brakes and turned into the driveway, relieved that neither Pam nor his dad was home yet.

What had she said exactly? Oh, yeah. *You can create your own special place in your head and heart. Then it can go with you wherever you are.*

What was that supposed to mean, anyway?

FOR THE NEXT COUPLE OF WEEKS school kept Pam so busy she didn't have time to think about much of anything except lesson plans, ordering play books for *Our Town,* writing the faculty pep skit for the Homecoming assembly and keeping up with her grading. She'd become a master of thirty-minute meal preparation and, so far, neither Andy nor Grant had complained. It helped when she could squeeze a quick nap in before she started dinner. Otherwise, she went to bed shortly before nine, amazed that pregnancy had sent her night-owl tendencies into total remission.

She worried about Andy. He still hadn't made any friends to speak of, except for Angela Beeman. It was as if he went out of his way to nurture the chip on his shoulder. She couldn't help but wonder if things would be better or worse between Grant and him if she wasn't there to defuse the tension. She could tell Grant was both baffled and hurt by his son's attitude. To his credit,

Grant was doing a fair job of standing back and giving Andy some space.

She'd come home from school this Saturday afternoon absolutely drained from helping judge the Keystone Invitational Forensics Tournament. But she had to rally for a command performance—dinner at the headmaster's with several other faculty couples. She stood in the bathroom applying fresh makeup, hoping she could keep her eyes open until after dessert.

Grant tapped on the door. "Are you about ready?"

She managed a tiny grin. He'd been too polite to say "Come on." If she'd learned anything about him so far, it was that he hated to be late. "Just a couple more minutes."

"I'll be in the living room giving Andy his marching orders."

When she emerged from the bedroom, wearing a lime-green dress with a bright blue linen blazer, she stopped in her tracks. The "marching orders" were not going well.

Andy's voice drifted down the hall. "Trouble? What trouble could I get into? Whaddya think? That me and Viola and Sebastian are gonna have a wild party?"

She waited, listening for Grant's response. "I care about you, that's all."

Andy said nothing, but she could imagine the cynical smirk he'd probably given Grant. She hurried toward the living room, where she greeted them with false gaiety. "Ready?"

Grant turned slowly, his eyes widening. "You look terrific."

It felt good to have a man notice her. "Thank you, sir." She smiled at Andy. "I left some cookies on the counter in case you feel like a snack later."

Andy flopped onto the couch and picked up the TV remote. "Cool."

When Grant took her by the hand and started toward the door, she turned back. "You have the number where we'll be, right?"

Andy sighed. "Yeah, yeah. Just leave, okay? I'll be fine."

"I certainly hope so," Grant muttered as they left the house.

They rode in silence, preoccupied with their own concerns.

"Are you sure you're up for this?" Grant asked as they approached the Campbells' house.

"I'd much prefer a bowl of soup, a video and an early night, but I wouldn't disappoint Connie for anything. She's been so excited about entertaining us."

"You'll understand then when I put my arm around you periodically?" His grin was that of a co-conspirator.

"And I'll crave your indulgence when I brush imaginary lint from your lapel."

"Anything to look convincing, huh, Mrs. Gilbert?"

"Is it getting easier?"

He pulled to a stop in the driveway, rested his arm along the back of the seat and studied her, his blue eyes seeking hers as if he wanted to communicate something, but then he merely smiled. "Infinitely."

The intimacy in his voice made it impossible to look away. When other people weren't around and she let down her guard, she could almost imagine that they really were starry-eyed newlyweds. That it wasn't all simply an act.

He picked up a tendril of her hair and rolled it between his thumb and forefinger. "Ready?"

"Lay on, MacDuff."

He held her hand as they walked up to the door. Connie opened it before they could ring the bell. "Welcome. Come on in. The others are in the family room."

Pam knew that Ginny Phillips and her husband, Jack and Darla Liddy and Ralph Hagood had been invited, but she didn't know who else would be among the guests. She was ill prepared, then, when she and Grant walked into the room and were greeted by a crowd shouting "Surprise!" She faltered, then felt Grant's steadying arm around her waist. Their friends looked so pleased and happy, confident they were doing a wonderful thing. On the coffee table were mounds of packages wrapped in white, silver and gold.

Jim emerged from the crowd and handed each of them a champagne flute. "Here's to the bride and groom," he said, as others echoed his words.

Pam looked up at Grant, who appeared almost as dazed as she felt.

Connie was practically jumping up and down by her side. "You didn't think you were going to get off without having a wedding shower, did you?"

Pam willed a smile to her face. How could she tell Connie or her guests that, within a year, she'd have to return all their heartfelt gifts? "Oh, this is too much. You didn't need to —"

"Nonsense. I know we didn't *need* to do anything. We wanted to."

Pam felt Grant's hand slide up her back to rest on her shoulder. "Thank you, Connie. This is very generous."

Pam allowed herself to be led through the throng of well-wishers. Along the way she set her champagne down behind a flower arrangement. Then there was nothing further to do except open the gifts. Benumbed, she picked up the first package and, with Grant's help, managed to fumble with the paper and ribbon.

"Be careful." Somewhere from the crowd Jessie Flanders's voice floated high and clear. "Every ribbon you break means another baby."

And with that, Pam pulled too hard and the first ribbon snapped in two. Laughter and catcalls erupted. Pam felt Grant's fingers massaging her neck. If they only knew.

That was bad enough. But then she opened the box. She'd only thought her face was red before. Nestled in fragrant lavender tissue paper was the flimsiest, laciest, most provocative nightie she'd ever seen. "Show us," trumpeted a voice near the window. "Ooh-la-la," someone else trilled.

She gulped, sensing a flush mottling her skin. When she held it up, she couldn't have felt any more exposed had she been an exotic dancer in a stag bar.

As if in a trance, she managed to get through the rest of the gifts. A soup tureen, a personalized welcome sign for the porch, a set of monogrammed bar glasses, a leaded crystal vase.

Well-meaning, thoughtful, generous. Her friends. Grant's friends. Their friends.

Until she and Grant would be forced to reveal their duplicity.

Until September.

GRANT CAST worried glances at Pam as they passed under streetlights on their way home. She reclined against the headrest, her eyes closed, her breathing measured as if she were deliberately trying to calm herself.

She had said not one word since they left the party.

From the stiffness of her smile and the studied way she had acknowledged each gift, he could tell she had barely held herself together. But once the curtain had rung down on this latest performance, she'd withdrawn into herself.

The wail of a melancholy saxophone on the late-night jazz station matched his mood. The outpouring of generosity and support from their friends and colleagues was humbling but at the same time, embarrassing. Neither he nor Pam was comfortable with deceit, and no matter how practical their motives for marrying might be, they had compromised their honor.

And yet...

He lurched away from a four-way stop. Damn it! There wasn't going to be any happily-ever-after. Like it or not, their arrangement was business. Spelled out by their contract.

Beside him, without opening her eyes, Pam stirred. "That went well, didn't it?" There was no mistaking the sarcasm—or the pain.

He restrained the impulse to pull her into his arms and reassure her. He had no right. "Tough night, wasn't it?"

She turned her head and opened her eyes. "I had no idea it would go this far."

"I know."

"They were so happy for us. I felt about two inches high."

He drove slowly through their neighborhood. Odd. He'd automatically thought of it as "their" neighborhood, not "his." Is that how it happened? Acceptance little by little? "Are you having second thoughts?"

"Second, third and tenth." Apparently sensing his discomfort, she laid a hand on his thigh. "And yet—"

she paused as if searching for the right words "—I'm feeling much more at home with you and Andy than I had thought possible."

He wasn't prepared for the sense of well-being that washed over him, drowning out the doubts that had surfaced during the party. "It's not all bad, is it?"

"No. And maybe it will get easier. Perhaps, with time, the roles will seem almost natural."

He eased into the driveway and shut off the ignition. Night sounds—katydids, a far-off barking, tinkling wind chimes—surrounded them. More than anything he wanted to pull her into his arms and convince her everything would be all right.

Just as he turned toward her to do exactly that, she took hold of the door handle. "The presents? I suppose we should carry them in."

"Andy and I'll get them in the morning. You're beat. You and Barney need to get to bed." He escorted her up the walk. Inside the house, one lone light was burning in the kitchen, casting the hallway in shadow. "Tonight you're sleeping in my bed. I'll take the den."

"Grant, really—"

"I insist. You're exhausted, and no matter what else is happening, you need to take care of yourself. Go on. I'll get my stuff after you're asleep."

She didn't argue, but headed for bed. He watched TV in the living room, the sound turned low. But he couldn't concentrate on the screen. Because, God help him, the picture in his mind was of a sleep-tousled Pam in that skimpy lace nightie, her full breasts straining the filmy material, her hips arched in desire. How in hell was he going to keep his fantasies in check for eleven more months?

Restless, he decided to check on Andy, not that he

would appreciate it. But Grant had a sudden, intense need to see his son, to stand quietly by his bedside and watch him sleep. To imagine what it would have been like if Andy had grown up with him. Would he have been so surly? So prickly? With a heavy sigh, Grant nudged open the door.

And felt his stomach rise to his throat.

The room was empty.

CHAPTER SEVEN

"ANDY?" Grant stepped into his son's room, desperately scanning for some clue to his whereabouts. A paperback thriller lay facedown on the bed, several CDs were scattered randomly over the desk and a Jacksonville Jaguars' sweatshirt lay on the floor as if flung in the general direction of the closet.

Grant whirled from the room and raced downstairs. "Andy?" he whispered, unwilling yet to wake Pam by raising his voice. But when a search of the downstairs and backyard turned up nothing, he began to feel sick. Where could the kid have gone? He didn't seem to have any friends. Nor had he given them any indication before they left for the Campbells' that he had plans. Anger, hot and immediate, clutched at Grant's gut, followed just as swiftly by panic.

Standing helpless in the middle of the kitchen, he broke into a cold sweat. God, what if something terrible had happened to his son? He'd never forgive himself.

The hell of it was, he didn't even know where to begin to look for him. How could they have lived together for a month without his learning more about Andy?

He hated to alarm Pam, but he clung to the hope she'd know something he didn't. Without further thought, he strode into his bedroom. Under other circumstances, he'd have been struck speechless by the sight of Pam curled up in his bed, her hair tumbling across her sleep-flushed cheek. But he didn't have that luxury tonight.

He turned the bedside lamp on the lowest setting. "Pam." He touched her gently on the shoulder. "Pam, wake up."

Slowly her lashes fluttered and she propped herself up on one elbow, brushing back her hair. "Huh?"

"Sorry to wake you. We've got a major problem."

She sat up abruptly, her eyes wide-open. "What—"

"It's Andy. He's gone."

"Gone?" She threw back the covers and swung her legs over the side of the bed. "What do you mean, 'gone'?"

"He's not in the house. Do you have any idea where he might be?"

She shook her head dazedly. "I can't believe it. Where would he go?"

"My point exactly."

She stood up, slipping her feet into fuzzy slippers and grabbing her robe from the foot of the bed. "Give me a minute." She scrubbed her face with her palms. "You don't think he's run away, do you?"

Run away? He hadn't even thought of that possibility. But it made perfect sense. "I knew he was miserable, but I never imagined—"

"Don't jump to conclusions. Let's think." Pam laid a hand on his shoulder. "Are his clothes still in his room?"

"Yeah, I think so."

"And his music?"

"Yes."

"Then there has to be some other explanation. Maybe he's made friends at school we don't know about."

"That's possible, I guess. Still, he should have told us where he was going." He had a sour taste in his mouth. "*If* he was going."

Pam started toward the kitchen. "I have an idea. Come on."

Grant trailed her through the house and out the back door. The yard light illuminated the empty patio, the basketball hoop, the detached garage.

"See if the bike is missing," she suggested, standing to the side of the garage door.

And if it was? Or, worse, if it wasn't? Slowly he raised the door. "It's gone," he said. "Now what?"

"What time is it?"

"A little after eleven."

"Let's give him a half hour or so."

"Before we call the police?"

She took him by the arm and walked him toward the house. "We won't have much choice."

As they sat in the living room eyeing the clock, Pam didn't try to make small talk, but rather sat quietly stroking Viola. He couldn't have said why, but having her here worrying with him somehow made the waiting bearable.

At eleven-thirty, he ran a hand through his hair and, feeling as if the bottom had fallen out of his world, he picked up the telephone. Something—a noise—stopped him before he could begin dialing. He hurried into the kitchen and peered out the window. There, under the yard light his son emerged from the garage, then paused to pull down the door before trudging toward the house, eyes downcast.

Grant threw open the back door. "Where have you been, young man?" His bellow caused Sebastian to seek refuge under the kitchen table.

"Grant, go easy." Pam materialized by his side. "Listen to his story."

"I guess I'm busted, huh?" Andy said as he slithered past his father.

Grant took a shuddering breath. "Busted? Do you have any idea how worried we've been?"

"I'm back. You don't need to make a big deal out of it."

"I'm glad you're safely back. But that doesn't excuse the fact that you left the house without telling us you had plans or when you'd be back." Grant was controlling himself only because he felt Pam's hand in the small of his back.

"Something came up."

"What, for Lord's sake?"

"A buncha guys I know," Andy mumbled.

"Who are you talking about?" Pam asked, her voice amazingly calm.

"Just some guys."

"Andy, give your dad a break. It's late, you're in a strange town, and we don't know your friends. Any caring parent would be worried sick."

Andy shifted uncomfortably before looking past Grant to Pam. "Some kids from the neighborhood came by. We went to the park and just hung out. I didn't think you'd be home yet. Nobody needs to get in an uproar."

Grant shoved his hands into his pockets to keep from pounding the table. "Son, this is unacceptable behavior. We need to know where you're going, who you're with. Imagine how we felt coming home from the party to find you missing."

"So what're you gonna do? Vote me out of the family?"

Grant cursed silently. He wasn't making a dent in Andy's so-what attitude. "Certainly not. But there are going to be consequences."

"It's not like you could ground me. I already feel like I'm under house arrest."

Before Grant could react to that remark, Pam stepped forward. "I'm sorry you feel that way, Andy. You know, lots of the kids at school have been inviting you to do things, trying to make friends with you."

"So?"

"Why are you making it so difficult on yourself? The only one truly holding you back is you. What have you got to lose?"

Grant began to breathe again. Andy was studying Pam, not antagonistically, and maybe even a bit thoughtfully.

"You wouldn't understand," Andy said in a low voice.

"I'd like to try," Pam replied.

"So would I," Grant added.

Andy merely shrugged. "So what's my punishment?"

Grant wanted desperately to make everything all right for his son. But he knew he couldn't shield Andy. Whatever he was going to learn, he had to figure out for himself. "Let's get the ground rules straight. From now on, when Pam and I go out at night, we need to know your plans. If something comes up unexpectedly, we expect you to check in with us or leave a note. Understood?"

Andy nodded, his mouth set in a grim line.

"And you're right. Grounding is no solution. Instead, I expect you to spend the next several days preparing a flower bed. Then Pam will give you some bulbs to plant. A little spade work ought to help remind you we're a family.''

"Some family,'' Andy mumbled before slipping off upstairs.

Grant started after him, but Pam restrained him. "Enough,'' she said softly. "He's gotten the message. Don't do anything you'll regret.''

Grant raked a hand through his hair. "I don't get it. He's my own son and he's driving me nuts. Jeez, you're probably wondering what in hell you signed up for here.''

"You're upset. But remember he's just a kid, a displaced, angry adolescent.'' She nudged him toward the bedroom. "Come on. Things'll look better in the morning. Let's get some sleep.''

A half hour later Grant lay with his knees practically grazing his chin on the painfully short daybed. Wide-awake. What if Pam hadn't been here tonight to temper his anger? He was supposed to be the adult, the expert on teenage boys, the responsible parent.

Yet he'd never felt so totally out of control.

ANDY FLUNG one tennis shoe, then the other against the wall. He stepped out of his baggy shorts, wadded them into a ball and rifled them toward the dark maw of his closet. Damn!

He threw himself down on his bed, with his hands under his head, staring out the window at the coldly luminescent moon. He wasn't a baby. And he sure as hell hadn't done anything wrong. Not really. It wasn't like he was bashing mailboxes, smoking pot or humping some girl. For the love of Mike—all he'd been doing was shooting hoops with Andre, James and the guys.

Who would have thought his dad and Pam would be

home so early? Not him. Shit, no. He was used to Mom and Harry, or whoever, straggling home blitzed and all lovey-dovey long after the late, late show was history.

He couldn't get over his dad pulling the big "Son, I'm the parent, let me show you the error of your ways" stunt. Flower beds. Jeez, Louise. What did he know about gardening?

If it hadn't been for Pam, he might've told his dad just what he was thinking. Like where do you get off telling me what to do after all these years? Like how come you never parted with the bucks to let me come spend summers with you? Like why do you care more about the guys on your team than you do about me? But what good would that have done?

Now his mother was gallivanting all over the Middle East with a guy practically old enough to be her father. Sure, she called once a week. But so what? All she could talk about was Harry this, Harry that.

And his dad? It was like he didn't even know how to talk to his own son. He'd asked Andy again about trying out for the basketball team. Why couldn't the guy understand? It wasn't brain surgery. If you couldn't get along with the man as a father, why would you give him power over you as a coach? No way.

Crazy as it sounded, Pam was about the only thing keeping him from walking out. She didn't give him a hard time the way everybody else did. But she didn't let him off the hook either. She'd asked him a hard question tonight.

Was he being a dork by treating the kids at Keystone like pond scum? He hadn't liked moving to Florida, either. But guys like Brady Showalter had been kinda fun to goof off with. Every day at school Chip Kennedy, the question guy, kept hanging around. He wasn't so bad, really. Andy flopped over on his stomach. The truth was, he wasn't giving Keystone a chance. He didn't want to give his father the satisfaction. After all, he'd be gone in a year. Out of Texas, back to... wherever. And then what?

A cold lump, like mucilage, rose in his throat. Crap. He hadn't cried in years. He sure as hell wasn't going to start now.

PAM PUNCHED HER PILLOW, then cradled the extra one against her abdomen. It was as if the thirty minutes' sleep she'd managed before Grant had awakened her had been it for the night. She'd been exhausted even before the party, but the surprises of the evening had left her feeling edgy, wired.

The house held a taut silence, as if its occupants were breathlessly awaiting certain doom. She tossed restlessly. Poor Andy. He was one of the unhappiest kids she'd ever seen. And Grant, so full of love for his son, so hopeful that things could be worked out with him, had overreacted.

Somehow she needed to find a way to help Andy spit out the source of his resentment. Nothing could be solved until father and son opened up and shared their emotions honestly. In the dark, she managed a wry smile. Right, like males were so good at expressing feelings.

If Andy was hurting, so was Grant. The fear and anguish in his eyes tonight, when Andy had gone missing, had been heartbreaking. The man loved his son. It had taken guts for him to lay the gardening chore on Andy, knowing he'd resent the exercise of paternal authority.

Would she have such courage when it came to her own child? Right now, it was hard to imagine anything other than a helpless infant cooing in her arms. But one day would that lovable baby be replaced by a teenager arching his or her brows and uttering a scathing "Mo-ther, you're so old-fashioned"? Grant must be in a world of pain.

She stilled her breathing and strained her ears. No sound. Was Grant lying awake rehashing their handling of Andy, too?

On an impulse too sudden and potent to ignore, she left her bed and tiptoed into the den. She had the strongest urge to comfort him, to tell him everything would be all right. Grant lay on his back, one arm flung off the cushion, a tangled sheet covering the lower half of his body. In the faint moonlight, she sucked in her breath. His broad naked chest, lightly dusted with tight dark curls, tapered to his trim waist. Although the sheet prevented further examination, her imagination wasn't so hampered. A wave of desire crested inside her. Pregnant women weren't supposed to...or were they? This was a bad idea. She needed to go back to bed.

"Pam?"

The whisper caught her off guard. She'd thought he was asleep. "Yes?"

"What are you doing?" He took hold of her hand and drew her down to sit on the edge of the bed.

"I—I couldn't sleep." Her bare arms prickled with gooseflesh.

"There's a lot of that going around." Tentatively he reached out and touched her shoulder. "Cold?"

"A little." She should move, leave. Why was she still here, lost in the sensation of his fingers lightly tracing her skin?

"Here." He settled an arm around her and nestled her against his warm body.

She was tinglingly aware of the feel of his flesh, of his fingers still stroking her arm.

"We don't want you catching cold," he said, but the tone of his voice was more sultry than therapeutic.

She shivered. "Grant, I—"

He tilted her chin and his eyes were dusky in the moonlight. She held her breath, fascinated by the planes of his cheeks, the light stubble of his beard, the nearness of his lips. "Shh. I know," he murmured. "It's been a heck of an evening, but we need to get you back to bed." He stood and pulled her to her feet. She was acutely aware of his powerful body, sheathed only in boxer shorts. "C'mon. I'll tuck you in."

And he did. Gently. Thoroughly. As if she were precious.

When he left the room, she experienced a stabbing sense of loss. What would it be like if he were her husband—*really?*

PAM CRACKED OPEN her lids, simultaneously sensing the spinning bedroom and harsh sunlight spearing her through a slit in the drapes. Trying not to move more than necessary, she snagged the container of soda crackers on the nightstand and forced herself to eat one. Then another. Slowly her stomach settled enough so she could ease up and lounge against the pillows. When she turned her head, she was surprised to find a pot of tea and a mug on the nightstand. Gratefully she poured half a cup, then let the warm brew soothe her stomach.

How had Grant known she'd need it? She squinted at the clock, then flopped her head back. She couldn't remember the last time she'd slept this late.

But then, with alarming suddenness, she remembered. In the cold light of day, it seemed incomprehensible that she had gone to Grant, that she had let him hold her, that for one wild moment she had actually thought—hoped—he was going to kiss her. Surely that last part had been her imagination. While she appreciated his care of her, like the gesture of the tea, he hadn't signed up for more than a housekeeper and she needed to remember that, however comfortable, theirs was a temporary arrangement. She had to be careful not to take advantage of his goodwill. Even if last night she'd experienced what could only be described as intense sexual desire.

The hormones of a crazy pregnant woman. That had to be it.

When she heard a knock on the door, she pushed her hair back and said, "Come in."

"Hi, sleepyhead." Grant stood in the doorway, wearing a gray Keystone practice T-shirt and snug, worn jeans that did nothing to help her recover from her hormone-induced urgings. "How're you feeling?"

"Thanks to the room service, I think I'll live." She managed a smile.

"It was the least I could do for you and Barney after your help last night."

"Is Andy up yet?"

Grant leaned against the doorjamb and folded his arms over his chest. "Oh, yeah. Not only up, but at 'em."

"The flower beds?"

"You got it. I wouldn't describe him as a particularly happy camper, though."

"And how about you, Dad? Are you okay?"

He shrugged. "I've been better. I don't think Shelley's kept a very tight rein on Andy. I suppose it's natural for him to resent me."

"Expectations are good for him," Pam said.

"In the long run, I know you've got a point, but—"

"Right now it's hard."

"It's not going to get any easier. Preseason basketball practice starts in another couple of weeks. I won't have as much time for him then." Grant approached the bed and refilled her teacup. "Darn, I wish he'd come out for the team."

"What if he didn't make it?"

"You've got a point there, but I keep thinking it might be a way for us to bond."

"Don't force it, Grant."

"Well, anyway, thanks for your support last night. I was glad you were here." He paused near the bed as if waiting for her to say something else.

Surely he didn't expect her to comment on her nocturnal visit to his room. Feeling uncomfortably warm, she needed a change of subject. "I promised my father we'd come see him." She ducked her head. "He wants to meet you and Andy. Do you suppose we could drive out over the Columbus Day break? It'll be awkward, but—"

"Of course. He must think it's odd we haven't been there already."

"I'll call him today, then."

"Later, if you feel up to it, maybe you could go to the nursery for some bulbs."

"I'd like that, Grant." After he left, she remained in bed a few minutes longer, trying to figure out what she'd done to deserve such an accommodating make-believe husband.

ANDY SAT in old man Jeffers's study hall staring at his reddened hands, raw from holding the damn spade.

Thank God he was finished with the digging. Now all he had to do was pull a "hunchback of Notre Dame" routine planting the stupid bulbs. He didn't know why his father had had to get all parental over his going to the park with the guys. The time had gotten away from him. But still, he'd never dreamed Dad and Pam would get home so early. In the future, he'd have to watch his butt.

Yawning, he stared at the slow-moving minute hand of the wall clock, then idly scanned the assignment sheet again. Ms. Carver had given out a list of suggestions to help with journal writing. She'd yapped on and on about the value of free writing, about topics in which they could let their "imaginations soar," about how these would be ungraded in the usual sense.

All this touchy-feely stuff made him want to puke. "I am happiest when…" "My most embarrassing moment was when…" "The person I most admire is…"

He supposed he'd have to do it. It was an easy way to help his grade, tons better than figuring out the difference between a gerund phrase and a noun clause.

He could write a damn volume about how it was the pits being a teenager. What it was like, all of a sudden, to have his dad acting like a real father. "Acting." That said it. He could remember when he'd desperately wanted his dad to come to Florida for his twelfth birthday. He should've known better because it was basketball season. His mother hadn't even put it tactfully. "Andy," she'd said, "your father is never going to be there for you. That's a fact. But you can always count on me." Famous last words. The only person he could count on was himself.

Across the aisle two girls started giggling, and when old man Jeffers fixed his evil eye on them, that made them laugh all the harder. "Quiet, you two. Respect the fact that others are trying to study." Andy swallowed a grin. The guy in front of him was flipping through a *Playboy* concealed in the middle of a library book, and the kid across the aisle was drawing juvenile-looking rocket ships on a piece of notebook paper. Two freshmen, under the guise of working on a group project, were playing Hangman.

For something to do, Andy opened his spiral notebook and started writing in his journal. Not one of the assigned topics, though. No way.

Let me tell you about being a new kid at Keystone. You're invisible, at least to the kids you might have a chance of liking. Some of the geeks are so desperate they look at me with these puppy-dog eyes hoping that maybe I'll actually sit with them at lunch. The popular girls practically have ski slopes for noses, they're so busy looking down them. And the jocks? Well, they think they're hot stuff. I'll bet none of them could bump and run with Andre or James.

Crap! He crossed out that sentence. The last thing he needed was Pam getting nosy about his hoops buddies.

You know what you said the other day about trying to make friends? It sounds good, but in the long run, what difference does it make? I'll be gone in a year. You probably think I'm pretty negative. You know, one of those guys who sees the glass half-empty. But there are some okay things about being here. I like your class. I hope you don't think I'm sucking up by saying that. And Viola is all right. Not to hurt your feelings, but I really like dogs better, though. Not that I've ever had one. Something I'm kinda curious about, if you don't mind my asking. You're a smart lady. How come you married my dad? If that's none of my business, just say so. But, to tell you the truth, I was kinda blown away that Mr. Deliberate got married all of a sudden. I guess this is enough for one entry. Maybe more than you ever wanted to hear.

He scrawled his name and class hour at the top, then stuffed the notebook into his backpack. When he glanced up, he was elated. Only five more minutes in this holding pen. Finally the bell rang. He took his time going to his locker. No need to rush to biology, where the odor of formaldehyde about made him gag.

"Gilbert?"

There he was again. Chip Kennedy. Andy slumped against his locker door, morbidly curious about the next inevitable question.

"What're you doin' Friday night?"

"Not much. Why?"

"Since the football game's in Houston, a bunch of guys are comin' over to my house to play pool. Wanna come?"

Andy thought about it. He didn't plan to form any of those lifetime guy-friendships here, but what else did he have to do Friday night? It beat watching his Dad and Pam watch him. Besides, maybe the old man would get off his back if he hung around with some of the Keystone kids. He shrugged. "Sounds good. Thanks."

"Great. Danny Martinez said he could pick you up about seven."

Danny Martinez? Oh yeah, the dark-haired, intense kid in his English class. "Okay, see ya."

Andy grabbed his biology book, slammed his locker and started down the hall. Maybe Chip wasn't such a bad guy after all.

FOR ONE OF THE FEW TIMES in recent memory, Pam ventured into the teachers' lounge the next week, waiting until after lunch when she was reasonably certain her stomach would cooperate. Connie sat at the corner table grading papers, Carolee Simmons huddled by the phone, obviously deflecting a parent complaint, and Jessie Flanders, true to form, was crocheting, as if school were the least of her worries. Which, sadly, it probably was.

"What's up?" Connie mouthed.

Pam waved a sheet of paper before tacking it to the bulletin board. "The faculty pep skit cast."

"Pamela, re-ally. When will you outgrow this infantile nonsense?" Oblivious to Carolee's frantic shushing motion, Jessie spoke in her normal trumpet blare.

"The kids love it," Pam whispered by way of justification. The irony was that Jessie would have been the first one to get in a snit if she wasn't cast.

"I'm sorry you feel that way, Mrs. Piper, but this *is* a conversational French course." Carolee held the phone at arm's length in disbelief, before dropping it onto the receiver. "Lord help us. Jerry's got enough trouble without a mother making excuses for him."

Jessie sniffed indignantly. "Children just aren't like they used to be."

"Phooey," said Pam. "It's the parents who are different these days. All too eager to help their kids avoid responsibility for their actions."

"Speaking of teens," Connie piped up, "how are things going with Andy?"

Pam slipped into the chair next to her friend. "It's been tough on him." She lowered her voice. "He's his own worst enemy, daring everyone to love him at his most unlovable."

Connie laid a comforting hand on Pam's forearm. "Kind of reminds me of Jim's challenge to us at the first of school."

Pam smiled ruefully. "Only mine's a twenty-four-hour-a-day challenge. But I'm seeing a ray of hope."

"That sounds promising."

"He went over to Chip Kennedy's house to play pool Friday night and Sunday Angela Beeman called to invite him to her church youth group meeting. I think he may screw up his courage to ask her to the Homecoming dance."

"Now that's progress."

"One other thing. Although he clams up at home, he's starting to open up to me in his journals. He's harboring a lot of anger, but at least we're communicating through his writing."

"He must trust you, Pam."

"It's a heavy responsibility."

Jessie stood by the bulletin board, her owl eyes the size of fifty-cent pieces. "Pamela, how could you have cast me as a munchkin?"

How could I not? "Our theme this year is the Wizard of Oz. You know, unmasking the Porter School Warriors as impostors."

"Jessie, thank your lucky stars. It could be worse. I'm a flying monkey," Carolee offered with a grin.

"Humph."

Connie arched a brow at Jessie. "Typical," she muttered under her breath.

Pam rubbed her temples in an attempt to soothe away the headache gathering there. "But somehow the show always goes on." She scooted back her chair and stood. "Duty calls."

"You look tired. Are you okay?"

Nothing a long nap wouldn't cure. "I'm fine. Just bogged down in midterm deficiency reports, college recommendations, a few hundred papers to grade and a list of suggestions for the curriculum committee. Business as usual, in other words."

Except it wasn't business as usual, Pam reflected as she walked back to her classroom. She was pregnant. And worried.

She, Grant and Andy were leaving Saturday for the trip to West Texas to visit her dad. Her father's opinion and goodwill mattered more than she cared to admit. They shared a special bond—the lonely widower and the motherless child doing their best to carry on, despite their loss. She had no way to anticipate how this meeting with Grant and Andy would go.

Nor did she have any way to anticipate how she and Grant would handle the sleeping arrangements. She pictured the home where she'd grown up. There were two guest rooms. Neither had twin beds.

CHAPTER EIGHT

HE WAS A *LONG* WAY from Florida, Andy thought, as he studied the miles of dusty wasteland out the car window. It was a monumental event to spot a grove of trees. Add to that the gross smell from the feedlots. The good thing, though, was his dad had asked him to sit in front so he could give him some driving instruction along the way to Will Carver's. They'd gone to the school parking lot a coupla times last week for his first actual lessons, and even his old man had said he'd done pretty well. The trouble was, he wouldn't have wheels before the Homecoming dance. But if Angie turned him down, it wouldn't matter anyway.

He was kinda curious to meet Pam's father, even if he did live in this barren place. He'd never been to a real ranch before. It could be cool.

He'd figured it would be weird to have Pam for a teacher, but it was turning out all right. He liked that she wrote back to him in his journals. He'd thought a lot about her answer to his question about why she'd married his father so suddenly.

She said she'd always admired his dad and hoped that while Andy was living with them, he'd learn what a fine man his father was. Well, never mind that part. Then she'd said sometimes when a certain relationship exists, like hers and his dad's, it can change just like that and you realize you're supposed to be together.

The funny part was he guessed old people who got married weren't as hot to trot as young people. He sure didn't notice any lovey-dovey stuff. You'd think his dad wouldn't be able to keep his hands off a babe like Pam. Go figure.

PAM EXPERIENCED a flood of emotions when they pulled up in front of the one-story brick ranch house. The trim needed paint and the flower beds her dad had always carefully tended were overgrown. He stubbornly refused to get help and even though he'd leased the cattle operation, he clung to the home place. She worried about him, particularly now that his knee was giving him so much trouble. Then there was the immediate concern— passing off hers as a marriage made in heaven.

While Andy stood awkwardly by the car, Grant opened the back door and helped her out, catching her hand in a steadying grip. "Are you ready for this?" she asked, checking his expression for signs of reluctance.

"Piece of cake," he said with a reassuring smile.

They were halfway to the door when Will Carver stepped onto the porch. "Welcome to God's country, ever'body."

Pam raced ahead and threw her arms around him. He smelled of leather, shaving cream and Ben-Gay. "Daddy, I'm so glad to see you."

"You're a sight for sore old eyes, dumplin'." He nodded over her shoulder. "And I thought you'd never bring these two to meet me."

Pam turned and made the introductions. Grant smiled broadly and extended his hand. Andy hung behind his father, muttering a "Glad to meetcha."

Will showed them inside. Pam sighed inwardly. Dust was thick on the furniture and old newspapers lay haphazardly stacked by the recliner, but in the middle of the dining table was a vase of fresh chrysanthemums and filling the house was the familiar aroma of her father's famous chili. "Let's get you settled, then we can chew the fat at dinner." Will turned to Andy. "Son, you're in the first room on the left. Grant, I figured you and Pam'd like a little more privacy—" he winked "—so you're at the end of the hall."

Pam groaned. The room with the extralong double bed and the private bath. When she'd mentioned the limitations of the guest quarters to Grant, he'd simply said, "We'll make it work, somehow."

But she didn't know how.

After getting settled, Pam helped dish up the chili and they gathered around the table. "Now tell me all about how you got hooked up with my daughter," her father said to Grant.

Maybe it was because the story had now been oft rehearsed, but Grant almost made her believe they'd been struck by a lightning bolt, realizing with swiftness and certainty that they were in love. He went on to make a convincing case for the need to marry before Andy arrived and school started. It all sounded so logical.

And so magical.

"Well, I couldn't be happier for you both," her beaming father said when Grant finished. "The main thing is you're happy."

She gave what she hoped was an enthusiastic smile.

"And I've got a new grandson, to boot. Can't ask for much better 'n that." Will helped himself to a spoonful of chili, then turned his attention to Andy. "Ever been on a ranch, son?"

Andy shook his head. "No sir."

"Tell you what. After supper, you and me and your dad'll take a little tour. Would you like that?"

Pam had to hand it to Andy. He was being a lamb. Her dad had always missed having a son and, in the summers, used to hire all kinds of strays from the local high school who needed a father figure. Maybe his spell would work with her stepson, too.

She was grateful when the dinner ended and the menfolk left for their ranch tour. Doing the dishes was a small price to pay for a little peace and quiet—and the opportunity to get ready for bed before she had to share the room with Grant.

One niggling thought ate away at her calm. Although he'd tried to hide it, her dad had winced when he'd stood up from the table, and had moved slowly, favoring his left leg. Hardly the loose, athletic gait of an expert horseman.

How much worse, exactly, was his knee?

GRANT WAS FASCINATED by Will Carver's running commentary about ranching and the glories of West Texas, and it was clear Andy was equally enthralled. With his broad paunch hanging over his large silver belt buckle, a salt-and-pepper mustache and silver-rimmed glasses, Will looked like a crusty version of Wilfred Brimley. Every now and then he'd stop the Jeep, peer out over the pastureland and point to a particular herd, commenting on its bloodline.

Back at the barn, he eyed Andy's baggy shorts. "You got any jeans with you, son?"

"Yeah. Why?"

"Those duds you got on aren't real suitable for riding. You like horses?"

"I dunno."

"Figure you'd wanna find out?"

"You mean go horseback riding?" Caution and elation warred in Andy's tone. "I, uh, I've never been."

"Then it's high time. Sunup, boy. I'll wake you."

After a tour of the barn and an introduction to the horses, Will led them back to the house. Andy ran ahead. "Didn't think to ask, Grant. You wanna ride, too?"

"I think I'll pass."

"Yeah, I expect it wouldn't be too good to roust a newlywed at the crack of dawn." He chortled, then clamped a calloused hand on Grant's back. "I like you. And I like your boy there, too." He paused at the foot of the porch steps. "I figure we'll keep you both."

Later, when Grant entered the bedroom and stood watching Pam hugging the edge of the mattress, seemingly asleep, he thought about Will's words. The man's acceptance had been straightforward and complete. As if he had no doubt that Grant would take care of his daughter—always. It was getting harder and harder to face the reality that they would disappoint so many people who believed in them.

Grant eyed the cramped bedroom. A gun cabinet and bookcase took up the only available wall and there was scant room between the window and the bed. He sat gingerly on the edge of the bed and began removing his shoes.

"Grant?" Pam sounded sleepy.

"I didn't mean to wake you."

"It's okay." She turned on her side to study him in the half-light of the moon. "I'm sorry. About the bed. I'll try not to move."

Damn. Why did she have to smell like a bower of roses? Just thinking about climbing under the covers beside her was making him hard. What if, in the middle of the night, half-asleep, he forgot where he was and reached out for her?

It wasn't just that she was a woman and he'd been a long time without. No, that wasn't the half of it. The trouble was, this was Pam. Pam, who was becoming *way* too important to him.

He shoved his shoes under the bed, then went into the bathroom to finish getting ready. He hadn't worn pajamas in years, preferring to sleep in his boxers, but he'd brought them for this trip. Putting them on only served to remind him how different this night was.

Back in the bedroom, he started to pull the covers back when Pam whispered to him. "You get under the sheet. I'll stay between the top sheet and the blanket."

So that was her plan. The twenty-first-century version of bundling. He supposed it was the best they could do under the circumstances.

Unless, of course, he ripped off the covers and pulled her into his arms and loved her the way he wanted to, the way his body was demanding.

Instead, he dutifully climbed beneath the sheet, cradled his head in his hands and stared at the ceiling, careful not to move. He could hear her measured breathing, feel her body warmth, inhale her special fragrance.

Pure torture.

IT WAS THE EVERLOVIN' crack of dawn. Andy squinted at the luminous dial of his watch. Five-thirty. Crap. He'd thought when the old man said "sunup," it was one of those figures of speech Pam talked about in class. Only the smell of bacon kept him from chucking it in and going back to sleep. He stepped into his jeans, pulled on a sweatshirt and ran his fingers through his hair.

In the kitchen, Pam's dad handed him a cup of hot chocolate, then asked him how he liked his eggs. "You always get up this early?" Andy asked.

The man's eyes widened. "You call this early? Why, in my heyday I was up by four-thirty every day but Sunday."

Andy couldn't imagine it. "Gosh, Mr. Carver, that had to be the pits."

"Let's get one thing straight, pardner." Will set down two plates of eggs and bacon and joined Andy at the table. "You can't go on callin' me 'Mr. Carver.' Not now that I'm your stepgrandpa."

"I guess that would be kinda weird." He thought for a moment. "But I don't know what—"

"How 'bout plain old Gramps?"

"Sounds good."

Gramps eyed him over his coffee cup. "So you've never been on a horse at all?"

"Once on a pony at this kid's birthday party, but I figured that didn't count."

"You're right. Now shovel that food in, son. We've got lots to do if we're gonna make it to the Ghost Gulch pasture in time."

"In time for what?"

"A glorious West Texas sunrise. I guarantee you haven't seen anything like it."

At the barn Andy tried manfully not to reveal his fear, nor to think about the lump of eggs and biscuit sliding around in his stomach. Pepper, the horse Gramps was saddling for him, was big, and his ears twitched kinda funny, and he stared at Andy with these big rolling eyes. "There," Gramps said, drawing the belt-thing tight around the animal's stomach. "All cinched. Ready to mount up?"

No way was he going to let Gramps see that he was scared shitless. "Sure." He put his left foot into the stirrup and swung up into the saddle. Feeling the horse shift beneath him, he grabbed the handle on the saddle and tried not to think about how high off the ground he was.

"Here's how you hold the reins." Gramps wrapped his fingers around skinny strings of leather, then stood back. "Just talk nice to ol' Pepper. He's as gentle as they come."

When the old man pulled himself into the saddle atop a brown-and-white spotted horse, Andy couldn't help noticing how he grimaced and let out a sharp moan, but, recovering, clucked his tongue and the two horses started walking side by side out the corral gate. It was just light enough that the buildings were dark silhouettes against a light gray sky. Around them, Andy heard the twitters of birds and, farther away, the lowing of cattle.

Gramps pulled up the collar of his denim jacket and rode alongside him, not saying anything. Yet it wasn't like he was ignoring him. More like they were compadres who'd known each other so long they didn't need words to communicate.

Andy was doing his best to concentrate on steering Pepper, but the horse kinda knew what to do without being told. Gradually Andy gained confidence. Until they broke into a trot and everything changed. He felt as if his teeth were loose marbles and his butt, a punching bag. Thank God for the handle on the saddle. He gripped it for dear life. Beside him he heard Gramps say, "Try not to bounce. Keep your hind parts in touch with the saddle.'' Surprisingly, when he tried it, he didn't bounce as badly as before.

Finally they stopped beside a watering trough in the middle of nowhere. Gritting his teeth, Gramps dismounted, then tested his left knee. ''Hanging in there,'' he muttered to himself. Then he walked over to Pepper, took the reins from Andy and helped him get off. When his feet hit the ground, Andy's legs nearly buckled. ''Not too bad, son, for your first ride.''

Even though his butt was sore and his knees refused to cooperate, Andy was exhilarated, and when Pepper turned his head and gave him an affectionate nip on the shoulder, Andy considered himself a regular John Wayne.

Gramps tethered the horses and then turned to Andy. ''C'mon, son.'' He led him to a rotted tree stump where they sat down. As far as you could see, there was nothing but land, undulating, then flat, marked by an occasional tree or outbuilding. ''Watch.''

They sat silently. Then, like an eruption on the horizon, the earth gave birth to a giant red-orange ball. Wisps of gray-blue clouds drifted across the face of the sun and in the distance the bird and animal noises intensified.

''Pretty amazing, huh?''

''Awesome,'' Andy said. Did they have sunrises like this in Florida? How would he know? He was never up this early.

The old man tilted back his Stetson and sat motionless, his gnarled hands folded between his legs. After several minutes, he spoke. ''You must feel like a lost dogie.''

At first Andy didn't know what he meant, but then

he hazarded a guess. "You mean being new to Texas, school and all?"

"Yep. That, and havin' a new stepmama. Could be tough on a fella. Lotsa change."

Weird. He'd only known this old guy a little more than twelve hours and already he felt more comfortable with him than anybody he'd met in Texas. It was like Gramps could read his mind. "Pam's okay."

Gramps merely nodded his head.

"School's...different."

"Kids already in their own packs, I reckon."

"Yeah."

"Takes time to break in."

"A coupla guys are bein' okay. And there's this one girl..."

"Sounds like you're doin' fine, then. Day at a time. That's the way to do it."

Andy realized Gramps made a lot of sense. Each day lately had been getting a little better. The guys he'd met at Chip's house were cool, and he and Angie were talking on the phone quite a bit. Even his dad had been better lately, what with the driving lessons and all.

"Whaddya do for fun?"

"Just hang out, I guess."

Gramps turned to look at him, his eyes kindly, but his mouth set in a firm line. "That's fool's talk, son. Waste of time. A man has to have a passion." He gestured at the prairie. "Mine's the land. Cattle. Horses." He turned back to study the horizon, plucked a weed from the ground and chewed on the end. "Out with it. What's your passion?"

Andy's chest tightened. He knew. But could he tell? He clenched his knees. "Basketball," he said softly.

"Basketball, huh? Your dad know about that?"

"No."

"Any particular reason?"

Andy felt confused and tried desperately to gather his thoughts. "It's *my* thing, you know? And at Keystone, he's the big basketball hero. Championship-winning coach and all that stuff." Andy hesitated, but when the old man didn't say anything, he continued. "I don't want to play for him. It's complicated, but—"

"You just want to play for yourself, huh? For your own pleasure?"

"Yeah, I guess that's it."

"That sounds fine. Unless you're missing out on some of the richness."

"Richness?"

Gramps continued chewing the weed for a long time. Finally he flicked it aside and spoke. "The team spirit, for one thing. The work ethic, testing yourself against competition, the sense of accomplishment." Then, with a grunt, he rose to his feet. "But that's all up to you. Your decision." He motioned to Andy to get up. As they walked toward the horses, Gramps put an arm around Andy's shoulder. "You've got plenty to sort out, son. But I'm betting on you."

Andy did better swinging into the saddle. He was even developing warm feelings toward Pepper. But best of all, from that tight, locked place in his heart, affection for Will Carver surged. Even if it didn't make sense, Gramps was already his friend.

PAM COULDN'T HELP HERSELF. She was fussing with Andy's tie, smoothing the shoulders of his new suit, just like a regular mother. He looked quite handsome—and very young and tentative. She could tell he was trying hard to maintain his air of bored sophistication, but it was clear this Homecoming dance was a big deal to him. "Don't forget the corsage," she cautioned.

"Oh, yeah," he said, breaking away and heading for the refrigerator.

Grant came out of the bedroom, car keys dangling. He looked around, then whispered, "I can't believe he's letting me take him and his friends to the dance."

She chuckled. "The good stuff happens on the way home, dummy. That's Chip Kennedy's father's responsibility."

"I don't even want to think about that."

"Ain't parenthood great?" Pam teased.

Andy entered the room, holding the florist's box as if it were a time bomb. "Can we go now?"

"Sure." Grant pecked her on the cheek in a great Ward Cleaver imitation. "See you later, honey."

Pam waved them goodbye, grateful that by some miracle she and Grant had escaped chaperon duty. Andy would have been mortified.

She settled on the couch, joined by Sebastian and Viola, vying for the choice position on her lap. She smoothed her hand over her tummy, aware for the last several days that it was rounding and that elastic waistbands were now dictating her clothing choices. She'd been for her second appointment with Belinda Ellis last week, and so far, her pregnancy was progressing right on schedule. "What do you think, kitties? Will you be jealous of Barney?" Sebastian reared up and looked at her, but Viola merely purred. She liked the way their warm bodies pressed against her, almost as if they were helping nurture the baby.

She closed her eyes, basking in a rare sense of peace and well-being. Her morning sickness had abated and the faculty Homecoming skit had gone off without a hitch. She grinned remembering how the kids had roared at Grant's comical rendition of the scarecrow. She knew he hated doing the part, but, as always, he'd been a good sport. The Keystone Knights had trounced their opponent and Brittany Thibault had reigned as Homecoming Queen. Best of all had been the change in Andy since their visit to the ranch. He was more cooperative and spent less time in his room, though he often left on his bike to explore the neighborhood, he said. The driving lessons were working miracles between him and Grant. They were actually having real conversations. Maybe things were falling into place. Finally.

Reluctantly Pam picked up from the coffee table the stack of senior exams. It was tempting to postpone grading them. But when would she have a better time?

Most of the students had enjoyed their study of Shakespeare's *Macbeth*, but, true to form, several had balked big time, ''Why can't the dude speak English?'' being one of the most amusing of this year's comments. After an hour, she laid the stack aside. Several had done high-caliber work, but then there was Beau Jasper. She sighed.

Just when she'd thought life was getting easier. The young man seemed to think being a football star made him exempt from studying. She doubted he'd read a word of the play. It was pretty hard to miss the fulfillment of the witches' prophecies. But he had. Before marking a fifty-two percent at the top of his paper, she scanned the exam again, looking for any redeeming responses. Grant would not be happy. He had to be counting on the kid for basketball, but if he became academically ineligible... The rules were clear.

To elevate her mood, she switched to the sophomore

journals, deliberately searching out Andy's, hoping it would corroborate her sense that he was adjusting. Sebastian woke, stretched, then draped himself over her shoulder. "Listen, buddy. This is pretty neat." She read Andy's words aloud.

"I didn't use to feel like I really had a grandfather. I hardly ever see Grandpa Gilbert and Mom's dad is dead. But your father is kinda like I always pictured one would be, you know, sort of a cross between Santa Claus and one of those old cowboy actors. I know he's not really related to me, but when he asked me to call him Gramps, I figured it didn't make much difference. Kinda like you said about home being in your head and heart. I think maybe that's the way it is with Gramps. He's the grandfather in my heart.

Pam sat for a moment, then shifted the cats and rose to her feet. "Sorry to disturb you guys, but I need a tissue—majorly." What was going to happen to her when Andy ultimately returned to his mother? With every passing day, he was becoming more and more the son "in her heart."

GRANT TOSSED his windbreaker onto the back of the chair and faced Pam.

"Well?" she asked with a quizzical smile.

"Now I know what the Invisible Man feels like." He flopped down beside her on the sofa. "Lord, I remember so well what it was like to be fifteen and embarrassed as hell that adults had to drive me and my friends on dates. Half the challenge was figuring out how I was going to kiss Tracey Camparis without being spotted in the rearview mirror.''

Pam chuckled. ''Do you think Andy's going to try for first base—or more?''

''He seems pretty stuck on Angela.''

''She's a nice girl.''

''That's what they always say.''

Pam raised an eyebrow. ''Don't tell me you're worried.''

''Worry is a way of life for a parent. I've worried about that kid ever since the divorce.''

Pam sensed Grant was trying to tell her something. ''Want to talk about it?''

He leaned back against the cushion and expelled a deep breath. ''Shelley has never given me a chance. And the way the custody arrangement turned out, well...'' He shrugged. ''When Andy was twelve, I sent a round-trip plane ticket so he could come here for the summer, but she had this big excuse that she'd already enrolled him in camp. I don't know whether she'd actually signed him up or not. Unfortunately, that was not an isolated instance. Another summer she claimed he needed tutoring in reading. It was as if she didn't want Andy doing anything with me. At least, until now.''

It was hard for Pam to believe Grant would have married a woman like Shelley in the first place. ''Was she always like this?''

He shook his head dazedly. ''Not at the beginning. Hell, we were just a couple of lovesick kids who didn't have a clue about life. We were struggling on my teaching salary, then Andy came along. Pretty soon I realized I'd never be able to give her what she wanted.'' He cleared his throat. ''Material things are important to her.''

She couldn't bear it. He must think Shelley was another person for whom he didn't "measure up." Pam returned to the subject of Andy. "You think she's been using him as a weapon to get back at you?"

"Get back at me for what? Being a coach? Making a living? Caring about my son?"

Grant's pain was evident. "How much do you think Andy suspects?"

"Who knows? It's not like I want to turn him against his mother. But I get tired of being the bad guy."

"Can you tell him that?"

"What? And play the same game Shelley does?"

"Surely, without trashing his mother, you can help him realize how much you've missed being with him."

He put his feet up on the coffee table. "Maybe. But the timing has to be just right."

"Don't you think things between the two of you are going better lately?"

"I do." He turned to face her. "That's why I'm afraid of blowing it." He picked up the remote. "Mind if we watch the news?"

Knowing he'd signaled "end of discussion," she shook her head, then turned back to the sophomore journals she'd been grading when he came in. Such love, and yet his hands had been tied, not just by the courts but by a woman who sounded shallow and vindictive.

It seemed at the same time both inconceivable and comfortable that they should be sitting here waiting for their child to return from his first dance.

Like any pair of concerned parents.

ANDY ROLLED OUT OF BED, aware his stomach was grumbling like mad. The house smelled like pancakes and, man, was he hungry. They'd had all this food at the dance, but he'd been too nervous to eat much. What if he spilled punch on Angie's dress? Or got spinach dip stuck in his teeth? Or developed onion breath?

He ran a hand through his rack-hair, remembering Angie in her pretty blue dress. It was strapless and fit her like a glove and was made out of this shiny stuff. When he'd first seen her, he'd panicked. What if he got a boner? But he hadn't. Not then, anyway.

Grinning, he pulled on a pair of shorts and struggled into a T-shirt. Yeah, later, in the very back seat of old man Kennedy's van, she'd let him kiss her, and the neat thing was, he forgot all about her braces. Her skin felt warm and soft when he put his arms around her, and when she made this little moaning sound, well, all he could say was he was glad for the dark so she couldn't see him standing at attention.

He didn't know what falling in love was like, but he hoped it was something like this. Angie made him feel like a real stud. He'd call her this afternoon. See if they could meet at the park, maybe. Unless his dad was going to take him driving. When he had his own car, it would be so cool. He and Angie could go tooling around and—

"Andy? Breakfast." Pam wasn't just a good teacher, she was a dynamite cook. He hoped she had blueberry syrup for the pancakes.

When he got to the kitchen, his father was already eating. "How're you doing, sport?"

"Great."

"Did you have a good time?" Pam asked as she dished up his serving.

Jeez, he felt like he was in a Disney movie. Wouldn't they be surprised if he told them exactly what a good time he had had? How hot he was for Angie? "Yeah. The band was cool."

He straddled his chair and was reaching for the syrup bottle when suddenly a plate clattered to the floor. He turned to see china and pancake and sausage all over the place and Pam doubled over, clutching her stomach.

Before he could react, his dad had leaped to his feet and was helping Pam to a chair. "Pam, what is it? Are you all right?"

Her face was pale and big tears stood in her eyes. "Oh, Grant. I—I think something's wrong with the baby." Then she grimaced again. "Call the doctor."

Doctor? Andy couldn't make sense of what was happening. What were they talking— Suddenly he knew, and bile replaced the void where his appetite had been. He faced them, his face turning fire-red. "Baby?" he croaked. "What baby?"

CHAPTER NINE

"WHAT'S WRONG?" Grant was frantic.

"I'm not sure. Just this sudden sharp pain." Pam twisted in the chair, her expression anguished. "I'd been having these little twinges all morning, but this one was...different."

Cursing the fact he hadn't yet memorized Dr. Ellis's number, Grant grabbed the phone and tore open the directory, his finger racing down the listing for physicians. There. Once he managed to dial, he looked up and simultaneously became aware of two things— Pam's pained expression and the stunned, hostile look on his son's face.

He got an answering service. The cool, detached voice of the operator infuriated him. Damn it, this was an emergency, not some routine medical question. Tersely he explained the situation, listened briefly, then hung up and addressed Pam. "They'll have Dr. Ellis phone soon. Luckily, she's on call this weekend." He knelt beside his wife. "Can you go into more detail?"

She nodded almost imperceptibly toward Andy. "Later," she whispered.

"Don't mind me," Andy said sarcastically. "Were you ever planning to tell me, Dad?"

"Not now, Andy, please." Grant, torn between his immediate concern for Pam and the obvious crisis with his son, felt his composure slipping. "Go to your room.

I'll be up after the doctor calls and we figure out what's going on.''

Pam lifted her head. "Andy, believe me, we didn't want you to find out this way. We were waiting until later to tell you, just in case something like this—'' she struggled to go on, her voice breaking "—happened.''

God, was she having a miscarriage?

Andy remained frozen, then finally shrugged, deliberately avoiding looking at Grant. "Whatever.'' Anger and concern flitted across his face. Finally he turned to Pam. "I hope you'll be all right'' Then, in a strangled voice, he added, "And the baby, too.''

Grant struggled to his feet. "Son?''

"Forget it, okay?'' Then Andy rushed from the room. The only sound registering with Grant was that of feet taking the steps two at a time followed by the shuddering explosion of a bedroom door slamming.

"Oh, Grant, I'm so sorry.'' Pam's eyes were full of tears.

"Sorry?'' He laid a comforting hand on her shoulder. "You don't have anything to be sorry for.''

"Just when you and Andy were starting to get close—now this.''

"Well, he'll just have to grow up.''

She placed a gentle finger on his lips. "Shh. None of this is his fault.''

"We're not talking 'fault' here. When we made our commitment, we knew it wouldn't be easy.'' He leaned over and placed his palm on her stomach. "But this? Oh, God, it has to be all right.''

Gently Pam placed her hand over his and he closed his eyes, praying for the baby to be okay. Then she got to her feet. "I—I think I better check to see if there's any bleeding.''

Bleeding? That could be bad.

After she disappeared into the bathroom, he stared at the phone, willing it to ring. Pam had to be terrified.

But maybe no more frightened than he was. He hadn't admitted it to himself before, but he'd been counting on this baby as a reason for them to stay together. Beyond their agreement.

Forever.

ANDY SOCKED A FIST into his pillow. Why did everybody always treat him like a little kid? His dad should have told him. A brother or sister, for cripe's sake. Great. Some little snot-nosed rug-rat he'd never get to know anyway. Now the old man would have the basketball star he'd always wanted. Andy could see it all clear as day. His dad would prob'ly give the kid a basketball when he was two years old and drill him all the time, coach his Little League team, take him to Mavericks games—all kinds of shit like that.

He paced around his room. A baby. You didn't have to be a genius to know they were a hell of a lot cuter than a dorky teenager.

Ha! Just when he'd begun to think his old man might be kind of okay. At least he hadn't embarrassed him driving his friends to the dance. And he'd let him try parallel parking.

But now he and Pam would be all goo-goo over some squalling brat.

They'd forget about him.

Screw it! He bounded down the stairs, ran past Pam and his dad, pausing only to grab up a cold pancake, and made it to the garage before his father could come after him. He vaulted onto the bike and pedaled like crazy down the street. So what if he hadn't told them where he was going. What did they care anyway?

God, why was he crying? He swiped at his eyes, hoping like hell no one had seen.

He wanted them to care. For a while he'd thought Pam did. And lately, maybe even his dad.

But now? How did a guy compete with a baby?

THE MINUTE SHE HEARD Belinda Ellis's voice, Pam sagged against Grant in relief. Shakily she gripped the phone and answered the doctor's questions. "No, no bleeding. Yet. Do I need to come to the hospital?"

"That's not indicated. Usually cramping at this stage is mild, but occasionally a mother will experience more pronounced discomfort. This is not unusual, Pam, and the fact you've had no bleeding is a big plus. Probably you're experiencing an anomaly, but I'd like to see you in the office tomorrow to be sure. Call my receptionist for an appointment. Any other questions?"

Pam knew the next twenty-four hours would creep by, but she appreciated the doctor's calm, methodical approach. "No. Thank you, Dr. Ellis."

"Well?" Grant's eyes were murky with concern.

"I'm supposed to take it easy and see her tomorrow."

"Are you going to be all right?"

She leaned her head against his chest. "I hope so," she said in a small, quivering voice. "Oh, Grant, I don't want to lose this baby."

She felt his hands tighten on her arms. "Of course you don't," he said, his voice sounding as ragged as hers felt.

She took a deep breath, then stood back. "What about Andy?"

"I don't know what the hell's the matter with the kid, racing out of here like that."

"Go find him."

"I won't leave you."

"I'll be fine. I promise." She sank into the closest chair.

"He'll come back eventually. I'll talk to him then."

"Are you avoiding him?"

Grant frowned. "Why would you say that?"

"Because I think you feel guilty that we hadn't already told him about the baby."

"I—I didn't have a clue how he'd take it."

"I know. It seemed easier to let him get used to the idea of us before we laid that on him."

"Did we make a mistake, Pam?"

He looked so distraught she'd have stood and hugged him if she hadn't felt so weary. "Maybe. We didn't mean to hurt him."

"Where do you think he went?"

She shook her head. "Where he always does, I suppose. Riding around. Hanging out with the neighborhood kids." She paused. "You know, maybe it's best to let him be. He may need some time to himself."

"When he comes home, I'll talk to him."

"Or both of us could." Pam couldn't think clearly. Andy needed reassurance, but it wouldn't be fair to delude him into thinking theirs was a forever-after family.

Grant ran a hand through his hair. "Both of us. Yeah." He hesitated, then hunkered beside Pam's chair. "There's one other thing."

"What's that?"

"Now that Andy knows, we'll have to tell other people. Your dad. My parents. The folks at school. Given his reaction, it's not fair to expect him to keep the news to himself.''

She felt old beyond her years. Where would this charade end? How? She nodded, her mind blank. "You're right. After I see Dr. Ellis, though.''

He clasped her cold hands. "Okay." His eyes held hers for a long moment. Then he stood. "C'mon, now. Let me get you settled in bed.''

He led her down the hall and into the bedroom, where he sat her down, slipped off her shoes, then tucked a lightweight blanket around her. Before he left the room, he said something that filled her heart, yet made her tremble with self-reproach.

"I care about this baby, too, you know.''

Then he quietly shut the door.

ANDY KNEW IT WAS COMING. The lecture. He'd always thought playing basketball could cure any problem, but even after beating the butts off the other pickup team, he still felt crummy. Drenched in sweat, he watched the guys heading home from the court for supper, knowing that sooner or later he'd have to face the music.

Finally he straddled his bike and rode slowly through the streets, wishing he were like the little kids he saw along the way riding trikes and playing in sandboxes. They had it made. No worries at all.

All afternoon just when he thought he'd forgotten, the truth would stun him. A baby. He knew he was supposed to be happy, but, jeez Louise, it felt weird. He liked Pam okay and he'd always heard women had this biological clock thing. Maybe that was it.

But how could his dad do this? He was too old to start all over again. Wasn't he?

He dismounted and walked up the driveway, set the

kickstand and left the bike in the garage. He'd hardly opened the back door to the house when, sure enough, there stood his father, hands on his hips, this big frown on his face. "Son, we need to talk. Now." He nodded in the direction of the living room. "In there."

Ooh, boy. Could it get any worse?

FROM HER POSITION stretched out on the sofa, Pam observed the two males—Grant, righteously indignant, and Andy, long-suffering and mutinous. How had a simple living arrangement become an emotional Waterloo?

"Have a seat, Andy," Grant said, gesturing to one end of the sofa. He himself pulled up a desk chair. Andy sat stiffly, arms folded across his chest, hands tucked in his armpits. "Where have you been all day?"

"Around."

"I thought we had an understanding. You agreed to tell us where you're going when you leave the house."

"That was before," Andy mumbled.

"Before what?" Grant's voice sounded self-consciously controlled.

"Before you left me out of the loop."

Grant exhaled. "The baby."

Andy feigned an incredulous expression. "Duh."

Pam couldn't stand it. "We should have told you, Andy. I'm sorry."

"Was it some big state secret?"

"We were waiting—" Grant began.

Not knowing how he intended to finish his sentence, Pam interrupted. "To be sure I wouldn't miscarry."

For the first time, Andy looked directly at her. "What did the doctor say?"

"She's cautiously optimistic."

He grunted.

Pam continued. "Believe me, we didn't want you to find out like that. You must've been shocked."

"Uh, ye-ah," he said, scorn dripping from his lips.

"But that doesn't excuse your bolting out of here without a word," Grant said.

"I was supposed to stick around and take it like a 'big boy,' is that it?" Andy glared at his father.

"That would've been nice."

"Sorry to disappoint you."

"It's not a matter of disappointment. Look, we've all got to get along here. Running out on problems doesn't solve anything. Anyway, a baby is hardly a problem."

Andy snorted. "Not for you."

Pam couldn't stand the pain she heard in his voice. "Oh, Andy, having a baby doesn't mean we'll love you any less."

Andy faced her again, the pure need in his eyes betraying the smirk on his lips. "Sure," he said.

"Pam's right. A baby doesn't change that."

"Is that all?" Andy stood. "Can I go now?"

"I love you, son."

Andy merely shrugged and walked from the room.

Pam squirmed. They hadn't reached him. He was neither reading the misery in his father's eyes nor acknowledging the heartbreak in his voice. She got to her feet and laid a hand on Grant's shoulder. "Let me talk to him."

He looked up, his face ravaged. "You can't do any worse than I did."

She took her time going up the stairs, searching for the words that might somehow get through to Andy. She rapped lightly on his door.

"Go away."

"It's Pam."

Andy opened the door, his face a mask of indifference. "Sorry. I thought you were Dad." He slumped against the doorjamb, his eyes following her as she entered his room, which smelled faintly of corn chips and dirty socks.

She gestured to the bed, where Viola lay curled in a ball sound asleep. "Mind if I sit?"

He didn't move. "Go ahead."

She shoved aside a couple of textbooks and lowered herself beside Viola. "Andy, why are you so determined to take on the world?"

"Whaddya mean?"

"You're a pretty nifty kid, if you'd only believe it. But it seems to me you're fighting all of us—your dad, me, the kids at school, your mother, and who knows who else. Why?"

He gave another of his who-gives-a-darn shrugs.

"People are reaching out to you all the time. Let them in. Take your dad, for instance. He's tried harder than a lot of men would to keep in touch with you, even though you were halfway across the country. From what I can tell, he's missed you terribly. For instance, he told me how disappointed he was that summer you went to camp instead of coming here."

Andy's body tensed and his eyes zeroed in on hers. "What summer?"

Pam had gone too far, but there was no backing off. "When you were twelve. You didn't know?"

He shook his head and she continued. "He'd already bought your airplane ticket."

"It's news to me."

"I think quite a few of the ways your dad's been trying to be a good father might be news to you. But that's between you and him. Right now, what I want to say is this. Grant is a good man. Even though he may care for this new baby, that doesn't mean he'll stop loving you. He will never do that. You mean the world to him.''

He slid down the wall until he was sitting on the floor, knees bent, hands bracing his body. Maybe, just maybe, she had his attention. "And for all your anger and hurt, I have a suspicion you love him, too." She took a deep breath and, without censoring herself, rushed on. "It's okay to love him, Andy. Really.''

Watching the boy chew on her words, she began to suspect something more. It might be okay for her to love Grant, too.

But she had no right. None at all.

GRANT PACED, waiting for Pam to return. Then he charged into the kitchen and mixed himself a stiff Scotch and water. No matter what he did, he blew it with Andy.

And now what kind of fix was he in? He'd had to send Pam to smooth things over. At least Andy listened to her. Sometimes. He swallowed a slug of his drink, letting the alcohol warm his gut. The reality was, he couldn't continue depending on Pam to bail him out. It wasn't fair putting her in the middle, and there'd be hell to pay with the kid when she was no longer around. Damn. The rapport Pam had with Andy was just one more thing that had lulled him into thinking the marriage could last. But given his lousy track record with family, what had made him think this situation could be any different?

He poured the rest of the whiskey down the sink. Alcohol wasn't the answer, nor could it help him avoid an unpleasant truth—he was a huge jerk to use Pam like that. She had her own child to worry about. She didn't need to take on his.

Yet he'd heard her say to Andy, plain as day, "Having this baby doesn't mean we'll love you any less." *We.* Did she mean it?

Then he regretted tossing the drink. Because an even grimmer truth surfaced. What would it do to Andy to lose her? When the time came. In September. Would that be one more blow to his relationship with his son? The final one?

"There you are." Pam slipped into the kitchen. "I wondered where you went."

"Where I went was straight to a fifth of Scotch." He held up the empty glass in a mock toast.

"That bad, huh?" She opened the refrigerator, helped herself to a bottle of water, then leaned against the countertop studying him.

"I'm not used to failing." The words were out before he realized he'd said them aloud.

"No, I don't suppose you are. In this case, though, 'failure' is a pretty harsh word."

"What am I doing wrong with him?"

She took a long time prying off the cap, then drank slowly from the bottle. He wondered what it was she was avoiding putting into words. "He needs something to keep him busy, something to help him feel good about himself."

"If he'd play basketball—"

"Give it up, Coach. That isn't going to happen. Maybe part of the trouble is your expectations. Andy's asserting himself. He's going to do things his way. Not yours." She bonked herself on the forehead. "Is that a recipe for conflict, or what? Heaven deliver me from two stubborn males.''

He could swear somewhere in there she was chuckling at him. ''I'm desperate, here. What do you suggest?''

''I have an idea. But I don't know if he'll go for it.''

''What's that?''

''I need help with the props and scenery for the play. Maybe I can dangle Angela as bait. She's an understudy.''

He mulled over the idea. ''Pam, you didn't bargain for all of this. He's my responsibility.''

''It's no big deal. I *like* him.''

''But what if he gets too attached? I don't want to make it harder on him...later.''

She focused on the water bottle as if it held the oracle of Delphi. ''It's a problem, isn't it? We didn't have the foggiest notion what we were getting into, did we?''

He stared at her, at first unable to reply, confused by her mixed message. She'd said she loved Andy, but just now... Was she having second thoughts? He felt sick. ''I guess not.''

She went on. ''So what do you think? About the play?''

He struggled for a normal tone. ''It makes sense. I'll be at practice while you're in rehearsal, so we won't have to leave Andy unsupervised very often.''

''Okay. I'll give it a shot.''

''You sure didn't need all of this today on top of everything else.''

''I'm fine. Or at least as fine as I can be until I see the doctor.''

He didn't know what to do with his hands, because he wanted to pull her into his arms, to thank her, to reassure her. Hell, to reassure himself. "I'm hoping for the best," he managed to say.

She smiled tenderly. "I know you are." Then she pushed off the countertop, walked past him, brushing her hand briefly across his chest, and left the room, leaving behind the faint fragrance of roses. A far more potent comforter than Scotch.

THE NEXT AFTERNOON Pam drove slowly down Connie's street, barely registering the brilliant fall foliage. She'd called from the obstetrician's office to ask if she could drop by. Dr. Ellis had examined her, checked the fetal heartbeat and then concluded that what Pam had experienced, though irregular, was nevertheless not a threat to the baby.

Now, more than ever, this child was important to her. She would lose Grant and Andy the following fall. With each day, she felt herself becoming more involved with them, more dependent upon them, more concerned for them. But surely loving and caring for her baby would help make losing them bearable.

She pulled into Connie's driveway, turned off the motor, then closed her eyes briefly. If only Grant hadn't been so quick to agree with her yesterday when she'd suggested they might not have known what they were getting into.

Yet who could blame him? He hadn't bargained on the problems her pregnancy presented, not to mention the triangular family dynamic.

One thing was for certain. No matter how tempted she was, there would be no more late-night excursions to his bed. Even if the memory of his warm, strong body often interfered with her sleep.

That decided, she slung her handbag over her shoulder and walked from the car to Connie's porch.

Connie greeted her effusively. "It's been way too long since we've had a good chat, unless you count those brief snatches of conversation between classes, which I don't. Jim's at a meeting, so I have all the time in the world." She ushered Pam to the glassed-in sunroom, shaded by a huge pecan tree and decorated in bright yellows and greens. "Iced tea? Wine? Soda?"

"Iced tea sounds wonderful." While Connie disappeared into the kitchen, Pam sank into a wicker Bombay chair and curled her feet under her. She needed Connie's support, because tonight she was calling her father and Barbara to tell them about the baby. Her lips curled in distaste. She had no doubt Barbara would react in the same way she had when she'd learned of the marriage. Indifference thinly disguised by disapproving surprise. Even though she'd made up her mind long ago that there was no changing her sister, Pam admitted to herself that she kept trying, hoping for a glimmer of sisterly affection. How could a childhood loss, no matter how devastating, continue to cause such bitterness?

"Here we are." Connie breezed into the room, bearing a tray with tea, lemon, sugar and a plate of gingersnaps.

Pam accepted her glass and took a refreshing sip, then grabbed a cookie before Connie sat down on the floral-upholstered glider.

"This is such fun," Connie said. "Between getting Erin off for college, settling Mother and Vernon in their new condo and dealing with all the usual school stuff, I haven't had much time for girl-talk." She grinned suggestively. "So let's get right to it. How's married life?"

"Uh, different from what I expected."

"How so?"

"For starters, there's Andy."

Connie chuckled. "Not exactly a honeymoon cottage, then?"

"Privacy is in short supply." That, at least, was the truth.

"Can't you give the kid a few bucks and send him to the movie?"

"We manage," Pam said, blushing. She wasn't used to white lies. They managed, all right. Managed to avoid each other.

"Seriously, how are things working out with Andy? He's pretty quiet in homeroom, but he seems like a nice enough youngster."

"It's taking time for him to adjust, but kids like Chip Kennedy and Angela Beeman are helping. I'm more worried about him and Grant."

Connie stopped her gliding motion. "Oh?"

"They're like two circling grizzly bears, each one afraid to actually engage the other."

"That surprises me. Grant is so good with kids."

"It surprises him, too. He has such a stake in earning his son's respect and love."

Connie shook her head. "Men. I don't suppose they could just talk it out?"

"What?" Pam raised her eyebrows mockingly. "And actually risk emotional disclosure?"

"I hope Grant knows how lucky he is to have you by his side just now."

Pam lowered her head, wondering whether, in fact, Grant felt lucky or burdened. "I'm pretty fortunate, too." Who else would have come to her rescue? But what she couldn't confess to Connie—or anyone—was her own fears. She was becoming way too involved with Grant and Andy. Somehow she had to detach herself and deal with her own burgeoning emotions.

"So now you're getting all geared up for the play production?"

Pam pounced on the change of subject. "Rehearsals start next Monday. I'm tickled with the cast. And, believe it or not, I've even talked Andy into helping backstage."

"With his height, I though he'd be playing for Grant."

"That's part of their problem. Andy doesn't want anything to do with Grant as a coach."

"Any reason why not?"

"I think Andy's punishing his father for not being around for things like Little League and shooting hoops after dinner."

"Poor kid. As if it were totally Grant's fault."

"I know. And now, of course, the poor guy has my pregnancy to contend with."

"What do you mean? Is something wrong?"

Pam filled her in about Andy's lukewarm reaction to the news and her recent scare.

"Give yourself a break, honey." Connie's eyes were warm with sympathy. "Your pregnancy is no burden to Grant. Quite the contrary. And Andy will come around once he gets used to the idea."

"I hope so." Connie's optimism was a welcome antidote to her own doubts. Before her friend's kindness could undo her, Pam shifted gears. "I could use your help, if you're willing."

"Auntie Connie's standing by. Anything. Shoot."

Pam raised up her sweater, revealing a safety pin barely holding together the waistband of her skirt.

"Would you go shopping with me? I have no idea what I'll need."

Connie clapped her hands. "I'd love to go, but bear in mind, it's been twenty years since I was pregnant."

"That's still more experience than I've had." She couldn't tell Connie, not yet, that she was going to need all the help she could get. Once Grant was gone.

AFTER SUPPER THAT EVENING, Pam sat on the edge of Grant's bed, clutching the receiver in her hand. She'd decided to deal with Barbara first, get the worst behind her. True to form, her sister hadn't disappointed her. "A little quick, isn't it?" was her initial response. Not "That's great news," or even a "When are you due?" Pam tried to ignore the implied judgment by sharing her own pleasure. Barbara wasn't buying it. "Motherhood is lots of work, you know." Giving up then, Pam inquired about her nieces, her brother-in-law's new clinic. Safe topics. At the conclusion of the conversation, Barbara uttered begrudgingly, "Take care of yourself."

With a clunk, Pam dropped the phone into its cradle. What had she expected? If there was fault to find, Barbara would seize on it. And, in this case, there was fault. Lots of it. But damned if she'd let Barbara rain on her parade. There was joy, too, in abundance.

Straightening, she dialed her father's number, waiting patiently while the phone rang five times. Finally he picked up. "Daddy? How are you?"

After the "Fine" that masked the truth about his knee, he went on to tell her about one of the horses that had gone lame and about a neighbor's sciatica. "Those fellas of yours okay?"

"They're great."

"And you?"

"That's partly why I'm calling. I have some news."
She drew in a deep breath.

"Well, don't keep me on tenterhooks."

She looked up to see Grant lounging against the door frame, a smile tugging at the corners of his mouth.

"I...I hope you'll be pleased."

"Can't be pleased if you don't spit it out."

"I'm going to have a baby." She bit her lip, anticipating his reaction.

"Well, why didn't you say so in the first place, girl? Whoo-ee. Isn't that somethin'? I'm going to be a grandfather. Goldurn."

Air whooshed out of her lungs. "Oh, thank you, Daddy."

"For what?"

"For being pleased."

"Why in tarnation wouldn't I be?"

"Well, Barbara thought it was a little soon."

"Barbara." He snorted. "Don't pay her any mind. She's my daughter, but I gotta tell you. I love her, but I don't always like her. I dunno. She just never was the same after your momma—"

"I know, Dad."

"But let's not talk about that." It was as if he'd realized that a reference to the manner of her mother's death might not be timely. "When's this little fella comin'?"

She laughed. "You and Grant. The 'little fella' could be a girl, you know. And *she's* arriving in late spring."

"You tell that husband of yours, I'm proud of him. He's done good work."

Pam looked up at Grant, beaming down at her as if he *really* had done the "good work." She couldn't let those warm blue eyes get to her. He was her friend. Period.

"What about the boy? How's he takin' the news?"

"Er, I'm not sure."

"Kinda shoves him out of the showring, huh?"

"You could put it that way."

"Honey, why don't you put him on? Lemme talk to him."

What could it hurt? "I'll go get him."

To Pam's surprise, Andy seemed eager to talk to her father and quickly picked up the extension in his room. However, he looked pointedly at her, not acknowledging her dad until she edged from the room. Only then did she hear him say, "Hey, Gramps. Whaddya know?"

Grant waited for her at the foot of the stairs. He grinned. "Well?"

"Daddy thinks you're quite a man," she said wryly.

His grin faded. The look in his eyes sent shivers from the nape of her neck to the tips of her toes. "I wish I had been."

She stared at him, speechless. It wasn't fair of him to have said that. He was being polite. Gallant.

She couldn't dare hope. "But you weren't," she said firmly.

"I know," he said, before turning and disappearing into the living room.

She couldn't move. Not until she heard the voice of the *Monday Night Football* play-by-play announcer. Not until she put the pieces of her heart back together.

TUESDAY THE WORD WAS OUT at Keystone. Grant had talked with Ralph Hagood and the athletic director and, of course, after Connie had told some of her friends, the news had gone forth from the teachers' lounge with the immediacy of a town crier. Students burst into her classroom, eyes alight, voices crescendoing. "Awesome, Ms. Carver, er, Ms. G.!" "A bay-bee, ooh, that's so cool." Then to her utter astonishment, one of the boys asked if he could touch her stomach. "Does it hurt?" another asked. She felt laughter bubbling inside of her. She was going to provide a one-woman sex-education-and-parenting course.

"Seats, everyone. After your test, I promise I'll answer all your questions." Catching some of their mischievous looks, she amended her statement. "Or at least most of them."

After she had finally settled the students and distributed the exams, she walked around the room, monitoring their work, filled once more with the pleasure she took in working with young people.

Today she owed this pleasure to Grant. Without him, she'd be pounding the pavement looking for a job.

DURING HER PLANNING PERIOD, she decided to look over the journals her sophomores had turned in that day. She couldn't let her grading pile up, not with rehearsals starting the following week.

In the room next door, laughter erupted, and from outside she could faintly hear the middle school gym class counting cadences. With a pleased grin, she acknowledged the fact she wasn't even tired. Then counting back, she realized she hadn't had morning sickness in over a week.

Turning again to the journals, she read several more before picking up Andy's. Her heart sank. His first entry since he'd learned about the baby. This one even had a title—"The Lost Dogie." She rested her chin on her fist and began to read.

The lost dogie. That's me. Gramps called me that since he figures I'm kinda displaced. Well, he's right. I know it's not your fault, but my mother's halfway around the world and now my dad's all excited about this baby. It's not like I'm jealous, exactly. I mean, there's no baby yet, right? So what's to be jealous of? Anyway, you'd have to be some kind of heartless jerk to be jealous of a baby. I like your father. He helped me last night. Said I had a chance to be like a role model. But I don't know if I buy something else he said. That I'd always have a special place with my dad, being his first kid and all. But let's face it. Teenagers aren't exactly cute. Babies are.

P.S. I'm really glad you're okay. It's not like I want anything bad to happen. I hope you understand that.

Pam set down Andy's journal and stared out the window. Did Grant have any idea how much the boy loved him?

CHAPTER TEN

ALTHOUGH ANDY HADN'T exactly jumped for joy about helping with the play, Pam noticed his attitude improved when Angela showed sudden interest in assisting him with props. By mid-November, the weeks had fallen into a comfortable routine. When she and Andy arrived home after rehearsal, he would go for a bike ride, giving her time to straighten the house, work on lesson plans, do laundry—all in peace. If you didn't count Sebastian and Viola, who vied for her undivided attention.

She was relieved, too, that football season was over and basketball was in full swing, helping to keep her arrangement with Grant more businesslike. He was gone more and more, and when he was home, he was busy. That left little time for conversation—or temptation. Since she was usually in bed long before he was, their paths rarely crossed. What little spare time he did have, she encouraged him to spend with Andy.

It was best that way, because she'd come to an irrevocable decision—she couldn't lull herself into depending on a husband, especially a short-term one. Especially one as attractive and appealing as Grant.

This particular afternoon, Pam had popped a roast into the oven and stood at the sink peeling potatoes and carrots, noting the lengthening shadows out the kitchen window. The trees were nearly bare of leaves and a cold northwest wind whistled around the corners of the house. The days were growing shorter and shorter as winter crept closer. Had Andy worn his jacket on his bike ride? She chuckled to herself. He'd be indignant if he guessed what a mother hen she was.

He and Grant seemed to have arrived at some kind of unspoken truce—they still went for Andy's driving lessons, but so far as Pam could tell, they weren't really communicating. It was nuts for Grant to protect Shelley at the expense of his son's understanding of the past. But then again, Pam wasn't the parent. Surely there was a way Grant could talk to Andy without putting down his mother.

Pam set down the vegetable parer and massaged the base of her neck. This was one of those evenings she'd love to be curled up in her flannel pajamas on the sofa of her condo, soft show tunes on the sound system, a pot of tea by her side, a cozy gas-log fire in the fireplace. Instead, she needed to finish dinner, clean both bathrooms and work on a staggering stack of college recommendation forms.

Today's confrontation with Beau Jasper hadn't helped her frame of mind. He'd barely passed her midterm exam, then his grades had gone abruptly downhill. He was a talented athlete with Division I college scouts on his trail, but arrogant beyond belief. Irritation welled up again as she pictured his insolent, oh-so-charming smile when he stood at her desk after school. "C'mon, Ms. C., we both know you're not gonna flunk me."

"Not if you turn in passing work."

"What's the matter with my work?"

She'd clenched her fists in the folds of her skirt, silently wondering if he was deliberately playing dumb or if he could really be so clueless. She'd taken out his latest paper and attempted to go over it with him, but he was far more attentive to his watch than to the intricacies of syntax. "I'm gonna be late to practice."

"Read my lips, Beau," she'd finally said. "No passing English, no playing basketball. Is that clear enough for you?"

She rarely descended to sarcasm, but he'd tried her patience once too often. The boy actually felt entitled to a passing grade based on his stature as an athlete. She'd tried talking to his mother, whose grip on reality, alas, was obscured by blind adoration of her son. He had no father.

Picking up the parer, Pam plucked the eyes out of a potato with irritated little thrusts. How would Beau ever learn responsibility for his actions? She'd like to have been able to motivate him herself. Now she'd have to use the last resort. Appealing to his coach to apply pressure.

It didn't help that his coach was Grant.

GRANT CROUCHED on the sideline, every muscle tensed, willing Chip Kennedy's free throw into the basket. This was the first home game of the season, and the Knights needed a lead going into halftime. His body uncoiled to a standing position when Chip's shot whooshed through the hoop. Now for the second attempt. He scanned the floor. Beau Jasper was on the line between the defenders, and Cale Moore, the point guard, stood poised at half court. When the shot hit the rim, Jasper, arms extended, grabbed the rebound and rifled it to Moore, who hit a three-pointer. Grant exhaled, barely conscious of the explosion of sound from the Keystone stands. A four-point advantage. Not much, but something to work with.

Walking, head down, to the locker room, he reviewed the remarks he needed to make. This was a team that could go all the way. But they had to do it game by game. He worried about their weakness from long-range and about Jasper's hotdogging. Winning consistently required a team effort. Jasper had all the skills, but he resisted coaching. Unfortunately, some of the other players relied on him when they should have been perfecting their own abilities.

Bottom line, though, they needed Jasper. Somehow he'd managed to stay eligible throughout the football season, but offhand remarks Grant had overheard the kid make at practice suggested he already had a terminal case of senioritis.

The familiar locker-room odors of rank bodies and liniment focused him. Several players sat with towels over their heads, and one emerged from the can. Beau Jasper stood front and center adjusting his jockstrap, a smug smile on his face. "I did good, huh, coach? Thirteen points."

Grant ground his teeth, for a fleeting moment imagining Pam correcting the self-absorbed kid's grammar. "Give your teammates some credit. Remember the game's only half over and the other team is good."

"Those pansies? We'll whip their asses. You watch."

"I hope so," Grant said dryly. "Meanwhile, gather 'round, men."

Grant outlined the strategy for the second half, then gave a short pep talk. Walking back out onto the court, he briefly searched the crowd. His wife, looking gorgeous in a new magenta maternity top, sat with Darla Liddy and her month-old baby boy. When Pam spotted him, she gave a broad smile and a thumbs-up. His heart thumped. One look and he was lost. With effort, he forced his concentration back to the game. Basketball could be all-consuming. Which was good, he told himself. So long as he was eating, breathing, sleeping basketball, he wouldn't be lured into thinking long-term about Pam. The one "game" he couldn't bear to think of losing.

PAM COULDN'T FIGURE Andy out. He bared his soul to her in his journals, but in person, he was deferential, though guarded. It wasn't unusual for students to feel safer sharing their feelings in writing, especially when she guaranteed them confidentiality. Sometimes she'd catch glimpses of him walking through the hall, holding hands with Angela, or loitering by his locker with Chip and think maybe he was beginning to fit in at Keystone. But at home, he preferred to be by himself, communicating primarily in monosyllabic teen-speak.

About once a week he perfunctorily asked her how the baby was. Her other students showed more interest and enthusiasm than he did. They'd even put a file box on her desk so they could all submit possible names for the baby. So far her favorite was Byron Milton Chaucer Gilbert.

But the other students didn't feel in danger of losing their fathers' affection. Andy did.

She looked again at his latest journal entry. Something needed to happen. Soon.

My mother calls me once a week. She wants to know all this stuff like how am I doing. I tell her, "Fine." Like she'd really understand about you or Dad or Angie. Usually she just tells me what she and Harry are doing. Her big "woo" is this new game she's playing. Maw-jong, or something like that.

I've been thinking a lot about what you said about Dad buying the airplane ticket for me to spend the summer with him. It must've been that time Mom sent me to this dorky camp in North Carolina. So I've been kinda wondering if there's more stuff she hasn't told me. Like maybe there were other times that he wanted me to come that I didn't even know about.

But probably not. It's maybe just me wishing he'd really cared. Well, I know you won't tell him. 'Cuz maybe I'm wrong. Probably I am.

Pam set down his notebook, carefully closing the cover. She'd promised to keep his confidences. But these two men needed to talk.

Much as she longed to, it wasn't her place to fix their relationship. That was up to Grant and Andy.

Whenever. However.

"I THINK MAYBE I'm taking advantage of you." Grant had just come in from a cross-town game, had helped himself to a bowl of chili warming on the stove and now straddled a chair at the kitchen table opposite her.

"Who me?" Pam adopted a puckish grin. "The housekeeper?"

"That's probably exactly how you feel." He paused, a spoonful of chili halfway to his lips.

"In case you've forgotten, Coach Gilbert, that's precisely what I signed on for. I suspect I'm not so different from a lot of actual wives."

"You're different, all right," he said before shoveling the chili into his mouth.

She leaned forward as if to urge him to tell her how she was different. But when he looked up again, there was no hint of flirtation. She must have imagined the nuance. ''I appreciate the attention you're giving Andy. I'm sorry I can't be more help.''

''Are you?'' She hadn't meant to be confrontational, but his apology was too smooth, too pat.

''What's that supposed to mean?''

''Do you really want to know?''

''I asked, didn't I?''

Logic told her he was tired, stressed from a game the team had barely won in overtime, but emotion overtook her. ''I think you're content to let me handle Andy. It's simpler. You can go on deluding yourself that he resents you because you've been, in your own words, a lousy father. For you, that may be easier than actually leveling with him. Or, heaven forbid, getting involved. Shelley is hardly mother-of-the-year material, yet you've let her get away with outright lies and manipulation. What's the matter? Are you afraid to let Andy know his mother isn't perfect? Or how much you've missed him? How much you care?''

She felt herself gaining a potentially fatal head of steam, but she couldn't stop now. ''What have you got to lose? Andy already thinks you don't care. That he can't measure up. But that doesn't stop him from hoping. So what's stopping you, Coach? Guilt? Fear of emotional attachment? What?''

She rose from her seat at the table. ''Whatever it is, you need to get over it. If you want to claim your son, that is.'' She stared down at him. ''Meanwhile, offering my services as the housekeeper is the least I can do.''

He stirred his chili, head bent over his bowl. For some reason, studying the few silver strands gilding his head, she wanted to run her fingers through his hair, take back all the harsh judgments, comfort him. Then he looked at her as if she was some stranger he thought he ought to recognize. "Are you finished?"

"Quite."

"Good." Without another word, he opened the box of saltines, extracted one and began chewing.

She waited, hoping for some reaction. When none came, she said as levelly as she could, "Help yourself to the cobbler for dessert. Good night."

She fled to the den, aware that she had just risked a great deal. And lost.

Sebastian joined her on the daybed. She lay awake for a long time, stroking him and wondering how she was going to handle her strong, unhousekeeperlike attraction to this man who seemed so afraid to love.

OVER THE NEXT FEW DAYS Grant couldn't stop thinking about Pam's outburst. He'd never regarded himself as a coward, or, worse yet, a victim. What was it she could see about Andy that he couldn't? Was she right? Had he harbored some misplaced notion of gallantry where Shelley was concerned? He'd figured, since Andy had to live with her, it would be easier if he didn't make too many waves. But was that rationalization? A throwback to his own childhood? Had he abdicated his responsibility?

The thought sickened him.

Nor did he feel very good about the accusation in Pam's eyes.

His aloof son with gangly legs and a suddenly deepening voice was a stranger to him. What had happened to the happy toddler with the Nerf ball? To his own dreams of creating the close-knit family he'd never had as a youngster?

On the Sunday after Thanksgiving, Grant happened to answer the phone when Shelley called. "How's your housekeeper working out?"

She was up to her usual tricks. She knew darn well he and Pam were married. "My wife, you mean?"

"Whatever. May I please speak to my son?"

My son. He grimaced. She'd like it that way, wouldn't she? But the more he thought about it, the last thing Andy needed was additional exposure to her itinerant lifestyle or her self-serving personality. No wonder the kid didn't say much. He'd probably long ago learned silence kept him out of trouble. Man, could Grant relate. He remembered all too well. You didn't talk to the colonel—you listened. "I'll tell him you're on the line."

After summoning Andy, he found himself pacing the living room, angry yet impotent. Pam was right. He'd been far too passive where his son was concerned and he intended for that to end. Today.

ANDY COULDN'T BELIEVE IT. He and his dad stood in the lot looking at used cars. Maybe after he turned sixteen he'd actually have wheels! When he'd gotten off the phone with his mother, his dad had told him to grab a jacket and come along on an errand. He hadn't wanted to—until he found out where they were going. Sunday afternoons were good for looking 'cause you didn't have to deal with those greasy salesmen with their fake smiles and "hot" deals.

"What do you think of this one?" His dad was standing beside a gray Honda.

"Okay, I guess."

"But?"

"It's not exactly a cool color. It doesn't have a sun roof."

"Is that a requirement?"

Andy shrugged. "I guess not. But it'd be good."

"Let's look over here, then." His dad walked toward a candy-red Firebird.

That was more like it. "Yeah, I can see myself in this."

Then his father gave him the spiel about considering more than looks—as if he was stupid or something. He knew about gas mileage, safety features and insurance rates. Not to mention price.

On the way home, his dad, kinda casuallike, said, "Has your mother talked with you about a car?"

"I guess she thinks you'll get me one."

"That's a pretty big assumption, I'd say."

Andy felt a squirmy sensation in his stomach. He'd never heard Dad use that tone of voice when talking about Mom. Then he went on. "Shelley and I haven't been very good at communicating. Especially where you're concerned."

No shit. What was this about anyway?

Dad was studying the road like he was in some Grand Prix race. "Did you know I used to ask your mother if you could spend summers with me?"

Summers? Plural? Pam had only mentioned the one. "Not exactly."

"I did. Up until a couple of years ago when I realized I was fighting a losing battle."

Andy didn't know if he bought this story or not. "What stopped you?"

Instead of answering the question, his dad glanced at him. "Did you ever know about those invitations?"

"No."

"Would you have come?"

"I dunno."

They'd arrived home. His dad parked the car but didn't get out. Instead, he put a hand on Andy's shoulder. "I wanted you to come, son. Always."

Andy felt queasy. "Why didn't Mom tell me?"

"She always claimed you had other plans—Little League, camps, trips." He cleared his throat. "I figured that you preferred it that way."

Andy erupted. "Like I had a choice? Like either one of you ever asked me what I wanted?" He grabbed the handle and leaped from the car, turning back for one last word. "And now what? You expect it to suddenly be okay? To fix it with a car? Hell, Dad, where've you been for sixteen years, huh?"

Blinded by a rage he couldn't express, Andy rushed past Pam and up the stairs to his bedroom. It was too late for some big father-son moment.

Even if it had prob'ly cost him his wheels. Son of a bitch!

"WELL, SO MUCH FOR communicating," Grant said, sinking defeatedly into his recliner.

Pam eyed him from the sofa, where she sat in her customary place, a pile of student papers in her lap. "What was that all about?" She nodded toward the stairs.

"Testosterone and one blown opportunity."

"Is it just today or do you always talk in riddles?"

"You were right."

"About?"

If a grown man could be said to be sulking, Grant was. "Shelley. Andy. Me."

She nudged the stack of papers aside. He must be upset—he hadn't even noticed Sebastian mewing plaintively and entwining himself between Grant's legs. Getting the story out of him was going to require delicacy. "For what it's worth, I take no satisfaction in being right."

"Where were you when I needed you all those years ago?"

Nice as it was to be needed, he wasn't going to lay this off on her. "A better question might be where were you?"

His frown deepened and he didn't answer. Pam smoothed her maternity top over her slightly rounded stomach, a sinking feeling making her distinctly uncomfortable. This was definitely not the way to let a man know you cared about him.

"Fair enough," he grunted. "I told him about the times I asked Shelley to send him for the summer." He looked at her. "He never had a clue."

"Is that surprising?"

"I can't believe I was so gullible."

"It's one of your most endearing qualities."

"Andy's angry. At both his mother and me. Justifiably. Shelley and I let our own egos get in the way of what was best for him."

"Anger could be good."

He gazed at her as if she'd lost her mind. "How do you figure that?"

"If he didn't care, he wouldn't be angry. He'd be indifferent. So long as he cares, you can reach him."

"I wish I knew how."

"By trying. Just like you tell your team. Keep practicing. No pain, no gain, right?"

He gave her an arch look that slowly dissolved into

a half smile. "You sound just like a wife." Then he tried to stand up, encumbered by Sebastian. "Jeez, a cat?" He shook his head. "I guess I'm learning tolerance."

She watched him leave the room, an amused grin twitching her lips. It had felt, for a few moments, like a real marriage. Full of troubles and strained relationships. But solid.

Which goes to show, she thought wryly, that appearances are deceiving.

THE NEXT WEEK was a whirlwind. Two basketball games, dress rehearsal and three performances of *Our Town*. Grant wished he could be more help to Pam. She had big circles under her eyes and he knew she wasn't getting enough sleep. Wednesday night he'd awakened and seen the living room lights on. She was curled up in his chair double-checking the ticket sales and seating assignments, her deliciously curved breasts pressing against her knit T-shirt in a way that sent him scurrying back to bed, full of libidinous thoughts.

Andy, too, was involved with the play. Probably a good thing, since they had both needed a time-out. Grant clung to the tiny ray of hope Pam had given him. Maybe Andy did care. If only they could find a way to communicate without anger and recriminations.

Sunday afternoon Grant finally attended an *Our Town* performance. He'd had games both Friday and Saturday nights. If it hadn't been for Beau Jasper's outstanding play, they'd have been outmatched. When the lights went down and the curtain rose, he found himself caught up with the residents of Grover's Corners, New Hampshire. By Act 3, he realized the tightness in his chest was caused by his identification with Emily, the heroine. Dying tragically as a teenager, she'd been permitted to choose one day to return to earth—to experience things anew, do things over. More than anything, he wanted "do-overs" with his son.

When the final curtain came down to thunderous applause, he joined the rest of the audience in a standing ovation. The kids had been terrific. Then the cast beckoned offstage for the crew, and there was Andy, holding Angela Beeman's hand, smiling, bowing and looking for all the world as if he, single-handedly, had been responsible for the success of the production.

Then the kids pulled Pam onto the stage and the male lead presented her with a huge bouquet of roses. Her eyes sparkled with tears as she turned to hug first one actor, then another. He was ashamed to admit that this was the first drama production he'd been to in several years.

Andy went with Angela and some of the others to a cast party. Grant lingered to help Pam secure the auditorium. As she turned the lock in the door and started to leave the building, a cool breeze ruffled her hair, coppery-gold in the fading light. He took her arm and tucked it into his. "You should be very proud of yourself. It was wonderful."

"Thank you, but it's the kids who made it happen."

"I understand. That's how I feel about my players. All the same, they couldn't have done it without you."

Her hand tightened on his arm. "It's moments like this that make us remember why we chose teaching."

"I know." He helped her into the car and drove slowly through the upscale residential area. Since confronting him about Andy, she had seemed guarded around him, and, in truth, he had resented her interference. But she'd been right. In the afterglow of her success today, maybe they could recapture their earlier closeness. He hoped so.

"Andy really enjoyed himself, I think." Her eyes shone and her skin, almost translucent, called out to be caressed.

"Thanks to you." He reached over and took her hand in his, grateful she didn't pull away. "You have a magic touch with kids."

"Not with all of them."

Something in her tone abruptly altered the mood. She had turned to look at him, her eyes telegraphing concern. "What do you mean?"

"You're going to have to talk with Beau Jasper."

Tightness banded his chest. "Beau?"

"Nothing I've said has made a dent. Not with him. Not with his ditzy mother."

"What are you telling me?"

"Short of a miracle, Beau is going to fail senior English."

He felt as if he'd just been socked in the stomach. "I need him, Pam."

She withdrew her hand. "I know you do. And I've tried to make him understand. Now it's up to you."

"Can't you help him? Figure out something?"

Her voice grew cool. "Take it up with Beau."

ANDY GAVE HOWIE an elbow, whirled and passed off to Andre, waiting under the basket. When he went up for the shot, James blocked it. Juan picked up the loose ball, bounce-passed it back to Andy, who hit a three-pointer. Andre strutted over, his palm extended. "My man!" he said, giving Andy a high-five.

Howie held the ball, surveying the others. "Wanna go another five minutes?"

"I'm freezin' my butt off," Juan said, picking up his windbreaker from the pavement.

"Pretty soon it'll be too cold to play after school," Andy said.

"Yeah, man, for dudes like us who aren't on the big team," James made two syllables of *team*, "winter sucks. Tomorrow?"

"Sure." Andy pulled the Keystone sweatshirt over his head, hopped on his bike and headed for home. Except for not getting to see Angie every day, he was glad the play was over so he could play basketball more. James was right. Winter sucked. For a few moments he allowed himself to wonder if he'd have made the varsity at his old school. He thought so. After watching the Keystone Knights, he was damn sure he could have played here. He and old Chipper would've made an awesome pair.

But that'd mean hours a day with his dad. Who didn't think he was good at much of anything. If he had, he'd have figured a way to get to Florida to watch him play.

Right. He'd had obligations as a teacher. As a coach. What about his obligations to the son he'd walked out on?

GRANT CLOSED his classroom door and, with a nod, indicated which seat Beau should take. The boy sauntered to the chair, only the high color in his cheeks betraying his nervousness. Grant remained standing, arms crossed, as the boy slid into the desk. "So what's up, Coach? Why'd you wanna see me?"

"I think you know. A little matter called English."

Beau's eyes were hooded. "What about it?"

"Ms. Carver tells me you're in danger of failing."

Grant thought he heard Beau mutter "that bitch" under his breath. "What'd you just say?"

The boy looked up, defensiveness in every feature. "I *said,* 'That's rich.' I do my work."

"Satisfactorily?"

"She doesn't like me. I know she's your wife and all, but she has it in for me."

Grant moved a step closer to Beau's chair. "That dog won't hunt, friend. Ms. Carver has showed me some of your papers and tests. If you gave that kind of effort on the basketball court, you'd be lucky to warm the bench. Are you trying to self-destruct?"

"Man, I never get a break. She loves to give me bad grades."

Grant felt bile sour his palate. There had to be a way to reach this kid. "She doesn't *give* you anything. She evaluates what you earn."

Beau shot him a skeptical look. "I don't need this crap. O.U., Baylor and Tech think I'm a hot prospect."

"You have to get there first. Not likely if you fail English."

"You think I'm stupid, or somethin'? I'll pull it out."

Grant ran a hand through his hair. "You better. You have a whole team counting on it." He paused. "Come to think of it, you have a whole future depending on it. Don't blow it. Understand?"

The boy stood up, eyeballing Grant. "No sweat, Coach. She isn't gonna flunk me. You watch." He ambled toward the door, then turned back. "Anything else?"

Grant stared at the insolent, blindly overconfident youngster. "No. That's it."

The only "anything else" he could think of was to

turn the kid over his knee and administer the long-overdue spanking he'd probably never had.

But he also knew the winning season had just walked out the door.

EARLY IN DECEMBER Pam sat at the kitchen table staring at the Christmas cards she'd purchased. "Warm holiday greetings to you and yours" read the message. Her family and friends would expect the cards to be signed "Pam and Grant," yet by this time next year, she'd be explaining about their divorce. She couldn't avoid a twinge of sadness. For all the awkwardness of their arrangement, this place felt like home. A very important home. The one where she would first bring her baby.

She picked up the pen and commenced writing a cheery note to her college roommate, then signed it, adding Andy's name to hers and Grant's. Heck, for now, this was her family.

Grant arrived home about seven-thirty, filling the kitchen with a blast of cold air and the scent of after-shave. His hair was still damp from his locker-room shower. Pam sighed. He looked downright gorgeous. He paused by her chair. "What're you doing?"

"I thought I'd better get a head start on our Christmas cards."

He grinned. "You're something else. I haven't sent cards in years."

"I'd like to include your friends."

He helped himself to a bowl of soup from the pot simmering on the stove. "Tell you what. I'll put Xs beside the names in my address book."

He sat at the far end of the table, making sure he didn't get food near the cards. She continued addressing them, sneaking looks at him from time to time. She liked the way he ate, with gusto but not sloppily. And she liked how his broad shoulders strained his blue ox-ford-cloth shirt. Best of all she liked the crinkly laugh lines bracketing his eyes.

He scraped the last of the bowl, shoved it aside, then sat back, folding his hands contentedly over his stomach. "You're cooking is spoiling me."

"Don't get too used to it." She'd meant it as a joke, but the remark came out as an unintentional reminder of their situation.

"I'll try not to," he said tonelessly.

"Grant—" As she struggled to lighten the mood, a strange thing happened. A twitch. Like a butterfly kiss. Her eyes widened and her hand went quickly to that spot on her abdomen. Another flutter. To the right. She moved her hand.

"Pam?" Grant was leaning forward, watching her with concern.

Almost as an aside, she felt the tears on her cheeks. At the same time, she smiled, filled with joy. "The baby," she stammered, "the baby…"

He'd gotten up and moved beside her. "What?"

"Oh, Grant, it moved. I could feel it."

"Where?"

And before she could stop to think, she placed his big, warm hand on her rounded belly. "There."

He frowned in concentration, and then there was a definite thump, stronger than before. His eyes were level with hers, warmed by genuine delight. "Awesome," he breathed.

They remained in that pose until the flutterings subsided. Then, as if on cue, the phone rang. Grant got to his feet and picked up. "Hello, Will. Yes, she's right here. I'll put her on. She's got some exciting news for you.''

Grant handed Pam the receiver. ''Hi, Daddy. Guess what? Your grandchild just made himself known. I felt movement.''

''I reckon that's plumb wonderful.''

''It is. Somehow, it makes everything more real.''

Her father chuckled. ''It'll get a lot 'realer' before all's said and done. How are you feelin', dumplin'?''

''Great. This second trimester is a breeze compared to the first. How about you? How's the knee?''

He didn't answer right away and Pam felt a twinge of apprehension. ''That's partly why I'm calling. I'm having the danged thing replaced.''

''Surgery? Oh, Daddy. Where? When? How can we help?''

''Slow down. Where? Fort Worth. When? I don't wanna ruin your Christmas plans, but how does December fifteenth sound?''

''I'm so glad you'll be here where I can keep an eye on you.'' She felt Grant's arm slip around her waist in silent support. She mouthed ''knee replacement'' to him. ''But what about the recovery? You can't expect to go home.''

''You asked how you could help. The doctor said I could go into a rehabilitation hospital or—''

''You'll come here, of course.'' Belatedly she searched Grant's face. He nodded. ''We won't hear of anything else.''

''I hate to impose—''

''You won't. Besides, maybe you can keep Andy company.''

''A fella could do a whole lot worse.''

After she hung up, she turned in Grant's embrace. "It *is* all right, isn't it? I mean, I forgot to ask."

"You didn't have to ask, Pam. This is your home. And Will is part of our family."

"Thank you for that." *Our family.* It had such a solid, comforting ring. If only it were true. "There will be some adjustments, though."

"I know." Then he grinned in a way that even the most innocent, virtuous maiden couldn't fail to interpret as flirting. "We'll have to give your dad the master bedroom. I doubt if climbing steps will be on his immediate therapy plan."

"But—" The implication set in. They certainly weren't moving Andy out. And there was only one spare bedroom upstairs. One small bedroom. With one very cozy double bed.

"Trust me. We'll work it out." Then he winked and kissed her on the cheek. He steered her back to the table and sat her down. "Merry Christmas," he murmured huskily just before he left the room.

CHAPTER ELEVEN

PAM COULDN'T HELP HERSELF. She picked up the sugary doughnut laced with colored sprinkles and took the first satisfying bite, oblivious to the early morning chatter and bustle of the teachers' lounge. One sinful indulgence. Surely it couldn't hurt. As if in agreement, a tiny kick nudged her tummy.

Connie edged up next to her, a teasing smile on her face. "Back to your evil ways, huh?"

"Caught in the act," Pam acknowledged, brushing crumbs off her maternity jumper.

"This is the big day, right?"

"I can't wait." Her ultrasound appointment was at eleven.

"Are you going to find out if it's a boy or girl?"

"No way. I love surprises." She finished the doughnut, wiped her mouth, then balled up the napkin and tossed it across the room into the wastebasket. "It's like opening night and Christmas morning all rolled into one."

"Good for you." Connie topped off her coffee. "Any further instructions about covering your class?"

"Just keep Beau Jasper's nose to the grindstone. Thanks for covering for me, Connie. I owe you one."

"What time are you and Grant leaving?"

"Grant?"

"Surely he's going with you?"

"He couldn't justify abandoning his calculus class. Besides, he has lunch duty today."

Connie searched her face, while Pam did her best to act as if going to her ultrasound alone was no big deal. Finally Connie simply said, "Men!" in a tone of voice that left no doubt which sex, at that moment, she considered inferior.

IT FELT LIKE playing hookey to be on her way to the doctor while her class was deep into a discussion of imagery in *Hamlet*. At least she hoped that's what was happening. Barney must be excited about the upcoming ultrasound, too. He beat enthusiastic tattoos all the way to Dr. Ellis's office.

Miraculously, the doctor was on schedule, and after the initial exam, Pam, uncomfortably bloated with all the water she'd had to drink in preparation, was sent down the hall to the ultrasound room. The technician helped her lie down, then bared her abdomen and applied a cold jellylike substance. "I'll get the doctor," she said, leaving the room. In her absence, Pam's excited anticipation turned more and more to apprehension. What if something was wrong with the baby? She closed her eyes against the thought. She'd already had one scare. She couldn't bear another.

"Pam?" Belinda Ellis, a broad smile on her face, peeped in the door. "Are you ready?"

"Most definitely."

"Good." She opened the door wider. "I have a surprise for you." She stepped inside, followed by the technician, and then by Grant. "Your husband was able to make it after all."

"Grant?" She turned her head and saw his big frame filling the range of her vision.

He hurried to the examining table. "You didn't think I *wanted* to miss this, did you?"

Pam was aware of Dr. Ellis, studying them with the delight of an approving parent. "But how—"

"When Connie found out I couldn't come, she turned into a one-woman dynamo, getting Jessie Flanders, of all people, to cover calculus and recruiting poor Jim to take my lunch duty."

Pam smiled wanly, aware of the bittersweet quality of the moment.

Dr. Ellis spoke up. "Are you ready to meet this baby?"

Grant clutched Pam's hand. "We sure are."

Was it only this morning she'd told Connie she liked surprises? She wasn't sure about this one, though. The more a part of this pregnancy Grant became, the more painful it would be when she had to leave him.

Then filling the screen was the image of a curved spine, a large head, and...

"See?" Dr. Ellis took the pointer and highlighted a blurry portion of the picture. "There are the hands."

"Wow," Grant said, squeezing Pam's fingers.

"It's pretty amazing, isn't it?" Dr. Ellis said, as if this was the first time she'd seen an ultrasound.

"Oh, honey," Pam addressed the screen, "I loved you before, but now..." She couldn't go on, over-whelmed with powerful maternal feelings.

When the technician finally turned off the machine, Pam slowly lifted her gaze to Grant. Another surprise.

Tears he made no effort to wipe away coursed down his cheeks.

IT WAS JUST AS WELL they had two cars, Grant thought, as he slowly drove back to Keystone. He needed time to take in what he'd just witnessed. Movement. Tiny skeletal features. Amazing. Had Shelley done this test with Andy? Surely he'd have remembered.

When Dr. Ellis had confirmed the pregnancy was proceeding normally, he didn't know who was more relieved, Pam or him.

But why hadn't she asked him to come to the appointment with her? Was she shutting him out? He had to admit it hurt. Yet what right did he have to be there? He wasn't the father.

The father. Just thinking about him caused Grant's gut to tighten. Did he have any idea how difficult he'd made Pam's life? Hell. No matter what was going on in his personal life, the man should've... Should've what? Not loved Pam? Damn difficult to do if his own experience was any measure. If Pam didn't blame the guy, how could he?

All he knew was he wouldn't have missed being there today for anything. Seeing the ultrasound had made the baby real in a way nothing else had. Most confusing was the fact that he could no longer think of it as *a* baby.

For reasons that had nothing to do with biology, a single notion filled his head—*you're* my *baby. Pam's and mine.*

Yet that could never be.

Weird. And cool, too. The pictures you brought home from the doctor, I mean. Did you ever see that fetus or embryo or whatever in the movie *2001, A Space Odyssey?* That's kinda what your baby looks like. I don't mean any disrespect. I'm sure it'll be lots cuter after it's born.

Pam stifled a smile. Bless Andy's heart, he was trying so hard to make her feel better, as if she'd been disappointed that her baby looked just as it was supposed to at sixteen weeks.

The other cool thing is that Gramps is coming to live with us for a while. I'm sorry he has to have his knee replaced, but this means I'll get to spend more time with him. You're lucky to have a dad like him. The kind that doesn't get on your case or talk at you all the time, but really listens.

Viola had crawled underneath the afghan Pam had spread over her legs and was rooting around, seemingly puzzled by the altered contours of Pam's lap. Eventually she settled her head right where the baby had been kicking a short time ago. Pam reread the last two sentences with mixed emotions. It was an accurate comment about her dad, but was Andy also saying something about Grant?

I need to ask you a big favor. I wanna get something nice for Angie for Christmas. Not anything too girly like perfume or bubble bath. But talk about clueless. That's me. So I was kind of wondering if maybe you'd go with me to help pick something out. But don't tell Dad, okay? It's no big deal.

Viola nudged the afghan aside and looked up at her with knowing eyes. "You're right, Vee. Those two guys are impossible." She leaned over and whispered in Viola's ear, "But I'm flattered Andy trusts me. I'm afraid trust is something he doesn't know much about."

THE NIGHT BEFORE Will's surgery, Pam perched at the foot of his hospital bed while Andy sat in the single armchair, one jiggling foot crossed over his other knee. From beyond the drawn curtain, Will's roommate's family prattled in overly hearty voices about that patient's recovery from a broken pelvis. "Grant said to wish you luck. He was sorry he couldn't make it."

"Big game?"

Pam caught Andy rolling his eyes. "This is the finals of the pre-Christmas Keystone Invitational Tournament, Dad. He was pretty keyed up."

"From what he tells me, they've got a good season going. After I get my sticks back under me, I'd like to take in a game or two before I head home."

"Grant would like that." Pam nervously smoothed the fabric of the bedspread.

"What about you, son?" Will turned a craggy smile on Andy. "Will you go along and fill me in about the players, all the inside stuff?"

"Not much to tell," Andy mumbled. "It's all about Beau Jasper."

"One-man team?"

Andy nodded.

"There's more to a rodeo than the bull riding. And it doesn't do to have men pulling in different directions. That only works in calf roping." He coughed dryly.

"Jasper's really good, Gramps."

"When he's eligible," Pam said.

Andy's jaw dropped. "What do you mean?"

Too late Pam realized she should have kept her mouth shut. Although it was inevitable Andy would pick up some school gossip, she'd been irresponsible to volunteer it. "Oh, nothing much. But he's struggling in English, that's all."

"You wouldn't flunk him?" Andy was incredulous.
Gramps scooted back against his pillow. "Why wouldn't she?"

"It'd screw the team."

"First of all, I doubt that, son. But more important, aren't there rules about keeping your grades up?"

"Well, yeah, but—"

"No buts, boy. A fella has to live by some sort of code. He's not much of a man if he doesn't play by the rules."

Andy put his foot down, then recrossed his legs. There went the other foot, fidgeting with the rapidity of a bird's wing. "Maybe."

"No maybes, either. Maybes can get you killed."

Pam watched their exchange with interest. Andy listened to her father in a way he listened to no one else. Despite the inconvenience of the upcoming sleeping arrangements, having Will in the house could benefit Andy.

The other patient's visitors departed, leaving only the incongruous sound of canned laughter from his TV. A nurse parted the curtain and excusing the interruption, began taking Will's vitals. Pam watched the blood pressure gauge, a tremor of fear eroding her composure. When the nurse finished, she smiled apologetically. "I'm afraid visiting hours are over."

Pam's stomach lurched. She couldn't think about tomorrow's "what if's." She approached the head of the bed and picked up her father's work-roughened hand. "I talked with Barbara today. She sends her love." Pam didn't add that Barbara had actually thanked her for taking care of their father. Maybe there was hope for the two of them. "Rest well, Daddy. I'll be here first thing in the morning.'' She leaned over and kissed his cheek. ''Everything's going to be fine.''

''Don't you worry, girl. No busted knee's gonna keep me out of action, hear?''

Andy levered himself out of the chair and stood awkwardly at the foot of the bed. ''G'night, Gramps. Good luck.''

''At least you didn't say, like Pammy always used to, 'Break a leg.''' He chortled at his own joke. ''Now, get on out of here.''

Pam picked up her purse and Andy started for the door.

''Son?''

Andy turned to face the old man. ''Yeah?''

''Remember what I said. A fella always has to be responsible. If he's a man.''

Pam averted her face before she alarmed Andy with the tears that threatened. Will Carver was a good man. And an extraordinary father.

And now, grandfather.

BOTH GRANT AND ANDY INSISTED on being with her at the hospital the next morning. Their welcome company helped keep her mind off the cold well of fear building inside her. Will had been both father and mother to her, and the thought of losing him was too hard to contemplate.

After what seemed an interminable wait, she crumpled with relief when the surgeon appeared to inform them Will had come through the procedure beautifully. When a nurse escorted her into the recovery room, her dad managed a smile, squeezed her hand and then drifted off.

Pam intended to spend the day at the hospital, but

urged Grant and Andy to return to school. For all their good intentions, neither was comfortable in the hospital setting nor was there anything for them to do. By late afternoon, Will had been transferred to a regular room, tired but glad to have the ordeal behind him, and they'd both talked with Barbara, assuring her all was well. When Will noticed Pam's eyes drooping, he mustered his strength and urged her to go home. "Nothin' you can do here, 'cept leave me in peace."

It *had* been a long day, she reflected on the drive home, marked by worry, boredom and relief. A warm cup of soup and her own bed sounded divine. Traffic was heavy and the late afternoon sun was in her eyes, so she exited the interstate and wound her way home, taking an unfamiliar route through her neighborhood. Stopping at a light, she recognized the park on the other side of the street. Not too far now. She fiddled with the volume control on the radio, then accelerated slowly through the intersection. Suddenly a dog darted in front of her. Braking, she watched it lope over the curb and off across the grassy area near the basketball court.

Then she saw it. A bicycle that looked like Andy's. A car eased up behind her. The driver gently tapped her horn. Pam collected herself, gave an apologetic wave and pulled over to the curb. What could Andy be doing here? It was nearly dark.

She got out of the car, buttoned her jacket and started walking toward the bike. That's when she heard grunts, shouts and the unmistakable words, "Gilbert, my man, awesome shot!"

She headed for the basketball court shielded by a stand of trees. Pausing there, she watched the pickup game in amazement. A couple of smaller, quick-handed boys and several taller ones were involved in a no-holds-barred contest. Bumping, leaping, dribbling, shooting with authority toward the basket. She watched for several minutes, her heart pounding.

They were good. Very good.

But the best was Andy, his eyes darting around the court, his jaw clenched in determination.

So this was where he mysteriously disappeared to. Grant clearly had no idea. Equally clear was the fact Andy didn't want him to know. What was she supposed to do about this? How could Grant not know his son was this talented? How devastated would he be to realize Andy couldn't share this with him?

"Pam?" Andy had seen her. The action on the court stopped abruptly, the lone sound a ball being idly bounced by a tall African-American youth who stood with the others in a huddle, watching Andy approach her. "What are you doing here?"

"I was on my way home from the hospital when I saw your bike."

"Crap!" He stood in front of her, eyes directed skyward as if imploring the heavens. Then in a gesture uncannily like his father's, he ran a hand jerkily through his hair. "This is all I need."

"What?"

"For you to tell my old man about this." He turned away. "Jeez!"

She stepped forward, knowing that what she said right now was crucial. "I haven't decided to do anything. Yet."

He slowly pivoted to face her, regarding her with stony eyes. "I don't want him to know."

"Why not?"

"I just don't."

What was her obligation here? Would it hurt to keep his secret? "I'll have to think about it, Andy."

"You said we could trust you to keep our confidences," he blurted out.

"In your journals."

"But no place else? Is that it?" The boy's voice was raw.

She laid a hand on his arm. "You've put me in a difficult position, Andy, but I'll tell you what. I won't say anything for now." His head drooped in relief. "But you and I are going to talk about this later."

He straightened and studied her warily. "How do I know I can trust you?"

She looked straight into his eyes. "Because I say so."

He held her gaze, then finally glanced at his bike. "I gotta go."

"I know. See you at home." She watched him walk toward his bike and, under her breath, added, "Please be careful."

She, too, would have to be careful. There was a delicate balance between keeping his trust and violating Grant's.

THE NEXT AFTERNOON Pam cleared off her desk, erased the chalkboard and grabbed the ungraded vocabulary quizzes. Maybe she could get to them while she visited with her father.

She checked her watch. Twenty minutes to drop Andy at home, then off to the hospital. When she leaned over to retrieve her purse from the bottom desk drawer, she heard a thump, like a dropped backpack. Looking up, she saw Andy standing a few feet from her. "You startled me," she said.

''Sorry.'' He made no move to leave. His hands were stuffed in his front pockets and she could hear the jingle of coin hitting against coin.

''Ready to go?'' When he still made no move, she felt a tic of annoyance. ''What *is* it, Andy?''

He jutted out his chin. ''Did you tell him?''

''No, I didn't. Not yet.''

''Are you gonna?''

''I don't know. It depends.''

''On what?''

''Whether you can figure out why you're so determined to punish yourself.''

His face colored. ''What are you talking about?''

''You love basketball, don't you?''

''What's the difference?''

Setting her purse on the desk, she summoned her patience. ''The difference is that you're denying yourself pleasure and accomplishment out of some misplaced notion of revenge.''

''That's crap.'' The coin-jangling grew louder.

''Is it? I think you've been blaming your father all these years for the divorce. Let me ask you something. Do you honestly think your parents would have been happy had they stayed together?''

He shrugged without looking up.

''Or that your father wanted to leave you? Walking out that door was probably the hardest thing he's ever had to do. Like you, he's been hurting every day since.'' Her voice softened. ''Can't you give him a break?''

''Why should I?''

Sighing in exasperation, she moved closer, settling her hands on his shoulders, forcing him to look at her. ''Darn it, Andy, why are you so hell-bent on turning your back on love?''

"Love?" He mocked the word. "Who gives a shit?"

Her eyes held his. "You do."

He wheeled away, picking up the backpack he'd dropped by the door. She grabbed her purse and followed him down the hall. When she caught up with him, he glared at her. "So you're gonna tell him, right?"

"No, I'm not." Before he could react in relief, she hurried on. "*You* are. Just don't wait too long."

All the way home not a further word was spoken.

GRANT FELT like a pack mule, schlepping stuff up to the guest bedroom he and Pam would now share. He nearly tripped over the top step wondering how he was going to manage to keep his hands off her. And more importantly, how they were going to fool Will Carver into believing they were in love.

Before Will was released from the hospital, Grant needed to grade his finals and get the Christmas tree up. Then there was the shopping. He and Pam were giving Andy a laptop, so that when he returned to his mother, he could take it with him. Grant mentally counted the months. Only eight and a half left. He felt like a failure as a father. Heck, maybe he was.

He heaved the armload of clothes onto the guest-room bed. He needed a special Christmas gift for Pam. But what?

She and Andy were way ahead of him. Yesterday they'd gone to the mall. When they'd gotten home, Andy had volunteered nothing about their shopping excursion. When Grant had inquired of Pam, she'd merely smiled wisely and said, "Did you tell your father everything when you were fifteen?"

Sure, the kid had a right to privacy, but Grant felt

totally out of the loop. Maybe he and Andy would have been forced to get along if Pam hadn't moved in.

But he couldn't imagine his home without her.

And now she was going to be in his bed. Every night.

He groaned in frustration just thinking about the self-control *that* would require.

"YOU DANG WELL DON'T have to give up your bedroom, kids." Will eased down onto the straight chair, his left leg extended, then propped his crutches in the corner of the living room.

"We'll manage," Pam said, wondering how.

"It won't be forever." Grant set Will's overnight bag in the hall, then eyed the staircase. "You don't really want to be confined upstairs, do you?"

"Heck, I can get up and down the steps."

"Dad—"

Will held his palms up in surrender. "I know, honey. Slow and easy." He looked around the room. "It's nice to be out of the hospital. Pretty tree," he said, gesturing to the six-foot Scotch pine in the corner. "Sorry I couldn't do much in the way of presents. But there are a few things I left in the trunk of my car before I went to the hospital."

"We'll bring them in later," Grant said.

"I'm glad the boy'll be here with us for Christmas. Nothin' like a kid around to make the holiday." His eyes twinkled. "And next year, just think. Gilbert Junior."

Pam turned her back, pretending to adjust a tree ornament. Next year's Christmas would be vastly different. No Andy. No Grant. No cozy little family. Steadying her voice, she answered. "It could be a girl, you know."

"That'd be all right. Reckon I know a thing or two about female critters."

Pam trusted herself to face him. "That you do, Daddy." She crossed to him and laid a kiss on the top of his head. "Now, how about some lunch and then a nice long nap?"

"I am kinda tired. Sounds good."

Settling him in front of the TV, Pam busied herself in the kitchen, heating some soup and grilling cheese sandwiches.

When Grant came through the kitchen carrying several wrapped packages, he paused. "How do you think he's doing?"

Pam shrugged. "Okay, I guess. But he seems pretty weak."

"Yeah, I thought so, too." He started to leave, but then stopped. "I think I'll sleep in the den these first few nights. To be right there if he needs help."

Pam noticed he couldn't quite bring himself to look directly at her. Nor did she want him to. She picked up a spatula and flipped the sandwiches. "That's a good idea," she said not trusting her emotions. "Thank you."

So. She had a reprieve. A few more nights sleeping alone. But the questions remained. Was Grant merely being solicitous of her father or delaying the inevitable? Was he as nervous as she was about what might happen when they shared a bed night after night?

Housekeeper. Think housekeeper.

CHRISTMAS MORNING. The turkey was in the oven, the table set, hot cider simmered on the stove. Satisfied, Pam surveyed the tree where Viola and Sebastian playfully pawed at the ornaments and colorful ribbons.

Grant was helping Will shave. Once they were finished, she'd wake Andy if he hadn't yet emerged.

He'd been all nervous excitement yesterday after delivering to Angela the delicate gold locket Pam had helped him select and returning with a boxed set of CDs he'd been wanting.

He stumbled down the stairs, rubbing his eyes, just as Grant helped Will into the living room. The older man greeted them exuberantly. "Merry Christmas, everybody."

"Yeah, Merry Christmas." Andy stood at the base of the stairs in his bare feet. "Anything to eat?"

After Pam served him a banana and warm cinnamon roll, they gathered around the tree, soft Christmas music playing in the background. Pam fought a pang of wistfulness. The scene appeared so festive, so homey.

Andy seemed tickled with his laptop, and the sweater she'd bought Grant turned out to be exactly the shade of his blue eyes, just as she'd hoped. Everything was greeting-card perfect until Andy opened his present from Will.

"Gramps, you're the greatest!" Andy's face was as animated as she'd ever seen it. "Wow!" He handed around the lettered certificate inside the box. "This entitles Andy Gilbert to one hand-tooled leather saddle and a half interest in Sagebrush Pepper Boy."

Pam watched the spectacle in disbelief.

"Now, I know, you'll be living with your mother some. But I reckon when you visit your family here, you'll be comin' to the ranch. A fella's gotta have his own mount."

Grant, his lips thinned in a grim line, caught her eye. She slowly lifted her shoulders in bewilderment. She'd known nothing of her father's intentions.

Then Will pointed to a package wrapped in red foil. "Get that for Pam, would you, Andy?"

She examined the card, then looked up, confused.

"You're seein' it right. Barbara sent it. Asked me to give it to you."

She and Barbara hadn't exchanged gifts since Barbara had left home immediately after her high school graduation. They'd talked briefly on the phone several times following Will's surgery, but...why in the world would her sister suddenly be giving her a Christmas present?

With trembling fingers, Pam opened the card and read the brief message. "My children used this. Now that you're having a baby, I suppose Mother would've wanted you to have it. Barbara. P.S. I hope all goes well for you with your pregnancy." Silently she handed the card to her father.

"Reserve judgment till you see what it is, honey. I think maybe Barbara's trying."

Pam slid her hand under the slick paper and slowly pulled it off. All she had to do was lift the lid of the box. But it suddenly seemed too much. She sensed the eyes of the men on her and knew she couldn't delay further. She removed the lid and parted the layers of tissue paper.

Lying in the box was something she hadn't seen since she was a tiny girl, but which was, nevertheless, comfortingly familiar.

"What is it?" Andy asked impatiently.

She gathered the pink-and-blue quilt against her breast and said with tear-filled eyes, "It's the baby quilt my mother made for my sister and me. See?" She pointed to the embroidered "LC" in the corner. "Lillian Carver."

Grant looked at Will, then at Pam. "That's quite a gift."

"I know," she said, holding it against her where Barney lay quietly at rest. She took back the card from her father and studied it. *I hope all goes well for you with your pregnancy.* Could it be? Maybe, just maybe, it wasn't resentment that had held Barbara in its grip. Maybe it was fear. Fear of loving and losing someone else as she'd lost her mother.

In that instant, Pam made a decision. It couldn't hurt, could it, to invite Barbara to come help after the baby came? And it might make all the difference.

Just when she thought Christmas couldn't get any better, Grant nodded to Andy, who disappeared toward the garage. "Andy and I have a little something for you, too," Grant said.

Pam could hear Andy banging through the kitchen, clearly carrying something large. An elfin helper couldn't have looked any more pleased with himself than did her tall, beaming stepson when he entered the room bearing an exquisite wooden cradle and a huge flat package.

Happiness flooded through her. She turned from one to the other. "Grant, Andy, I'm overwhelmed." She walked over to the cradle and crouched beside it, imagining her child rocking to sleep. She rubbed her fingers along the maple wood. "It's beautiful," she said softly. "Just beautiful."

Andy bounced on his heels. "Do you like it?"

The two men exploded in laughter. "That's what the woman said, son," Gramps shifted in his chair. "You came up with a winner."

"What's this?" Pam lifted the large package from the cradle. "It's heavy."

Grant sat forward expectantly, elbows on his knees. "Open it."

When she removed the wrapping and saw what it was, she turned to Grant. "A wallpaper sample book?"

"Don't we need a nursery?"

The reds and greens and yellows of the Christmas tree lights blurred in front of her.

"I thought we could fix up the spare bedroom," Grant continued. "But I wanted you to pick out the paper, the color scheme. You're the decorator, not me."

"You can say that again," Andy added.

She turned from the cradle and gazed at this warm, generous, thoughtful man. Realizing that Andy and Will were anticipating some kind of reaction, she knelt in front of Grant and took his hands in hers. "Thank you," she breathed before leaning forward and kissing him tenderly.

When she pulled back, he squeezed her hands. "You're welcome." Time seemed to stop. No matinee idol had ever looked at his leading lady with such intensity. "There's one thing more," he said, clearing his throat.

"There can't be. You're spoiling me."

"Oh, but there is." He winked at Andy. "While you're at it, for God's sake, pick out some paper to replace that abomination in the kitchen."

ANDY HAULED HIS LOOT up to his bedroom. The laptop was way cool, and he couldn't wait to start the Anne Rice vampire books Pam had given him.

But the best was Gramps's gift. It would be great to see Pepper again, even if a ride meant he'd have a monumentally sore butt. And his own saddle—that was really something. He'd bet not too many of the Keystone kids had their own—what had Gramps called it?—yeah, their own "mount."

But then there was the package from his mother and Harry. He peered warily into the box as if it contained a nest of vipers. Jeez, how could Mom think he'd wear those smarmy Italian silk shirts or those skintight pants with the buttons? They might be okay in the Mediterranean, but in Texas? He'd be laughed off the streets. Or called names he didn't want to think about.

He supposed his mother would phone sometime today. She'd want him to gush about the new clothes. Why couldn't she have sent him the boom box he'd asked for? But that was just like her. She always thought she knew what was best for him.

Well, it hadn't been best to keep him from spending summers with his dad, now had it? Of course, Pam and Gramps wouldn't have been there then, so maybe it would've been different. Worse?

But it had been kinda fun going with his dad to shop for the cradle. At first it had felt weird to be in that big baby store. Cripes, how much stuff could one little kid need? The cradle they picked out was one of the most expensive, but like Dad said, "Pam's worth it." Then they'd gone to eat Mexican food, and on the way home, Dad had actually let him drive. It had been a really okay day.

How many more might he have had if his parents had just asked him what he wanted to do in the summers? Was that too difficult a concept?

But at least he had this year. And it was getting better and better. He and Gramps had plans to watch a bunch of old cowboy movies. Stuff like *Shane* and *High Noon*. He and Angie were getting along great and he even thought he'd done all right on his exams.

And Pam hadn't told about the basketball.

But she expected him to. When he was ready.

He dumped the box of pretty-boy clothes in the back of his closet and shut the door. He reviewed again the great Christmas morning. One of the best ever. But he still felt nervous, anxious.

He wasn't ready to tell his dad. Not yet.

THE DAYS IMMEDIATELY AFTER Christmas fell into a comfortable routine. Grant worked on some house repairs, set up his course outlines for second semester and spent early afternoons conducting short practices with his team.

Will was making a valiant effort with his therapy and bending over backward not to be any trouble. Grant was glad he'd decided to sleep in the den. Twice he'd caught the old man trying to get to the bathroom by himself and had been able to assist him. Will was a trouper and great company, especially for Andy, who might've been bored without their movie marathons. Grant was grateful for the mellowing he observed in his son.

Christmas had been a great day—harmonious, sentimental. Vastly different from the perfunctory observances of his past. Yet it had left Grant with an unsatisfied longing. Almost every gift had been a painful reminder that the good times couldn't last. How would Will feel when the truth came out? Or Andy, whose relationship with Pam and Will was deepening daily?

Betrayed, no doubt.

New Year's Eve, while Pam and Andy were running errands, Will limped into the kitchen where Grant was fixing the two of them bologna sandwiches for lunch. "Ever try fryin' that dog meat?" Will asked as he lowered himself into a chair. "It's mighty good that way."

Grant smiled at the man's colorful expression. "I'll give it a try." He placed a small skillet on the stove and began heating the bologna.

"That's one good kid you've raised."

"I wish I could take more of the credit."

"Don't be so hard on yourself. It's natural for kids to pull away."

Grant turned down the heat and pulled out a loaf of bread. "I just can't reach him. It's almost as if he's afraid to get close."

The old man looked up, a gleam in his eye. "Think about it. Remind you of anyone?"

Grant leaned against the counter, pointing the spatula at Will. "You know men almost as well as horses, don't you?"

Will chuckled. "There's not much difference."

Afraid to get close? Grant thought fleetingly about his own father, cold and rigid, then more intently about himself and his son. There wasn't going to be a pattern here. Not if he could help it.

"Great fried dog," Will said, after swallowing the first bite of his sandwich. "Pass me some more of that hot mustard."

Grant savored the fresh bread, the tang of the sauce and the surprisingly rich flavor of the bologna. "It is good."

"Say," Will said, pausing to swallow another bite, "there's one more thing. A man oughta start the new year with his bride, not with his gimpy father-in-law. So tonight, it's upstairs to bed with you, son."

The bologna suddenly took on the consistency of rubber. "Tonight?"

"You heard me. You gotta bring in the new year right, know what I mean?" Then Will winked broadly, suggestively, and Grant realized he'd developed a galloping case of pregame jitters.

PAM LAY ON HER BACK, the blanket pulled up to her chin, her eyes following Grant as he moved around the end of the bed to his side. "It feels strange, doesn't it?" she said.

"I'm trying hard to think about it like Boy Scout camp."

Her eyes twinkled. "Roughing it, you mean?"

He slid beneath the sheets, aware, with a jump in his pulse rate, that the "bundling" layer was gone. "In a manner of speaking." He stretched out cautiously, crossing his arms over his chest.

"The light?"

"Oh, yeah." He rolled onto his side and reached the bedside lamp. The darkness made him uncomfortable. Things could happen in the dark that didn't happen in the light.

When he lay back down, she reached for his hand and laced her fingers through his. As if she could read his mind, she said, "We're friends, Grant. We can do this."

Do what? "You mean get through this with no sex?"

"It's probably harder for a man."

You've got that right. "We have an agreement. I haven't forgotten."

"Well, we've got Barney on our side. It can't be too appealing to be in the same bed with a butterball."

If you only knew. "Are you comfortable enough? I could go back down—"

"Grant, we'll have to sleep together sometime. We may as well start now. When Dad goes home, then we can go back downstairs."

Roses. Damn. The whole bed smelled of her. "Yeah." He couldn't continue this conversation, not if he didn't want to develop a bigger hard-on than he already had. "Have you completed all your grading?"

She withdrew her hand and seemed to stiffen beside him. "Yes."

"And averaged your semester grades?"

"I finished this evening."

"So?"

"What?"

"What about Beau? Did he pass?"

In the silence, he found himself counting the individual ticks of the alarm clock on the bedside table. Finally she answered. "No, Grant, he didn't."

Faster than he could mark F on a report card, his attention turned from sex to basketball. This was a disaster. "Are you sure? Can't you do something?" She turned her head, and in the light from the streetlamp, he could see her one eyebrow raised. "No," he said, expelling a deep breath, "I guess you can't."

At midnight he was still awake, marveling that there were revelers all over Fort Worth celebrating the new year with hope and promise, while all he could think of was that stupid line from "Casey at the Bat." There was definitely *no* joy in his Mudville this night.

CHAPTER TWELVE

WHEN PAM awoke on New Year's Day, her first thought was—*this* is the year. She rubbed her hand over the rounded flesh of her belly, seeking the protrusion of a tiny foot. *This year my precious baby will come. And nothing will ever be the same.*

She spread her arms in a huge, contented stretch and then encountered the empty pillow beside her, still bearing the lingering scent of Grant's aftershave. Her heart plummeted as the memory of last night's final conversation surfaced.

In one fell swoop, she'd dashed his hopes of a winning season. She corrected herself. She wasn't responsible. Beau Jasper, perfectly capable of doing acceptable work, had been the instrument of his own destruction.

She'd have done almost anything not to have hurt Grant, but she couldn't change an undeserving student's grade.

She closed her eyes, picturing again the pickup game in the park. If Andy were on the team, maybe Beau's abrupt departure wouldn't be such a disaster.

Would Andy tell Grant, as she'd advised? She could give the boy another nudge. She hugged Grant's pillow against her chest. No, she wouldn't. It had to be Andy's decision.

AT THE END of the final vacation practice, Grant had the team huddle up. He hated making his announcement this way, but Beau Jasper had ignored his request for a private meeting. Denial or arrogance? Who could tell? "Gentlemen, I'm afraid I have some disappointing news." Heads shot up, but Jasper leaned over, hands on his knees, as if winded. "I wanted to pass this on before you get back to classes and hear rumors." He paused, knowing full well the devastating effect his next words would have on team morale. "We'll be playing one short next semester."

Cale Moore interrupted. "Whaddya mean, Coach?"

"Jasper will be ineligible."

Beau's head shot up, his face turning a fiery crimson. "The hell you say!"

The thin thread of Grant's patience snapped. "Watch your language. You failed English."

The other boys looked shocked. Several shook their heads in disbelief, and one muttered an emphatic "Crap!"

Beau edged a step closer to Grant, his lips curled, his eyes a stormy gray. "What's the matter, Coach? You whipped? Get her to change it."

Grant jerked his thumb toward the locker room. "Out! Now."

Jasper glared at him. The others were dead quiet. A moment later, the boy turned and sauntered toward the locker room, but not before everyone heard his hissed "This is bullshit!"

When the locker-room door slammed shut behind Jasper, Grant took a deep breath, then turned to his team. "This is a blow. I'm going to be asking all of you to suck it up and play harder than you've ever played before. There'll be some shifts in assignments, but we won't worry about that until Monday's practice.

Then we'll start fresh.'' He paused, studying each stunned face. ''Anybody got anything to say?''

''We're trashed,'' the substitute center mumbled.

''Only if we let ourselves be,'' Grant responded. ''I know you're disappointed. I am, too. But you're a team, and together you can accomplish a whole lot more than you think you can. Believe in yourselves and each other.''

Cale drew circles on the gym floor with the toe of his shoe, then looked up with watery eyes. ''We'll do our best, Coach.''

''That's all I ask.'' There didn't seem anything more to say. ''Hit the showers, men.''

They started for the locker room, but Chip Kennedy lagged behind. ''Can I talk to you a minute, Coach?''

''Sure. What's on your mind.''

The boy picked up his shirttail and wiped perspiration from his forehead. ''I dunno if I should say somethin' or not.'' He hesitated, searching Grant's face as if for an answer.

''Shoot, son.''

''We need another forward, right?'' Grant nodded, wondering what the heck the kid was getting at. ''I think I might know somebody.''

''I'm open to any reasonable suggestion.'' Hell, yes. He was desperate.

''Over Christmas me and my cousin Howie got together. He's a senior at the public school near where you live.''

''Go on.''

''He says there's this great basketball player that plays pickup games with him and his buddies.'' He paused.

Grant bit his lip in frustration. What was the kid driving at? "And?"

"He goes to Keystone."

"Great, let's get on it. What's his name?"

The boy couldn't look at him. "That's just it, sir. It's, well, it's Andy."

Andy! Grant struggled for breath. "What?"

Kennedy looked straight at him. "Howie says he's awesome. Really awesome. He could help us, couldn't he?"

Help them? There wouldn't be any eligibility problems and if he was good... Then, like an engulfing red sea, rage hit him. Damn it! Why had Andy held out on him? His son didn't hate basketball. Hell, no. He hated his father! In a choked voice, Grant said, "Thanks, Chip. I'll look into it."

If he hadn't been afraid the team would hear him, he'd have howled in pain.

PAM TOOK ONE LOOK at Grant when he came in from practice and knew something awful had happened. His whole body was tense, and the expression on his face was at the same time shattered and resolute. She scooped up Sebastian and held him close. The man was in no mood for cats.

He threw his jacket across the sofa. "Where is he?" he said in a cold voice that sounded nothing like the man she knew.

"Who?"

"Andy."

"In his room. Why?"

He didn't answer, but took the steps two at a time. She hurried to the bottom of the stairs, clinging to the newel post with a growing sense of dread. Grant knocked loudly and flung open the door.

Without even straining, Pam made out his first words. "What kind of crap have you been pulling? Why didn't you tell me?"

Then came Andy's defensive reply. "What are you talking about?"

"What am I talking about?" Grant's voice had a metallic edge, like flint striking on steel. "Basketball. That's what I'm talking about!"

Pam swayed, momentarily dizzy. Dear God. Grant had found out.

THIS WAS FRIGGIN' GREAT. Pam must've told on him after all. Damn. "What's the big deal?"

His father stood over him, making him feel like a cornered rat. "What's the big deal? I'll tell you. For starters, you lied to me. Apparently you've been playing a lot of ball in the park." His voice grew eerily sarcastic. "Kind of odd for a guy who professes to hate the game, wouldn't you say?"

"It was somethin' to do."

"A pretty amazing something, from what I hear."

"What'd Pam say?"

That stopped his father dead. The color drained from his face and he looked momentarily confused. "Pam? What's she got to do with it?"

"Who else could've told you?"

"She knew?"

"Well, yeah, but—"

"Wonderful. The whole family's involved in this conspiracy."

"It's not like that!"

"I'll deal with her later. The important thing is that I *did* find out."

Andy hated himself for the tears he felt threatening. "How?" he managed to ask.

"Chip Kennedy from his cousin Howie. That name ring a bell?"

Howie. Jeez, what a crappy coincidence. "Yeah."

"So do you want to tell me about it or do I have to get it some other way?"

"I'll tell you." Damn, his voice was cracking like an eighth grader's. Maybe Pam had been right. This wouldn't be happening if he'd just told his father first.

His old man settled on his bed, folded his arms and waited. "I'm listening."

"You prob'ly won't believe this, but I was gonna tell you. It didn't feel right sneaking around. But I was afraid you'd get mad."

"So what kind of basketball player are you?"

Andy wiped his hands on his jeans, then looked straight into his father's implacable eyes. "A good one." He let that sink in, then added, "A damn good one." He noticed a perceptible slump to his father's shoulders.

"Why couldn't you tell me?"

"I was afraid you'd make me play for you."

"And you didn't want to do that?"

"No."

"Why not?"

What could it hurt to tell the truth? He was screwed anyway. "I didn't think I'd be good enough to please you." His dad looked like an old man all of a sudden. "I—didn't want you on my case...any more than you were already."

"On your case? Is that how I come across?"

Andy felt like a lower life-form. "Not always."

His father got to his feet and with a hangdog look just stared at him. "I never meant to make you feel that way." He started from the room, but paused at the door and turned back. "I'm glad you don't hate basketball. It's a great game." He looked up at the ceiling like there was something written there. Then he sighed. "Andy, I was angry when I came in here. Maybe I shouldn't have gotten so carried away. I want to ask you whether you'd consider coming out for the team now."

Andy stared at him. What was going on?

"Jasper lost his eligibility. We're desperate for a good shooting forward." He cleared his throat. "I need you, son. Think about it."

He waited several beats, then left the room, shutting the door softly behind him. His old man needed him? On the team? Andy closed his eyes, picturing himself in the crimson-and-gold uniform shooting the game-winning bucket, the fans going wild.

But what if, instead, the ball caromed off the rim into the opponent's hands?

He couldn't risk it.

"YOU KNEW." Grant slumped into the recliner, exhaustion written all over his face.

Pam continued dusting, desperately needing to keep her hands occupied. "Yes, I knew."

"Any reason you chose not to tell me?"

She couldn't stand to look at him, nursing his wounds like a defeated bear. "Andy asked me not to." She picked up a small figurine she'd always liked and dusted beneath it.

"Don't you think you owed me the truth?"

She set down the figurine and turned to face him. *"Owed?"*

"He *is* my son. I might've liked knowing how he put in his spare time."

"Especially since it was basketball." Pam perched on the arm of the sofa.

"Makes sense to me."

"He trusted me." She gathered her thoughts. "He needs somebody to trust."

He stared at her as if she were daft. "And you think he can't trust his own father?"

"To the contrary, I think he most certainly can. But he doesn't know that. History—whether manipulated by Shelley or not—has taught him otherwise. With time, though, he'll discover he can trust you. Most of all."

"I asked him to come out for the team." His words were flat, toneless.

"What did he say?"

"Not a thing, Pam. Not a thing."

She longed to go to him, to shield and embrace him. But it wasn't her place. In keeping Andy's trust she'd betrayed Grant, just as she had feared. She hoped Andy appreciated what she'd done, because right now she felt totally miserable.

"SOMETHIN' GOIN' ON HERE I should know about?" Will sat at the kitchen table watching Pam flour pork chops.

"Why?"

"The herd seems kinda restless, that's all. Grant's outside in this cold weather pounding nails into the fence like there's no tomorrow. Andy didn't wanna watch *Silverado* and you, well, you're mighty quiet."

He tucked his thumbs into his suspenders. "It's downright unnatural."

Before Pam answered, she tested the temperature of the oil, then one by one placed the pork chops in the skillet. Unnatural? Grant was disappointed in her, hurt by Andy. Andy was under pressure from Grant, and as for her? She'd let them both down. She didn't blame Grant for being upset with her.

The aroma of browning pork chops filled the room. She turned the meat, then covered the skillet. "Daddy," she set down the fork and slid into the chair beside him, "I've made a mess of things."

"Anything you wanna discuss?"

She told him about discovering Andy playing basketball and agreeing, for the time being, not to tell Grant. "But Grant found out today. The same day he kicked Beau Jasper off the team."

"And he wants Andy to play?"

"Yes."

Will chewed his lip, as if considering the implications. "What does Andy want?"

"I don't think he knows. Except he doesn't want to fail."

Will snorted. "That's what life's all about. It's how a fella deals with failure that makes a man of him."

"He's so afraid of disappointing Grant that—"

"He doesn't risk a damn thing. That's hiding out. That's not owning up."

Pam found herself wanting to defend Andy, protect him. But her father was right. From the beginning, Andy hadn't given Grant a chance, and she sensed Grant was nearly to the limit of his understanding. "I don't think Grant will ask Andy to play on the team again."

"So it's up to the boy." He drummed his fingers on the table. "Don't you and Grant have someplace to go tonight?"

Pam frowned, puzzled. They not only had no place to go, but she couldn't imagine Grant would want to spend any time alone with her. Not after what had happened. "No, we—"

"Yes, you do. Take in a movie, bowl a few lines. Get out of here, though." Then he clucked his tongue and winked at her. "The boy and I have some palaverin' to do."

ANDY SCRATCHED HIS HEAD. Something was weird. His dad and Pam were going to a movie. Angie was always talking about her folks doing stuff together, kinda like dates, but come to think of it, Pam and Dad never did anything like that. They'd left right after dinner for the early showing of an action-thriller. That was weird, too. From stuff she'd said in class, he knew Pam hated those kinds of movies.

But he was glad they'd gone. He didn't want to have to talk to his dad anymore. He'd wanna dwell on basketball. Right now, Andy didn't care if he ever played again. It'd just gotten him into trouble.

He laid aside the book he'd been reading, figuring he oughta check on Gramps. He was watching an old World War II movie, *Twelve O'Clock High,* but Andy hadn't been able to get into it.

"Want anything to eat?" he asked, poking his head into the living room.

Gramps turned down the volume and looked up, a mischievous twinkle in his eye. "How about some kippers and crackers?"

Andy about gagged. Kippers smelled like dirty jockstraps. How could anybody eat one? "Okay, I'll get them."

By the time he'd arranged the crackers and offensive strips of putrid fish on a plate, Gramps's movie was over. When Andy appeared, Gramps turned off the TV, then helped himself to the snack. "Sure you won't join me?"

Andy held up a nearly empty bag of Oreos.

"Suit yourself." He proceeded to fix three more cracker sandwiches, not paying any heed to where the crumbs fell. "I understand you've got a problem?"

Andy was instantly alert. "What's that?"

"With your passion."

Passion? "Huh?"

"Basketball, son." The old man chewed thoughtfully, watching him through shrewd eyes.

"You know."

"Yep." He wiped his mouth on the sleeve of his flannel shirt. "What're you gonna do about it?"

"That's obvious. I'm not gonna play."

"Why's that?"

"I told Dad, when I got here, I wasn't going out for basketball."

"Fair enough. But the situation's different now."

"How do you figure?"

"He needs you. The team needs you. Not to mention that you need him. And the team." Gramps was arranging yet another kipper on a cracker, not even looking at him.

"I don't need anybody."

"Right. You're just gonna struggle on through life by yourself, is that it? The Lone Ranger?"

Andy shrugged. "Maybe."

"Well, I got news for you, son. Life doesn't work

that way. You gotta face what you're afraid of.'' The rheumy green eyes nailed him. ''And you're afraid you'll let your father down.''

''I already have,'' Andy mumbled.

''That's pure horse manure. You're punishing him because he didn't stay married to your mother, because he didn't jeopardize his job and *his* passion to indulge your idea of what a father is.'' Gramps leaned forward. ''Lemme tell you somethin'. Whether you believe it or not, that man loves you. But you're too busy manning the barricades to see that.''

Andy felt his face burning. More than anything he wanted to run from the room. But Gramps was still talking.

''You won't have a chance of a good relationship unless you spend some time with him. And I can think of a lot worse ways to spend time together than doing something you both love. Play ball, Andy.''

''But what if—''

''Baloney! Life's full of 'what if's.' A real man does what he has to do anyway. What's the worst thing that could happen?''

''What if I'm no good? What if I let him down?''

''Whaddya think he's gonna do? Disown you?''

''No, but—''

''Put it on the line, kid. Instead of focusing on the negative, try this on for size. You could help him out. Help the team out. And maybe, if you don't act like a stubborn cayuse, you'll gain a father out it. Somehow I don't believe playing a game you love and excel at is too big a price to pay.''

Andy looked at the bag of Oreos, then folded the sack. He wasn't hungry anymore. It sounded like

Gramps was calling him chicken. Was the old man right? Was he wimping out because he was afraid?

Gramps brushed his hands together, scattering crumbs all over the carpet. "Well?"

"I'll think about it."

"That's all I ask." He rubbed a finger under his nose. "You know, you remind me a lot of Pam."

"Pam?"

"You grew up without a father on the scene. She grew up without a mother."

"Whaddya mean?"

Gramps looked at him with big, sad eyes. "My Lillian died giving birth to Pam."

"You mean she never knew her own mother?"

"That's what I mean. It was tough. Still is, I reckon. 'Specially now she's havin' a baby." He paused. "I imagine it hurt not having your dad around, but you have a chance Pammy never had. You still have time to get to know and love your daddy. She never had that opportunity with her mama."

Andy swallowed the lump in his throat. He'd never really thought about what it'd be like if he didn't have a father at all. That idea sucked. What if Dad really did need him? He stood up, then went to Gramps's chair. "Lemme help you into bed."

He levered the old man to his feet and handed him the crutches. "Thanks, son. You're a good man."

Man? He wanted to be. "I hope I don't let you down, either."

"You won't. Just do what your heart tells you is right."

Andy settled his grandfather in the bedroom, then sat in the living room staring at the shelf laden with his dad's basketball trophies. He had a lot of thinking to do before morning.

IN JUNIOR HIGH SCHOOL, Pam had had her first movie date. Tongue-tied and uncomfortably aware of her awkward body, she'd been at a genuine loss for words for one of the few times in her life. But that was a breeze compared to the strained, overly polite conversation she and Grant managed before and after a movie so full of explosions and gunfire her head reeled. They had studiously avoided any mention of the basketball debacle, confining their remarks to fascinating subjects like car maintenance and the weather.

It was no wonder, then, that Grant delayed coming to bed or that she burrowed under the covers, praying she would fall asleep before he joined her. All evening, she'd longed to say something, do anything to ease the tension radiating from his clenched jaw. Maybe days ago there had been a time she could have ventured to touch him, comfort him.

But she'd lost that chance.

She didn't blame him, but deep inside her was a hollow place where regret found a home.

EARLY THE NEXT MORNING after four hours of fitful sleep, Grant tiptoed from the bedroom, leaving Pam snuggled under the covers. In the dark kitchen, he put on the coffeepot, moving quietly so as not to disturb Will. While he waited for the coffee to pcrk, he rubbed his hands over his face. It wasn't bad enough he had to retool the whole playbook and motivate a team who'd had the heart knocked out of them. Or that he had a son engaged in a game of "Now I've got you, Dad." Until

Will left, he had to sleep with a woman who'd kept an important secret from him.

And who still smelled provocatively of roses.

When the coffee was ready, he poured some into a mug, then sat at the kitchen table drawing plays and reconfiguring lineups. Before, they'd had a good shot at the league title. Now? Short of a miracle, the Knights would be lucky to win half of their remaining games.

As the weak winter sun filtered through the dark, he heard a rustling upstairs. Pam? He groaned. What was there to say? Maybe she thought she'd been justified in keeping Andy's confidence, but how long had she known? Didn't she realize how much he'd missed with his son?

Worst of all had been Andy's painful accusation, which still smarted. "I didn't think I'd be good enough to please you.... I didn't want you on my case." His own father's words came back as clearly as if the man stood glaring down at him right now. "What's the matter with you, Grant? Can't you do anything right?" No matter how hard he'd tried, he could never earn commendation from his soldier father. Was he doomed to repeat the same mistakes?

He buried his head in his hands. Basketball wasn't worth it. Somehow he had to convince Andy that he was okay whether or not he played basketball, tiddly-winks or anything else. That he was loved and accepted just as he was. His job as a father—and as a coach—was to build confident, responsible young men.

"Dad?"

Grant looked up, surprised to see Andy, fully dressed, standing in the kitchen door. "I heard noises. I thought it was Pam."

"Nope, it's just me." Andy crossed to the refrigerator, pulled out a carton of milk, filled a glass and joined Grant at the table.

"What're you doing up so early?"

"With school starting tomorrow, I figure you and I have a lotta work to do today. You know, before..."

Grant frowned in bewilderment. "Before what?"

Andy wiped away a milk mustache. "Practice."

For the first time in twenty-four hours, Grant permitted himself to feel hope. He leaned forward. "Son—"

"I figured maybe you and me could go over to the gym. I could show you my stuff. We could work out. See if I'm good enough."

A huge smile settled on Grant's face. "As a son, there's no question you're good enough. That's what matters." He chuckled. "But I've gotta tell you, I don't mind seeing if you can play basketball."

THE NEXT WEEK they fell into a routine. After school Pam took Will to physical therapy, then had dinner waiting when Andy and Grant came in from practice. Grant and Will watched TV together while Andy studied and she graded papers. She retired early and usually fell asleep before Grant came to bed. He was always up in the morning before she was. They hardly spoke unless it was to say "Pass the salt," or "What time will you be home?"

Several times Pam caught Will watching her, his eyes narrowed as if he was trying to solve a puzzle. She chafed that her life was so troubled, static. But at the beginning of this sixth month of pregnancy, Barney was definitely growing. She'd already had to move to the next largest buttonhole of her maternity slacks. Sometimes in the solitude of her bed, she whispered to the baby. "Are you a boy? Will you be as complicated as

Andy and Grant? Or solid and easygoing like your grandfather?''

Andy, preoccupied with making a contribution to the team, seemed oblivious to the strain between her and Grant. One morning, when she and Grant were first into the kitchen, she had asked him, "Is Andy good?"

He'd taken a sip of coffee before he'd answered her. "Better than good. By the time he's a senior, he could outdo Beau. And *Andy's* coachable." He managed a quirky smile that didn't quite reach his eyes. "Guess I have to give you credit, huh?"

She wasn't after credit, particularly not at the expense of Beau Jasper, who would have to repeat English in summer school in order to earn his diploma. It was reward enough that Grant and Andy were, at last, finding a common language in basketball. Will, too, had noticed the difference in their relationship. On the way to therapy yesterday, he'd said, "Reckon those two are mending some fences."

If only she and Grant could do the same.

The week ended on a better note, at least from one perspective. Andy's journal.

I don't know quite know how to tell you this, but I owe you an apology. When Dad found out about me playing basketball at the park, I thought you'd told him and I was pissed. But it wasn't you. I'm glad 'cuz I wanted to believe you'd keep my secret. And it turns out you did. Thanks. In a way, though, I'm glad Dad found out, even though I should've told him myself. Gramps was right when he told me to risk giving Dad a chance. Dad doesn't yell at the team like some coaches do and the other guys really respect him. I guess I needed to see a different side of him. You know what? I think I'm beginning to appreciate how lucky I am. I mean to have such a great father and stepmother. And a grandpa, too.

CHAPTER THIRTEEN

ANDY'S FIRST GAME WAS in Houston, so despite her eagerness to support him, Pam elected to stay home, not only for the baby's sake, but so she could keep an eye on Will, who had graduated to a walker. The two of them settled in front of the TV to watch a rerun of *Cheyenne Social Club,* but neither Henry Fonda nor Jimmy Stewart could draw her out of her funk.

She had grown all too accustomed to this family group, forgetting somewhere along the way that they weren't really a family—just a temporary merger, with Andy and Will as unwitting participants. It had all seemed so simple at first. Two friends joining forces for mutually advantageous purposes. Cut-and-dried. Except they'd overlooked one point. Emotions were never simple.

And hers were perilously close to the edge. The thought of losing Grant and Andy was more than she dared contemplate. Even her joy about the baby was tempered by the realization this child would never really know them as father and brother. Until recently, when she'd breached Grant's trust, she'd allowed herself to hope their arrangement could become permanent, based not only on their mutual need, but on love.

There. She'd admitted it. She loved Grant. Wanted him to be her husband in every sense of the word. Longed for him to be a real father to the baby.

She tried to concentrate on the figures moving on the screen, but all she could think was *How am I ever going to endure these next few months?*

When the answer came to her, she gave a tiny snort. *Play the part.*

With strident intrusion, a commercial came on at an ear-splitting decibel level. Will grabbed the remote and turned off the TV. "Thanks, Daddy. I hate those loud commercials."

"Me, too." He lifted his leg to rest it on the sofa. "How'd you like the movie?"

"Is it over?"

He chuckled. "Guess that answers my question."

"Sorry. I must've been woolgathering."

"I noticed." He gestured to the empty seat at the end of the sofa. "Come sit by me."

She moved, recognizing the "let's talk" in his request.

"You know," he began, "it's not too long till I'll be going home." She nodded, uncertain where he was headed with the conversation. "When I leave, I'd like to know things are all right with you."

"They will be. I love my job. I'll soon have a bouncing grandchild for you. I'll be fine."

"You don't say?" He fixed his eyes on her. She waited, sensing whatever he said next would make her uncomfortable. "Seems like you left out somethin' kinda important from your little list."

"What?"

"Unless my hearing's worse than I thought, I didn't pick up mention of your husband." She could feel his eyes boring into her. "Or your stepson."

She couldn't look at him. "No, you didn't."

"Some particular reason for that?"

She debated, knowing whatever she did would be wrong. Not to tell him would prolong a lie. Telling would destroy his illusions about her. About Grant.

"Cat got your tongue?"

"This is hard, Daddy." She gulped. "Things…aren't exactly what they seem."

"I figgered. Better get it out, dumplin'. It's not gonna get any easier."

"About Grant and me—"

"You're not married?"

"No, we're married all right. It's just that…it isn't going to last."

"You can't know that. Just because your marriage has hit a little trouble doesn't mean—"

"Daddy, listen to me. It's not a *real* marriage."

"What in tarnation are you talking about?"

Then, clenching her fists at her sides and without looking at him, she went through the whole story of their arrangement, ending with its termination in September. Even telling him about Steven and the baby. When she finished, she sat with her head bowed, waiting for him to speak. When, after a long silence, he hadn't, she looked up. "Say something, Daddy."

"That's quite a story. Not every man would marry a woman carrying another man's child. Does the boy know any of this?"

"No."

"Guess you hadn't figgered on him comin' to love you?"

"No."

"Or on Grant lovin' you."

"He doesn't—"

Will cut her off. "Or on you lovin' him." He sat up, carefully repositioned his leg and snuggled her against him. "Guess you got yourself in quite a fix, didn't you, girl?"

The soft nap of his shirt, the comforting warmth of his arm and the honey in his voice were more than she could bear. The tears came, not fast and furious, but slow and wrenching. He rested his chin on her head and patted her, as if settling a spooked horse. She eventually managed a muffled, "What am I going to do?"

He tilted her chin, then, stroking her hair gently, asked the question. "Do you love him?"

"Oh, Daddy, with all my heart."

"Well, then, that makes things a whole lot easier."

"I'm afraid there's nothing easy about this."

"Lemme tell you somethin', honey. I've spent my whole life around creatures. And I've seen one or two animals during the mating season. That husband of yours has picked out his mare, even if the two of you have been too contrary to see it. I'll be a tin-eared coyote if that man isn't crazy about you." He pulled back and studied her. "What in the world's goin' on with the two of you in that bed?"

"Not a thing."

He harrumphed. "That's not natural. I've seen the way Grant looks at you. The man must be bitin' bullets up there."

"So what are you suggesting?"

"There's nothin' wrong with lettin' him know you're willing."

"I want this to be about a whole lot more than sex."

"So does he, Pammy, so does he. But you can't keep living the lie. It'll only dig you in deeper and hurt all of you in the long run."

"So what do I do?"

He cupped his roughened hands around her face.

"Give the horse his head and he'll return to the barn every time. Just be sure you're waitin' for him with love in your eyes."

She put her arms around her father's neck and put her forehead against his. "I love you, Daddy."

"I know you do, sugar." His voice caught. "I know you do."

HIS NERVES TAUT AS a drumhead, Grant walked out onto the Keystone court after halftime. Somehow they'd managed to go shot for shot with the Porter Pirates in the first period, but whether his kids could run with them for another thirty minutes remained to be seen. If ever the Knights needed home-court advantage, this was it. Provided they could squeak by Porter, they stood an even chance of winning the rest of their conference games.

He allowed himself a glance at the home stands, crowded with kids and fans bedecked in the crimson-and-gold school colors. The cheerleaders had just completed the traditional cheer that brought the team onto the court. In the front row were Will and Pam, her hair accentuated by the red and gold of her sweater. He couldn't think about her. Not now. But, jeez, she looked pretty.

His stomach coiled tighter. They still hadn't talked through the situation with Andy. The timing was never right. And bed wasn't the place. It was all he could do each evening to slide in beside her and keep his hands to himself.

He paused on the sidelines, watching the kids take their warm-up shots. Cale Moore's leadership had been a big factor in the first half. Along with Andy's fourteen points, including a clutch free throw with ten seconds left. He still had awkward moments when he wasn't in sync with the play, but he'd shown a lot of heart and was improving with each game. When he and Chip Kennedy hit a rhythm, they were formidable.

The ref whistled the start of the second half, and Grant put everything except the game out of his mind. Porter scored first on a jumper from the keyhole. Then Keystone set up a give-and-go, but Chip's shot circled out of the bucket. Porter responded with a two-on-one fast break. Andy chased the ball handler, catching up with him to fight for possession of the ball. Coming down across the shoulders of the other Porter player, Andy was upended.

With a sickening thud, his head struck the hardwood floor.

Silence shrouded the gym. Grant heard only the pounding of his own heart as he raced to the prone body of his son.

He and the trainer reached the boy at the same time. The other players parted, then stood watching at a respectful distance.

The trainer checked Andy's respiration and pulse, then lifted his eyelids. "He's out cold, Coach. He needs to be examined for a concussion."

Grant signaled for the stretcher, then watched the practiced movements of the paramedics as they lifted Andy and bore him to the locker room.

Grant had never been so afraid in his entire life.

FROM FAR AWAY, as if they were under water, Andy could hear sounds. Muffled. Slurred. "Andy, can you hear me?"

He tried to answer the disembodied voice, but he was buried in cotton. He opened his eyes, then blinked them shut. The light. It hurt his eyes. When he tried to speak, it was as if he couldn't push the air through his lungs. So he quit trying.

A deep voice he didn't recognize said, "Call the hospital. Tell 'em we're bringing him in."

Andy remembered then. With supreme effort, he managed one word. "Game?"

Close above him hovered his father's face. "Don't worry about the game, son." His voice sounded funny. Scratchy kinda. "The main thing is you're gonna be fine."

"Fine," Andy echoed lazily, before closing his eyes and losing himself in a gray mist.

PAM TOOK WILL HOME, then raced to the hospital, her thoughts lashing in all directions. Andy had to be all right. He was a healthy kid, she told herself. Surely it was nothing more than a bump on the head. Not…something worse.

Luckily she found a parking spot near the emergency entrance. Inside, a nurse ushered her to an examining room. She paused in the doorway. Grant slumped on a stool, his head resting on Andy's bed. Andy appeared to be asleep.

Stepping inside, she whispered, "Grant?"

Slowly he reared up, his face ashen with worry.

"How is he?" She crossed to stand on the other side of the bed, gently caressing Andy's forearm.

"The doctor thinks he's had a mild concussion. He regained consciousness in the locker room and came to once more in the ambulance. They'll keep him at the hospital overnight for observation, waking him periodically to check his responsiveness. They're arranging for a room for him right now.'' He stood up and gestured to the empty stool. ''Here, you sit.''

Barney was riding low in her abdomen and the offer was welcome. When they circled the foot of the bed, Pam put her hands on Grant's shoulders. ''How are you doing, Dad?''

''I'm not gonna kid you. I'm shaky.''

As she slid her arms around his neck and whispered, ''You're entitled,'' he responded by gathering her in his embrace and then expelling a long, shuddering sigh.

''Thanks for coming,'' he said, his voice husky.

''Where else would I be? We're family.'' Then she added a silent prayer, for Andy, for Grant and for Will's wisdom to prove true.

BEFORE ANDY CRACKED OPEN his eyes, he heard people moving about. The clank of carts on rollers. Metallic clicks. Voices. His stomach growled. He was massively hungry. Finally he squinted through crusty lids. Whoa. He was in a strange bed, staring straight at this picture of windmills. Far out.

''Son?'' His dad vaulted out of a chair in the corner.

Then he remembered. He was in the hospital. How had he gotten here? He concentrated. Oh yeah, he and that big Porter center had collided in mid-air. ''Hi, Dad.'' He thought he even managed a smile. ''Did we win?''

''I don't know yet.''

How could his dad not know? ''Why not?''

''I didn't stay for the end of the game. I came with you in the ambulance.''

''But you're the coach.''

''I know.'' He felt his father's cool fingers on his forehead, smoothing back a lock of hair. Then his dad gripped the bed rail with both hands and leaned over. "But it was just a game. You're my son. Nothing is more important."

Andy tried to wrap his mind around that concept. "But the guys? The team?"

"The junior varsity coach took over for me. I needed to be here. With you."

"You *did?*" A warm glow flooded through him, easing the dull headache. His eyes fluttered. He was sleepy again. Just before he dozed off, though, he smiled and mumbled, "Cool. Way cool."

As he drifted away, he thought his dad was smiling, too, but he couldn't be sure.

IT WAS AFTER TWO when Grant and Pam pulled into the driveway at home. The nurse had assured them there was nothing they could do. By morning Andy should be much more alert, she said. Pam went on to bed while Grant took a quick shower, then slipped in beside her. Pam lay on her side, one hand curled beneath her chin, the other wrapped around her tummy, as if protecting her child. He turned his head and studied her, wondering how he would ever handle September. Take tonight, for instance. He'd been beside himself until she came to the hospital. Until she held him.

A raw breath escaped him. For one awful moment there on the court, he'd thought he'd lost Andy. That's what it would feel like when Pam left.

"Grant?" Her sleepy voice caught him off guard. Her eyes fluttered open, and in the glow from the streetlight, he could see the question in her eyes.

"He's going to be all right."

She scooped up the pillow and pushed it under her head. "It was scary, wasn't it?"

"Very."

She continued gazing at him. "Are you sleepy?"

"No."

"Feel like talking?"

No way could he tell her what his traitorous body really felt like. "Sure."

"I overstepped my bounds with Andy. I should've told you he was playing ball in the park. He's your son, after all."

He rolled onto his side, propping his head on his hand. "He trusted you."

"So did you. Then."

She sounded sad, wistful. "I still do. You did what you thought was best for him. And, Lord knows, you were succeeding with him when I wasn't."

"And now?"

"We're doing better. At practice, I try to treat him impartially. And he's controlled his mouthiness. The guys have been really great about accepting him."

"Dad's noticed the change in him. Andy was afraid of you before. About the basketball."

"I know. How could I have been so blind?"

"Shelley—"

"That's a cop-out. I should have made Andy my business. She's not responsible for my failings. I am." He flopped over onto his back. "From now on, I'll be the kind of father Andy deserves."

"He loves you, Grant." Unbelievably, he felt her fingers thread through his. Even this slight touch was enough to make him lose his bearings. Was it his imagination or had she inched closer to make hand-holding easier?

"He loves you, too." Then, unbelievably, he felt

wisps of her hair against his shoulder where she rested her head.

She didn't say anything for the longest while. He'd have thought she was asleep except for the way she feathered one finger up and down his forearm, inciting a powerful rush of desire. Jeez, all he had to do was move toward her, pull her into his arms and...

"Grant, what are we going to do?"

"About what?"

"About us? About Andy?" She let go of his hand then and surprised him by moving even closer, draping an arm across his chest, cradling her head between his shoulder and neck.

He couldn't find his voice. The warmth from her belly, the scent of roses, the tickle of her hair against his cheek were making it impossible to concentrate. He reined himself in. Desperately he sought an answer to the question so he could keep talking. "Carry on, I guess."

"Wait until September to decide?"

"That was the agreement." Oh, damn. Now she was making tiny circular motions on his chest. His nipples weren't the only part of him hardening.

"Just friends, then?"

It must be his imagination. She couldn't be kissing him in that vulnerable place under his ear. But what else could be sending shocks of current through him? "Uh, yeah. Friends."

She moved her head, and her breath was soft against his ear. "But what do I do about wanting you?"

"Wanting me?" If he didn't know better, he'd swear she was seducing him.

She moved again, and her breasts nestled against his chest. She drew one hand gently, tantalizingly across his cheek, all the time looking at him with this soft, tender expression. "Well?" she said.

Before he could formulate an answer, she sought his mouth, wantonly, fully. He gathered her to him, running his hands up and down her back, reveling in each plane and curve, lost in the sensations of her body, her kiss. Still keeping her lips on his, she rose up, lowered the blanket from their shoulders and, unbuttoning his pajama top, ran her hands over his chest. He fought for control. They'd had an emotional evening. She was vulnerable right now, that was all. For that matter, so was he.

Then she withdrew and, trailing kisses from his neck to his shoulder, settled back into his embrace. "Very good friends," she murmured throatily.

He waited until his heart rate was back in the high normal range. "You're a beautiful, desirable woman. But I could never take advantage of you." Besides, they had an agreement, even though right now he'd like to rip their stupid contract to shreds.

She cocked her head and stared at him. "You think maybe it's hormonal?"

He gritted his teeth. "It's possible."

"Or maybe you don't find a pregnant woman desirable."

Double damn. What could he say to that? "Desirable? You're about to drive me wild, woman."

A slow, lazy smile bloomed on her face. "But?"

"This can't be just about need. Er, wanting."

"It's been a long time for both of us, is that what you're saying?"

"Not exactly, but we *did* make a deal. We've been talking about trust with Andy. I want you to trust me. Especially about this."

She propped up so she could see him better. "Know

what I think? You're probably right. Now isn't the time. We're both stressed. Tired.''

What kind of masochist was he anyway, turning his back on this achingly beautiful woman? ''Maybe our friendship's more important than...you know...''

She lay back down, drawing her knees up, facing him. ''Could be.''

He waited for her to drift off, knowing he'd be second-guessing himself until dawn. Just when he thought she'd finally gone to sleep, she spoke again. ''Could I ask you a favor?''

''Shoot.''

''The childbirth classes start next month. Would you be willing to go? Be my birth coach?''

He'd walk to the ends of the earth for her. What was a little thing like a childbirth class? ''Sure.''

The next time he sneaked a peek at her, she was sound asleep, a tiny smile playing over her lips.

GRANT HAD REJECTED her advances. She shouldn't feel happy. But she did. The funny thing was it didn't seem like rejection. Not really. She'd awakened about six, aware that their bodies, for the first time, were spooned, that his hand was cupped around her breast, that his exhalations rustled her hair. She felt protected, secure.

They were both adults. Married, even. It would've been easy to fall into a sexual relationship. But like he'd said, their friendship was too important. He'd given his word.

Trust had to come first. Then commitment.

If she was very, very lucky.

GRANT ARRIVED at the hospital shortly after seven and was relieved to get a positive report from the nurse at the desk. He entered Andy's room quietly and stood at the foot of the bed observing his sleeping son—thick brown hair, sleep-induced rosy cheeks, an upper lip and chin sprouting early indications of manhood. Where had the years gone? How could he have been so oblivious? Surely there had been signals.

He hung his head. Parenthood was something he'd never learned from his own father. He sometimes wondered what would've become of him without Brian. Who else would've taught him the left-handed hook shot, paved the way each time they entered a strange new school or defended him against his father's tirades? God, he missed his brother. He'd have liked Pam and Andy and Will.

He supposed he needed to call Shelley, but that could wait until Andy was alert. No point alarming her unduly. He could fault her for the way she'd handled the custody issue, but there was no doubt she loved their son.

Settling in the only chair in the room, he began reading the newspaper he'd brought from home, containing a full account of Keystone's loss to Porter. Funny how that didn't seem nearly as important this morning. He looked up from the article. Instead of his son, *had* he made basketball his priority? He didn't think so, but it sure could've seemed that way to Andy.

When a nurse arrived to take Andy's vitals, he stirred, then tried to sit up. "Easy," the nurse said, laying her palm on his chest. "Get your bearings, then we'll try elevating the bed."

"Can a guy get anything to eat in this place?"

Grant smiled in relief. "I'd say you're feeling better."

"Dad?"

Grant moved to Andy's bedside. "How's the head?"

"I feel pretty good, considering. What about the game?"

"Porter won by nine."

"Damn."

The nurse put her arms under Andy's shoulders and pushed a second pillow under his head. Then she elevated the bed. "Any dizziness?"

"No. Does this mean I can go home?"

"That's up to the doctor."

Within ten minutes, scrambled eggs, oatmeal, toast, milk and juice arrived. Grant didn't know when he'd taken such pleasure in watching someone eat.

"The Knights mighta won if you'd been there to coach," Andy said between bites.

"Or if you'd been there to play. But we'll never know."

"Makes the rest of the season tougher, right?"

"We don't have much margin for error, that's for sure."

Andy concentrated on buttering his toast. "Dad, how come you didn't stay with the team? I mean, that's your job."

Grant perched on the foot of the bed. "Yes, that's my job. But it's not my life." *Now.* The time to say it was here. "I'm afraid I haven't been much of a father, Andy."

"But—"

"You deserved more attention through the years than I gave you. Oh, I had my reasons. And you're right. Many of them had to do with the school and basketball. It was wrong of me to expect a seven- or eight-year-old to understand.'' He studied his hands. ''Maybe the biggest factor, though, was fear.''

''Of what?'' Andy asked, his expression puzzled.

''That I didn't know how to be a good father.''

Andy shoved aside his breakfast tray. ''I don't get it.''

''Something you said the other day really got my attention. You said you didn't think you'd be good enough to please me. That you didn't want me on your case. It got me to thinking.'' Grant fell silent, picturing his own father standing in full dress uniform in front of the scared little boy whose shoes hadn't been polished to specifications.

A cafeteria worker entered the room and removed the tray. Summoning his courage, Grant went on. ''They say history repeats itself. In this case, I'm afraid that may be true. Your grandfather provided for me in several important ways, but, for whatever reasons, he was never able to give me his approval.''

Andy eyed him attentively, waiting for him to continue. ''When you came along, I hadn't had any practice at being a father. Nor had I had a very good role model. I...I felt helpless. To cover up my own insecurity, I made some serious errors in judgment. Not letting you know through the years how much I love you was one of them.'' He mustered a lopsided smile. ''Whether or not you played basketball.''

''You were okay, really.''

''Thanks for trying to make me feel better, son.'' Grant got off the bed and moved beside Andy, laying a hand on his shoulder. ''Mainly I want to say I'm sorry, and to pledge that from now on things are going to be different. Better.''

Andy's eyes brimmed. "I can go for that." Then he held up his palms. "Hit me, Dad."

It was the best high-five of Grant's life.

IT WAS GREAT to be home. And it was cool how he was sort of a hero. Angie had spent yesterday afternoon with him. She'd even made him a shoe box full of chocolate chip cookies. And when Gramps, Dad and Pam kinda disappeared, Angie'd cuddled with him on the sofa. Then last night some of the guys on the team had dropped by with a James Bond video. Before they watched it, though, he heard about the rest of the Porter game. It sucked that he'd gotten hurt. But the neat thing was how determined Chip and Cale and the guys were to bust the season open, game by game.

Dad had made pancakes for breakfast. Gramps told this funny story about a bull he used to have. And Pam looked...prettier somehow. A coupla times he even caught her sending his dad these special looks. Mainly, though, he'd been doing a lot of thinking about what Dad had said about being a lousy father.

But there was something that bugged Andy. Maybe he'd blocked it out before, but he could remember times he'd heard his mom on the phone with his dad saying stuff like, "That wouldn't be convenient," or "I don't think it's appropriate for him to fly alone." He'd heard about how divorced people sometimes used their kids as pawns. Was that what his mother had done?

But she sure didn't have any problem now, having him come live with Dad. He shuddered thinking what it might've been like to be in Dubai with Harry. The worst was, he was getting used to it here. Pam was the greatest and Gramps had practically adopted him.

Andy'd even started thinking of Keystone as his school. And then there was Angie. Lots of reasons to stay.

But that prob'ly wasn't an option. Mom had only agreed until September.

There was one other thing bugging him. It sounded kinda childish, he guessed. He picked up his notebook. Maybe he could tell Pam about it. She sometimes gave good advice. And he sure needed it. Because, of all the dumb things, he was jealous of a baby that hadn't even been born yet.

GINNY PHILLIPS CORNERED Pam outside her classroom. "You're looking fat and sassy this morning."

Pam patted her stomach. "Emphasis on the 'fat.'"

"Let me rephrase that. 'Contented' is more what I had in mind."

Smiling a secret smile, Pam nodded. "That's fair. I am happy."

"Grant being suitably attentive?"

"A veritable prince among men." One bound and determined to keep his word. At least Pam hoped that was why, though they continued to snuggle, he'd retreated from her not-so-subtle come-on. "We start childbirth classes next week."

Ginny wiggled her eyebrows. "Think Grant's up for the film?"

"Is any man?"

Students ebbed and flowed around them, banging lockers, shouting greetings. Ginny paused long enough to chastise one young man for inappropriate language. Turning back, she said, "The faculty women would like to have a baby shower for you. At my house. You just tell us when."

"Oh, Ginny, that's so kind, but you all participated in the wedding shower and—"

Ginny adopted her counselor's voice. "That baby can't wear place mats and monogrammed towels. We won't take no for an answer."

Pam held up her hands. "I surrender. I'll check my calendar and get back to you."

All day Pam felt buoyant, carried along by productive responses from her classes and appreciation for the thoughtfulness of her colleagues. During her planning period, she typed a quiz, then picked up the sophomore journals, chuckling over Chip Kennedy's account of his first date and wiping a tear away at Angela's description of her grandmother's lingering illness. Then she came to Andy's.

You know how sometimes you feel really good about yourself and then other times you feel like crap? Embarrassed or ashamed of yourself? But it's like you can't do anything about it? Can't change anything? Well, that's how I'm feeling. I don't wanna hurt your feelings, but I need advice. It's about your baby.

See, Dad's all excited about having this kid. And it'll be great and all, but I've got this big, immature worry. Okay, I'll just say it. I'm afraid Dad'll be closer to this kid than to me. This baby will live with him all the time. Grow up with him. They'll do kid stuff like go to Disney movies, rake leaves together and play hoops in the backyard. They'll build lots of memories. More than me and Dad have. It's not that I won't like this baby. I mean, it's not his fault for Pete's sake. But what about me?

Dear God, Pam thought as she laid Andy's journal aside. Things were better between Andy and Grant, much better than they'd been before Andy's concussion, but he still needed so much more from his father.

And what he needed most of all was the truth.

Somehow she had to convince Grant they had to tell Andy about the baby's parentage. And about their "marriage."

CHAPTER FOURTEEN

"No!" INCREDULOUS, Grant gaped at Pam. How could she suggest telling Andy the truth about the baby's parentage? About their agreement?

Pam sat calmly on a chair in the coach's office where she'd tracked him down over the lunch hour. He paced the narrow confines of the room, before finally coming to a halt. "This is not negotiable." He raked a hand through his hair. "Where did you come up with such a nutty idea, anyway?"

Pam gathered her skirt, crossed her leg, then neatly arranged the folds of material. "That doesn't matter. Trust me, though, Andy needs to know."

"Trust you? What is this? Another of your 'confidential' pieces of information about my son?"

"It's not like that."

"Well, what is it like? Have you forgotten *I'm* the boy's parent, not you?" He couldn't believe this was happening.

"That's exactly why we have to tell him." When she looked up at him, he averted his gaze from her plaintive hazel eyes. "He's had enough manipulations and half-truths in his young life. How can he trust either one of us if we aren't honest with him?"

"Why now? Just when I feel as if I'm getting close to him? The boy's been desperate for family. Why destroy his illusions?"

"He'll find out in September anyway."

Grant slumped against the edge of his desk. Her words had robbed his lungs of oxygen. Apparently he'd been fooling himself to think about a future with her. "Can't we give him this one year, at least?"

"And then what? Is it going to be any easier in September when he believes he has a half brother or sister and a real home?"

She had him there. All his rationalizations couldn't negate the fact that he'd lied to his son, by his words and by his actions. They both had—and the facts would eventually come out. Pam leaned forward in her chair. "It's important, Grant."

His anger faded, replaced by overbearing weariness. "And what about you?"

"What *about* me?"

"We've managed to keep the secret of the baby's parentage pretty well."

She lowered her eyes. "I told Dad."

That was news to Grant, but he wasn't terribly surprised. "I'd trust Will with my life. But do you really think we can burden a fifteen-year-old boy with such a momentous secret? It would take only one slip and it would be all over school."

"I've thought about that, but if we trust Andy, it's a risk we need to take. Whatever agreement the two of us may have made, I care for him. I don't want my personal situation to create any further barriers to your relationship with him."

"He'll be devastated."

"Yes, at first I imagine he will. But we can't go on living a lie. Your son needs to be able to trust you completely. He's your family." She stood slowly, one palm making small, nervous circles on her amply rounded stomach. "He needs to know he always has come first with you and always will."

He folded his arms across his chest and studied her face. In it he read concern, sadness, but above all, conviction. She'd been right about Andy in the past. Hell, her instincts had always been better than his. But this was asking too much. "Let me think about it," he said.

Never taking her eyes off his, she nodded. "Fair enough."

THERE WAS NO MORE CUDDLING in bed. After her conversation with Grant in his office, Pam hadn't expected there to be, but she desperately missed both their physical and emotional closeness. Despite their accuracy, his words had cut her. *Have you forgotten I'm the boy's parent, not you?* Somewhere along the way, the lines had blurred. At times they had felt so much like a family.

Not anymore.

Even her father had noticed, but she'd passed off his concern by saying Grant was intensely focused on basketball. Which was true. The team played a minimum of two games a week, above and beyond practices. Andy had become an integral part of the team, and his pride and satisfaction were evident. He was happier, more confident.

Ten days had passed since she'd broached the subject of telling Andy. Finally one evening, when Grant came to bed, he fluffed the pillows and sat, half reclining, his hands folded on his chest. "Okay," he said, as if carrying on from their original conversation. "I've thought about it."

Barney was tight against her rib cage, making it hard to breathe. "And?"

"I'd like to wait until after the season. Andy's got enough on his mind now with school and basketball. That'll still give him a month or more to get used to the idea before the baby comes."

They'd waited this long, what difference would another few weeks make? The main thing was that Andy would know he, and he alone, was his father's son. "That sounds reasonable."

"There's one more thing."

Even though the double bed was narrow, the distance between them seemed to grow exponentially. "What's that?"

"Could we wait until summer to tell him…about September? The baby's enough news to lay on him at one time. Anyway, by summer, he'll be thinking about going back to Florida and maybe the marriage thing won't seem so monumental to him."

Pam closed her eyes. Was this to be the never-ending drama? This final act would be even harder to carry off, because she stood to lose so much—a son, a father for her baby and, most important, her best friend, the man she loved. "All right. One piece at a time." She rolled on her side, hoping the baby would reposition himself. "You pick the time."

"Fine."

Regret for what might have been kept her wide-awake. Beside her, she sensed that Grant, too, lay sleepless.

At first, she wasn't sure he'd spoken her name. But then he went on in a tight, controlled voice. "About the childbirth classes. Do you still want me to go?"

Was he opting out? Or did he suppose she'd reject him now? She thought about the alternatives. Connie or Ginny would do it, but they'd wonder why her husband wasn't her birth coach. Going through the emotional experience of the classes and the birth with Grant would break her heart.

But without him?

Unthinkable. She wanted to share this special time with the man she loved, whether or not he could reciprocate her feelings. "Yes, Grant, I do."

GRANT HAD THOUGHT basketball practices were difficult. They were nothing compared to these childbirth classes. Bad enough were the graphic descriptions and films, but cradling Pam, breathing with her, torturing himself about the baby and the end of their marriage? It was like riding the bench with a career-ending injury.

No matter how hard he tried, two things Pam had said led him to the unmistakable conclusion that, for her, their marriage always had been nothing more than a mere arrangement. *He'll find out in September anyway.* As if it was a foregone conclusion. But the clincher was *He's your family.* So much for his grandiose visions of the four of them—Andy, the baby, Pam and him—coming together as the family of his dreams.

The chipper voice of the birth instructor intruded into his thoughts. "Next week we'll be showing some basic infant-care procedures. Feeding, burping, bathing, changing diapers. You fathers ready for that last one?"

Some of the other men managed hollow laughs, but all Grant could think was that he wouldn't even be around long enough for the baby's first tooth.

On the way home, both he and Pam were silent. What was there to say? Where was the happy anticipation? "Have you picked out the new wallpaper?" he asked. A safe, neutral topic.

"Yes, but it's your house. You should make the final decision."

His house. *His* son. "That's not necessary. I trust your taste."

"I'll call the paperhanger, then."

"Next week's our last game. Unless we get into the play-offs, which looks doubtful."

She looked sharply at him. "But if you'd had Beau Jasper?"

"Don't go there." He worked on mellowing his tone. "Watching Andy blossom has been worth a play-off berth." That didn't necessarily pacify the other team members, but it was funny how things had a way of working out. *Some* things, he added bitterly.

"How do you want to go about telling Andy?"

He didn't want to think about it. Things were so great for Andy right now. "I'll be there, but the way I figure it, the baby's your show." He cleared his throat. "Besides, you have a better touch with him than I do."

"It's not a competition."

"Right." But it sure felt like one.

SAYING GOODBYE to her father was harder than Pam had anticipated. He'd been such a comfort—and a much-needed buffer—but he had almost fully recovered, getting around with only a cane, and was chomping at the bit to get home. Until he saw with his own eyes, he said, he wouldn't believe his neighbor could take adequate care of his horses.

That Saturday morning in early March after Grant and Andy had loaded Will's suitcases in the car, they all gathered in the kitchen for the farewells. Will clamped his hands on Grant's shoulders. "Take care of these two," he nodded at Pam and Andy. "And lemme know as soon as that new young 'un makes his appearance.''

''Or hers,'' Pam reminded him yet another time.

Then Will turned to Andy. ''As for you? You have a happy birthday, hear? And just because you get that driver's license doesn't mean you have to act like a damn fool.''

''I won't, Gramps.'' Andy stood with his hands tucked in the back pockets of his jeans. ''After the baby gets here, I wanna come visit you and Pepper.''

''I'm countin' on it.''

Andy took a step forward. ''Uh, thanks for everything. You know. The advice and all.''

Will cocked his head, studying the young man in front of him. ''I'm right proud of you, son. Right proud.'' He hesitated, then pulled Andy into a bear hug. ''Aw, hell. I'm gonna miss you like the dickens.''

''Me, too,'' Andy whispered raggedly.

When Will drew back, he pulled out his bandanna and wiped his nose. ''Somebody musta spilled pepper in here.'' Then he turned to Pam. ''Come out to the car with me, dumplin'.''

She tucked her arm through her father's and walked alongside him. At the car he paused, squinting at her as if she were a specimen under a microscope. ''One day you're gonna have to tell the man.''

''What?''

''That you love him. Don't like to say this about my own kind, but men are dense. If you don't tell him, how else is he gonna know? No self-respecting male's gonna risk his pride if he thinks he'll be rejected. Or worse yet, laughed at.''

''But he could just as easily reject me.''

Her father put his arm around her, rubbing her back

as he continued. "Well, then, I guess you'll always wonder what coulda been, won't you?" He eyed her shrewdly. "Never knew you to be a coward, though."

"Oh, Daddy." She threw her arms around him, aware, with a wonderful intimacy, that his grandchild was sheltered between them. "I'll miss you."

"Take care, honey." He drew back. "And call me the minute you have that baby."

She stood, hugging herself against the strong early March wind, as his car disappeared from sight.

Now it was just the three of them.

And the moment of truth.

GRANT SAT on the sofa after lunch, hands clamped on his knees. Waiting. Dreading. Pam entered from the kitchen, trailed by Andy, who paused awkwardly in the door. "So whaddya wanna talk to me about?"

Pam gestured to the easy chair before taking her seat on the sofa beside Grant. She picked up an orange textured pillow and clutched it over her stomach, almost as if protecting the baby from the anticipated fallout from their discussion. Andy, looking warily from one to the other of them, perched on the edge of his chair, poised on the balls of his feet. Sensing the tension in the room, Grant rubbed his hands over his thighs and began. "We want to talk with you about trust."

"What'd I do now?"

"Nothing," Grant said. At the same time Pam murmured, "Not a thing."

Pam caught Grant's eye, signaling that she'd take the lead from here. "Remember when you asked me to keep your confidence about playing basketball in the park?"

Andy nodded, one leg moving up and down like a piston.

"And I did." She toyed with the fringe of the pillow. "But honoring your request meant I betrayed your father's trust."

"How do you figure?"

"He is your parent. I'm not. He had a right to know what you were doing after school."

"What's the big deal? Everything turned out all right, didn't it?"

"Yes, *this* time," Grant interjected. "But Pam and I have been talking." He looked at her to secure her support. She inclined her head slightly. "We've expected honesty from you, but we haven't been totally honest in return." He gulped, finding this whole scenario even more difficult than he'd imagined.

Andy threw up his hands. "I don't get it. What the heck are you guys talking about?"

"The baby," Pam said, her voice shaky.

Andy paled. "He's all right, isn't he?"

"He's fine, son. What we're about to tell you absolutely mustn't go any further. If it did, it could hurt all of us, especially Pam and the baby. Only one other person outside this room knows. Gramps. And that's the way it has to stay. Always. I guess the big question is, can we trust you to keep this confidence?"

Pam leaned forward. "I'm sure—"

Grant cut her off. "Son?"

Andy shrugged. "I guess so. Sure, I mean, if it's that important."

"It is," Grant said quietly.

Pam laid aside the pillow. "There's no easy way to say this, but the truth is—" Grant watched her falter, before going on ''—your dad is not the father of my baby.''

Andy's whole body stilled and his eyes widened in shock. Again he looked from Pam to his dad and back. ''Wait a minute. I don't understand. You guys are married.''

Pam hung her head. ''I was pregnant before then.''

Grant could almost see the wheels turning in his son's brain. ''Oh, it was one of those artificial insemination things, right?''

Grant could hardly bear to watch his son sorting through all the explanations, desperately trying to find one that would make everything right. ''No.''

Andy fixed him with a baffled stare. ''You mean it's someone else's baby?''

Pam laid a hand on Grant's leg. ''Let me tell him.'' She pushed her hair back and looked directly at Andy. ''This summer I had a loving, intimate relationship with a man who wasn't and isn't in a position to be a father to this child. I wouldn't consider adoption or...other options, even if it meant losing my job. I love this baby.''

''Jeez, Dad, you *knew* this? And you married her anyway?''

''I'd known Pam a long time. She was a good friend. She was in trouble.'' He turned then and sought Pam's eyes. ''Besides, I cared for her.'' If she only knew how much. ''It's not such a big deal to take on another man's child. Babies can be pretty easy to love.''

''I couldn't ask for a better husband or father,'' Pam said, her eyes glittering with unshed tears. ''But I...we...didn't want you to wonder where you stand.''

''You are my son. My only son.''

Andy simply sat there, saying nothing.

Grant continued. "I hope it's obvious how important it is to keep this in the, er, family. Pam is a great person. A wonderful teacher. Her reputation, her future, in a way, is in our hands. And, of course, the baby's. I'm counting on you to be man enough to understand the ramifications."

Andy stood. "Can I go now?"

Eyeballing his son, Grant got to his feet, too. "You will keep this to yourself?"

Grant sensed a smart remark coming, but then Andy looked at Pam, who was clutching the pillow again and simply said, "I told you already. *Yes.*" Glaring at Grant, he added, "Now, if you don't mind, I'm leaving for the park. See? This time I'm telling you where I'm going."

Andy whirled from the room, grabbed a basketball out of the hall closet and left the house. In the void Grant heard the cats playing tag in the upstairs hall, smelled the apple pie Pam had baked earlier, felt the churning of his stomach. When he turned to look at her, she was already on her feet. "I think I need to be alone," she said, moving past him to the den.

With a jolt he remembered. Will was gone. No more sharing the room upstairs.

It was as if all three of them had retreated to their separate corners.

And it was anybody's guess how Andy was reacting to the news.

SON OF A BITCH! Son of a goddamn bitch! Why'd they have to tell him that? It about made him puke. His legs churned, catapulting the bike down the street. Wind whipped his hair and his nose ran with the cold.

He couldn't picture it. Pam—*Ms.* Carver, for God's

sake—getting it on with some dude and then turning around and snagging his dad. Was his dad so hard up for a woman that he'd take used goods? That was sick!

Reaching the park, he plunked down the bike, relieved to find the basketball court empty. He bounced the ball savagely several times, as if he could pulverize it, then hurled it at the backboard, again and again. He'd thought they were a family. Oh, he'd noticed how Pam and his dad sometimes kept their distance, but he'd figured all parents were like that. But hell! They'd been keeping a secret. A big one.

He ran in under the hoop, made a layup, then dribbled the key and arched a twenty-footer. Catching his own rebound, he repeated the pattern over and over. How could his dad have gotten married like that? To somebody already pregnant?

When sweat dripped from his face, he tore off his jacket and kept shooting, not even caring whether the ball went through the stupid hoop. It didn't sound like Pam, either. He liked her. He'd almost felt closer to her than his own mother. She didn't nag and she did neat things for him like help get Angie's present.

Finally he stopped the frantic activity and stood staring into the distance, idly bouncing the ball. Slowly, inevitably, a thought formed in his head. Maybe he would never have found out except for that journal entry. The one about being jealous of the baby.

Well, Pam and his dad had certainly given him a solid reason not to be jealous any longer. The baby wasn't his father's.

But that meant it wasn't his brother or sister, either.

He didn't need to be jealous at all. He should be relieved.

But he wasn't. He felt like total crap!

THE WEEKS SPED BY. The warmer days of early spring were redolent with earthy smells. The upstairs bedroom, now papered in bright blue and white ticking with a border of teddy bears, was ready. The tiny onesies, booties and sleepers from the faculty baby shower were stacked neatly in the drawers of the recently acquired changing table. And thanks to the cheery new kitchen decor, making casseroles to freeze for after the delivery had been more pleasant.

At school, the Thespian Society had initiated its new members, spring-break tales were old news and Pam was working diligently on lesson plans for her substitute. Andy was busy with the tennis team, Brittany Thibault had been admitted to the college of her choice and Randy Selves had talked with Pam about subleasing her condo again for the upcoming school year. She'd put him off, of course, because by September everything would be different.

When the tulips in the backyard bloomed, she knew the time was close when Barney would make his—or her—appearance. The tulips. *Her* tulips. Would she ever see one again without thinking of Andy? Of Grant?

Was it any wonder Andy's wonderfully personal journal entries had dried up after they'd told him the truth? Now he confined himself to discussing movies, musical groups, current events. Anything except his feelings. He spent all the free time he could at Angie's or Chip's house and retreated to his room when he was at home. She and Grant didn't seem to have much to say to each other. They had never spoken about Andy's reaction to their news, largely, she felt, because it was hard to interpret how the boy really felt.

At least they'd pulled off one successful event— Andy's sixteenth birthday celebration. He'd invited the basketball team and their dates to a dinner party before they all went to a movie. Grant grilled hamburgers and Pam had made two chocolate sheet cakes, which were completely devoured. The isolated, uninvolved boy from the school year's beginning now had a host of friends who accepted him. That was something. And he had more freedom. He'd passed his driver's test.

Maybe, given the tension among them, it would be a relief when she and Grant told Andy the rest of the story.

It seemed almost surreal that at one time she'd thought she could tell Grant she loved him.

But Andy's disappointment in her made that impossible. Grant would never enter a relationship now that his son was so disillusioned about her.

Until the baby came, her only true companions in this home were Viola and Sebastian.

She found herself envying the unencumbered life of a housekeeper.

"WHAT ARE YOU DOING?" Andy, his hair sleep tousled, stood shirtless and barefooted on the back stoop, watching Pam string clothesline between two trees.

"It's such a beautiful morning. I love the smell of air-fresh sheets and towels. I'm bypassing the dryer today." Pam had awakened early full of energy that belied three nocturnal trips to the bathroom. She'd already done two loads of wash and cleaned the refrigerator. "Want to bring me the basket and help?" She nodded at the wicker container on the first step.

"What are these?" he asked, setting the basket down and picking up a clothespin.

"This, my young friend, is an ingenious device for

hanging clothes. See?" Selecting a hand towel, she demonstrated.

"Isn't it easier to use the dryer?"

"Easier, maybe, but not nearly as satisfying."

The look he gave her told her that he thought she was certifiable. "Where's Dad?"

She gestured expansively. "It's a lovely April Saturday. A man needs to be on the golf course." She didn't add how awkward weekends were when Grant stuck around the house—pure Kabuki theater of avoidance.

Holding a washcloth at arm's length, Andy fumblingly attached it to the line. "You really think this stuff's gonna smell better?"

"I know it. And if you're smart, you'll run upstairs and bring me the linens from that cave you call a room. I'll pop them in the washer and pretty soon your lair will smell like flowers."

"Yuck."

She giggled to herself as he left, unaccountably feeling more optimistic than she had in weeks. As if to remind her not to get too cocky, Barney did a tour jeté, nearly knocking the breath out of her.

After frying bacon and eggs for a ravenous Andy, she cleaned up the kitchen and started his wash. Reluctantly he slouched out to the garage, unearthed the lawn mower and began cutting the grass, as Grant had instructed him to do the night before.

Pam crossed items off her To-Do list, noting that only cleaning the oven remained. But it was too pretty a day to undertake that chore. She'd check the bag she'd packed for the hospital one more time. On her last weekly visit, Dr. Ellis had said the baby could come anytime. Pam was still teaching, although she desperately hoped her labor would begin at home, not at school, where a cast of hundreds would be involved in her private drama.

On her way to her room, she peered in Grant's, smiling at Viola snoozing on his bed. Apparently the contented feline had never gotten the message that she wasn't the master's favorite animal. Or else they'd achieved détente.

When she reached the den, Sebastian, who lay sunning on the windowsill, raised his head and licked his chops in acknowledgment. She'd given Grant and Andy strict instructions about the care of the kitties and had stockpiled cat food, just in case. Other than the oven, she couldn't think of a thing she'd forgotten to do.

Again Barney performed an amazing acrobatic feat, but then settled down. Pam lowered herself into the rocker, caressing her stomach, humming softly. Focusing on her baby made it easier to avoid thinking about the dreams that had died. Of being truly married to Grant. Accepting and loving Andy as a son. Creating a real family. Giving this precious infant a wonderful father and brother.

On the light breeze from the open window wafted the fragrance of newly mown grass. Birds chirped. Springtime. Renewal. Rebirth.

With bittersweet longing, Pam recognized the tune she'd unconsciously been humming. "What I Did for Love."

THERE. The stupid lawn was done. He'd even used the edger. Mowing was about the last thing he'd wanted to do today. The baseball team was playing in Dallas at one o'clock and he'd wanted to see Cale Moore pitch. He checked his watch. Too late now.

There was one other thing. Pam looked like a blimp and he'd noticed how she kept rubbing her stomach. Dad was playing golf. He didn't feel right leaving her home by herself. A shiver of dread coursed through him. But what help would he be if something happened? Like if she went into labor? Not that it was his problem. Or his dad's. This kid had nothing to do with him. Still he felt weird. The most he knew about having babies was what he'd learned in that dorky film they'd showed in fifth grade—the one where they separated the boys and the girls. It had some dumb title like *Becoming a Man.*

After lunch maybe he'd read the new Tom Clancy. Chill out. Call Angie about their date tonight. He stowed the mower in the garage, and when he went in the house, he found Pam pulling a big old casserole of macaroni and cheese out of the oven. It was hard to stay mad at her when she cooked so good.

He'd just finished his first helping and she'd gotten up to get him seconds when he heard her say something like "Woof." When he turned around, she was clutching her stomach and peeing all over the floor.

He was paralyzed. What the hell was happening?

"Towels, Andy. Get some towels quick." She was panting like a dog and leaning against the counter.

Towels. Think towels. He raced outside and grabbed four off the line, barely registering that they did smell kinda good. When he got back inside, she was still supporting herself at the counter. In a calm, scary voice, she said, "I'm okay. My water just broke." Whatever that was. He guessed it had something to do with the baby. "Call the golf course and leave word for your father to meet us at the hospital."

Us? Hospital?

He turned his head away. She was wiping between her legs with the towel. "Then hand me the phone to call Dr. Ellis."

His tongue wouldn't work to get the words out. "You're...you're having the baby? *Now?*"

She threw towels onto the floor to sop up the mess. "Not now, exactly. But soon. And I need your help, Andy."

"Mine?"

"Can you drive me to the hospital?"

Whoa. He loved to drive. But taking her to the hospital? What if she had the baby in the car, like in those movies where they don't make it to the emergency room? What if he had an accident?

"Andy?"

"Uh, yeah. Sure. Okay. I'm calling the golf course now."

He was scared shitless. But when she let out another breathless moan, he knew he had to be the man. There wasn't anybody else.

ANDY DROVE, white-faced, in a manner that would bring an approving smile to any driving instructor but that caused Pam to bite her lip in frustration. Couldn't he go any faster?

By the time they reached the hospital her contractions were about four minutes apart and she had a new appreciation for the word *travail*. A sweet-faced nurse, who looked like one of her students—what could she know about childbirth?—settled her in the labor room, decked out to deceive her that she was in a luxury hotel. She could see Andy hovering anxiously in the hall. Finally the nurse finished her ministrations and nodded to

Andy. "You can come on in now and keep your mother company."

Pam momentarily shut her eyes. If only that were true.

Andy peered nervously around the room, studying every detail except her mounded stomach. "What are those things?" he said, pointing to the fetal monitor apparatus.

She explained to him about tracking the baby's heart rate as well as the length and strength of the contractions. He leaned over to study the erratic scratches on the paper feeding through the machine. "Cool." Then he stuck his hands in his pockets and stared over her head. "That a boom box?"

"Yes. There are some CDs in my bag." Just then a contraction tightened her stomach, and she concentrated only on the crescendoing sensation.

"Pam?" Andy's voice sounded strained.

The pain ebbed. She smiled. "It's okay. Just a contraction."

"Isn't there something I'm supposed to do?"

"Not a thing, except cross your fingers all goes well." She studied his drawn face, his clenched hands. "You don't have to stay with me. Maybe you'd be more comfortable in the waiting room."

"No!" He seemed shocked at his own strong reaction. "I'm responsible. Until Dad gets here."

Pam smiled, then held out her hand. "Thanks, Andy. I'd like you to keep me company."

And, for the next forty minutes, that's exactly what he did, putting on some soothing CDs and holding her hand until Grant, face flushed, burst into the room. "Thank God, I made it in time."

Pam had never been so glad—or so sad—to see

somebody. The moment was here. But what she had
was a birth coach, not a husband.

THE NEXT COUPLE OF HOURS WERE a blur of reassuring
voices, intermittent examinations and the inevitable
surges signaling contractions. Dr. Ellis had arrived,
checked her and given Pam a big thumbs-up. "You've
slowed down some, but we should have a baby before
this youngster's bedtime." The doctor winked at Andy,
who had steadfastly refused to leave Pam's side, except
when the nurse asked him to step into the hall while
she did some tests. About four in the afternoon, he
picked up the bedside phone. Grant was feeding her
chipped ice and stroking her forehead. They couldn't
help overhearing.

"Angie, yeah, uh, I'm not gonna be able to make it
this evening. My stepmom's having her baby, and I
gotta be here.... What's it like? Well, it's not the easiest
thing in the world, you know?" He listened, then
grinned. "You're right. I guess that *is* why they call it
'labor.'... You, too. Yeah, I'll call you as soon as he
comes."

"She," Pam murmured just before another contraction crested.

"Deep breaths," Grant coached. "Atta girl. Just a
little longer."

When the pain passed, she gazed into his eyes, ar-
restingly blue and heartbreakingly full of concern. She
clutched his warm hand. "Thanks for being here."
Then she looked over at Andy. "Both of you."

"You're going to have a beautiful, healthy baby.
Keep focused on that." Grant's voice was like a lullaby.
He projected calm, confidence. No wonder he was an
effective basketball coach.

A beautiful, healthy baby. Tears welled and splashed down her face.

Grant leaned over. "Are you all right?"

She tried to smile through the tears. "Yes." *Except for the fact my baby will never know you as a father.*

AT DINNERTIME the nurse suggested Grant and Andy get something to eat. "You have a long night in front of you. Best to be fortified."

Grant didn't like the sound of that "long night." Labor was supposed to come more quickly when a mother's water broke. What was taking so long? Watching Pam's struggle was pure agony. He ached with love each time she endured a contraction, each time she gripped his hand in concert with her body's upheaval.

"Do we have time to run home?"

When the nurse learned they lived close by, she told them to go on, saying nothing much would change in the next hour or so.

"Dad, are you sure we should leave?"

"We won't be long. There's something I need to get at home. We'll grab a bite at the drive-through and be back in a jiff."

"What'd you forget?"

"Never mind. It's between Pam and me."

Andy shot him a strange look, but didn't question him further. Grant concentrated on his driving. And on thinking.

He'd missed Pam these past few weeks. Oh, sure, they'd occupied the same space, but the old intimacy was gone. Until today. Logic told him this wasn't his wife. Wasn't his baby. But with each contraction, each heartbeat ticking away on the monitor, he kept thinking, "I love you, I love you."

He left Andy in the car and raced to his desk in the den and pulled out the envelope. Maybe this was a crazy idea, but it was no crazier than his idea of getting married in the first place.

It was a desperate game plan, but winning meant putting everything on the line.

And, God, how he needed—wanted—to win!

DAD LOOKED SO SERIOUS, so worried, Andy figured he'd better say something. Help get his dad's mind off Pam. But that was hard 'cause that was all he was thinking about, too. About how tinkly her laugh was, about how she made him feel good about himself, about the way his dad stared at her when he thought nobody was looking. He'd been pretty much an ass about learning the baby was somebody else's. You had to look at it from the kid's point of view. He'd need a family. And it wasn't like Andy had any other siblings. Besides he couldn't believe he was actually going to be there when the baby came. Well, not *there,* like in the delivery room, but right outside. Like a regular brother. Andy gazed out the window. They were only a few blocks from the hospital. "Dad, I've been thinking."

"What about?"

"I'd like to stay."

"Well, sure, son. Pam and I want you at the hospital."

"Uh, that's not what I meant." Andy cracked his knuckles, desperate to make his dad understand.

"I'm listening."

"I want to stay in Fort Worth, go to Keystone, be part of your, uh, our family."

He'd thought his dad would break out one of those world-class grins. Instead, he looked pained. Didn't he want him? "Nothing would make me happier, Andy. It's been great having you here. But—"

"I know. Mom."

"I have no sense of how she would react."

"Couldn't we try?" Looking down at his lap, Andy realized he'd crossed his fingers.

His father's features relaxed and, with a sigh, he smiled. "Yes, son. We'll try."

"YOUR HUSBAND'S HERE," Dr. Ellis announced, peeling off her rubber gloves. "I'd say he's just in time. You're dilated to eight." When the doctor stood aside, Grant hastened to Pam's bedside. She was so relieved when he returned. His presence soothed her in a way back rubs and foot massages never could.

He picked up her hand and held it against his chest. "How're you doing?"

"I just want it over," she moaned. "Why can't this baby hurry up?"

"I guess he takes after his mother. Wants to make a grand entrance."

She couldn't hear the rest of what Grant said. She closed her eyes and screwed up her face. Through the red mist of a strong contraction, she made out his one word. "Breathe."

From the foot of the bed, a nurse said, "It won't be long, now, honey. But you've got to work with me."

Her body felt as if a battering ram had taken up residence in her pelvis. No sooner would one wave crest and break than another would take its place. The only constants were Grant's deep voice and his gentle hand tenderly wiping the damp hair off her forehead. "Please!" she heard herself call out.

Time stood still, yet rushed past with a fury, bringing with each movement of the clock hand another spasm.

"Don't push," the nurse admonished.

Dr. Ellis swept into the room, gowned and masked, her eyes dancing. "Show time, Mama."

"Thank God," Pam managed to say before becoming aware the room had suddenly been transformed into a brightly lit surgical theater.

"Breathe, then hold it," the doctor said.

Pam felt herself lifted and cradled in Grant's strong arms.

"Now—" the obstetrician's voice was emphatic "—*Push.*"

Pam gripped the sheet and bore down with all her might. She felt tears on her cheeks as she slumped against Grant, helpless to deliver the massive weight pinning her to the bed.

"Rest." The nurse sponged her face.

"One or two more," the doctor intoned.

Again the cataclysm—cramping, exploding.

"Okay, okay," Dr. Ellis murmured. "The head is crowning."

Pam knew she couldn't possibly do anything more. They'd just have to take the baby some other way. "I can't."

Suddenly Dr. Ellis stood over her. "Stay with me, Pam. Your baby wants to meet you."

Then Pam was filled with a fierce urge, magical in its intensity, followed by a rapturous kind of pain.

"Push!" the doctor ordered.

Then, as if a huge hole had been blown in the dam of her body, she felt release, and almost before she could process the change, the doctor held up a tiny, perfect infant, bawling its head off in greeting.

"You have a beautiful baby girl," Dr. Ellis said, beaming. "Would you like to hold her?"

Would I like to hold her? Pam held out her arms. "Thank you, thank you all." Then she welcomed her daughter, wrapped loosely in a warm blanket. A miracle. Amazingly, the baby quit crying while Grant cut the umbilical cord, and then through unfocused deep blue eyes studied her mother.

The medical personnel were busy doing something at the other end of the bed, but Pam didn't care. Her precious baby was here. Safe and sound.

Then she looked up at Grant, intending to thank him. The words died on her lips. He made no attempt to wipe away the tears streaming down his cheeks. "You're so beautiful," he said to her, his eyes awash with love. Then he looked at the baby. "You both are," he whispered.

Holding her daughter, gazing at the man she loved—a man who'd stood by her even through this miracle—she knew that her dad was right. She could no longer risk the pain of not knowing.

She offered him her daughter. "Here, you take her."

His eyes clouded with uncertainty. "You're sure?"

"Oh, yes." She placed the baby in Grant's arm, tucking the blanket around the tiny form. Then she found his eyes. "I'm sure, because I love you so very much."

For one heartbeat, she thought he was going to drop the baby, but he recovered, nestling her even closer to his chest. His voice caught. "Does this mean what I think it does?"

Her eyes never left his. "What do you think it means?"

Cradling the baby like a football, he reached into his pocket and withdrew an envelope. "I hope it means that

I can tear this up.'' It was their written agreement. ''That we don't have to wait till September to decide about the rest of our lives.''

Gently he placed the baby in her arms, catching one of her hands and kissing it reverently. ''I love you, Pam. I've loved you from the beginning, all along, and most especially right now.''

She felt a warm glow radiating throughout her body. She sighed contentedly, pointed to their contract, and then smiled into his dear face. ''Tear away, beloved.''

ANDY COULDN'T BELIEVE IT. They were letting him in the delivery room. Right away. ''Is it a boy or a girl?'' he asked the smiling nurse.

She winked. ''Why don't you come see?''

He opened the door carefully, peering around the edge. He didn't wanna walk in on, well, yucky stuff.

''Son? Come in.''

His dad sat on the edge of the bed, his arm around Pam. Cradled in her arms was this round-faced baby with squinty eyes, rosy-red cheeks and lots of black hair. Andy edged closer. ''Jeez, he's kinda little.''

Both his dad and Pam chuckled like they were in on some big joke. ''What's so funny?'' He didn't know crap about babies. Had he said something wrong?

''*She,* Andy, *she,*'' Pam said with one of those laughs like warm butter.

''You mean it's a *girl?*'' That was weird. He'd all along figured it was a boy. He hung his head for a minute, remembering all that energy he'd wasted being jealous of a brother.

His dad's eyes danced. ''Do you need to check the equipment?''

"That's okay." He took another step closer. "She's got lotsa hair, doesn't she?"

"She'll lose most of it," Pam told him. "The main thing is she's eight healthy pounds of baby." She motioned toward a chair. "Pull that over here and sit down. Then I'll let you hold her."

"That's all right. I don't know any thing about—"

His dad muscled the chair into position. "Nonsense. Every man's got to do it sometime. She won't bite."

The next thing he knew he was sitting there with this warm, squirming baby in his arms. She smelled good, like talcum powder or something. And she kept moving these rosebud lips and making little kissing noises. A *girl*. He still couldn't get over it. Just let any creeps try going out on a date with her. He'd show 'em. "She's awesome. It feels kinda like she's our baby, you know, Dad?"

"Yes, son, I do know."

"What's her name?"

Dad looked at Pam like he didn't have a clue. But she didn't seem perturbed at all. "She doesn't have one yet." Andy watched Pam gaze up at his dad with these really goo-goo eyes. Then she reached over and held his dad's hand. Andy might as well not have been in the room. Finally she turned back toward him. "That's your job."

For a minute he thought the baby would slip through his fingers. He held her tight. "My job? Whaddya mean?"

There it came again. The laugh that made him feel warm all the way through. "I want you to name your sister."

Sister. How could that be? This wasn't Dad's child. Maybe she'd made a mistake. But then like the sun rising after a stormy night, it came to him. "It doesn't matter, does it?"

"What?" His dad seemed really interested in what he was going to say.

"It's not biology that does it. It's love."

"That does what?"

Andy leaned down and nuzzled the baby's cheek. When he raised up, he had the answer. "That makes us a family."

"YEAH, GRAMPS, she's got all this fat, wrinkly skin and waves her hands kinda funny, like she's lookin' for something she can't find."

Pam lay back in her bed, gazing fondly at Andy, who stood at the foot of the bassinet, the phone at his ear while he studied his sister. She was exhausted, but she'd never been so happy in her entire life. Grant had already made a list of the people at school they needed to call and you'd have thought Andy had, in a matter of hours, become an expert on infants.

"It was really cool to be at the hospital. I drove Pam here, you know."

There was no mistaking the pride in Andy's voice. "You prob'ly wanna talk to her."

Andy handed her the phone. "Hi, Dad."

"A girl, huh? You hornswoggled me. I just knew it was a boy. But if she's half the little girl you were, you've got a genuine winner."

"She's a miracle, Daddy."

"How's Grant doing?"

She turned her gaze to her strong, handsome husband. "He's quite a man."

"Are you tryin' to tell me somethin'?"

"I sure am."

He chortled. "Got yourself a reg'lar little family there, then?"

"As regular as love can make it."

"Goldurn, dumplin', I couldn't be happier."

"Me, either."

"Say, I got the full physical description from Andy. But you've gotta register a name for that foal, don't you?"

"That's up to Andy."

"Andy? Put that young 'un back on the line."

Pam held out the phone. "I don't think Gramps is going to let you off the hook. It's name time."

Grant looked first at her, then at Andy. "This is special," he said as he moved to the bassinet and picked up his daughter, who grabbed his finger in her fist and held on tight.

Andy took the receiver. "It's me again…. Her name? That's easy."

Pam held her breath. Anything was possible with Andy.

"Ready?" Andy was playing the moment for all it was worth. "I figured she needed a name from both our families, since she's kinda the, whaddya call it—" he glanced at Pam as if for corroboration "—the symbol of our new family. My middle name is Paige. So I decided we could name her Pamela Paige Gilbert and call her Paige."

Andy looked at Pam again, a question in his expression.

"It's lovely, Andy. A beautiful…symbol."

Andy expelled a sigh of relief. "I did good, Gramps. They like it." Then he paused, before adding a comment. "But next time I'm gonna ask if they can try for a boy."

Pam's eyes welled with tears as she took in the scene, inscribing each one in her heart. Dear Andy. Precious Paige. Loving Grant.

Best of all, she knew that, at last, they were a family. A real one. The forever kind.

Men of Maple Hill

Muriel Jensen's new trilogy

Meet the men of the small Massachusetts town of Maple Hill—and the women in their lives.

Look for the second title in the trilogy,

Man with a Message, **May 2002.**

Cameron Trent has despaired of ever having the family he's wanted, until he meets Mariah Shannon— and love and two lonely children turn their worlds upside down!

The Men of Maple Hill trilogy tells heartwarming stories with a sense of humor, genuine charm and emotion and lots of family!

Available wherever Harlequin books are sold.